sign

Colin Dray grew up in rural New South Wales, where he fell incurably in love with Shakespearean heroines. He holds a PhD in the Arts and teaches English literature and creative writing from time to time. His short fiction has appeared in publications such as *Meanjin*, his criticism has appeared in *Australian Literary Studies* and *Antipodes*, and his poetry has been burned to ash for the sake of humanity. He now lives in the Illawarra region with two daughters who are the most delightful people he has ever met. *Sign* is his first novel.

sign

COLIN DRAY

ALLEN&UNWIN
SYDNEY•MELBOURNE•AUCKLAND•LONDON

First published in 2018

Allen & Unwin
83 Alexander Street
Crows Nest NSW 2065
Australia
Phone: (61 2) 8425 0100
Email: info@allenandunwin.com
Web: www.allenandunwin.com

Cataloguing-in-Publication details are available
from the National Library of Australia
www.trove.nla.gov.au

ISBN 978 1 76029 473 1

Set in 12/17 pt Fairfield Light by Post Pre-press Group, Australia
Printed and bound in Australia by Griffin Press

10 9 8 7 6 5 4 3 2 1

For Clara and Hannah

'Batman, because he doesn't have any super powers.'

HOME

1

The morning after his surgery, still wrapped, and giddy, and numb, Sam woke to find his mother sitting in the visitor's chair beside him, a magazine splayed open across her lap. At first she was little more than a blur, a brown smudge undulating on a sea of orange. He had to blink several times, slowly, to clear the stickiness from his eyes, watching the smears resolve into a thin cotton dress, hair pulled back in a loose bun, and her face, drawn but smiling.

His entire body felt somehow tender and deadened all at once, his lips cracked and dry, his neck throbbing beneath its bandages, his mouth tethered to a plastic tube. His nose itched. Right on the tip. But it was covered in tape, pinned by another, thinner hose, and his arms were still too heavy to lift. His hair was stuck to his forehead. His temples were pounding. His mother inched forward. Katie lay asleep on the floor, curled up under his mother's jacket.

'Oh, Sammy,' his mother whispered. 'You're here. You're with us. You're home.'

But he wasn't home. He wasn't sure why she'd said that. He was pinched beneath stiff sheets. His muscles were thick and soupy. He could feel the sheen of fluorescent lights above him on his flesh. Could hear how scrubbed clean the air was, voices echoing along concrete walls and lino. He blinked and lay in place. Feeling his nose itch. Already beginning to feel the pain that was to come rising in the back of his throat.

It had started when he was nine years old, after his father moved to Perth. Sam was having trouble swallowing and kept getting a sharp pain in his ear. When he was ten, by the time his father stopped sending postcards, he was bald, silent and blistered. Every other day for two months he had treatments— chemotherapy that made him tired; radiation that gave him mouth ulcers, turned everything he ate into a tasteless mush and condensed his saliva into snot. Long before anyone began talking seriously about surgery, a doctor had explained his condition by showing him a goofy cartoon filled with sneering blue monsters and sword-fighting white blood cells. But as Sam sat in the consultation room, feeling the tremble of his mother's hand as she rubbed his back and tried to smile through her tears, the animation became a jumble of colours dancing, and he forgot what all of it was supposed to mean.

As the weeks passed, as his hair grew back, a little patchy at first, his mother joked about how important he must be to have so many specialists wanting to see him—and at times Sam did indeed feel tall in their waiting rooms when the nurses remembered his name and slipped him lollies as he said hello. After an upper endoscopy that made him gag, two CT scans that made him feel like he was in a submarine, four ultrasounds, blood tests and an oral surgeon who kept prodding his neck and dipping his grey-flecked eyebrows in disapproval, the doctors decided at last. He was stage two. It meant the cancer had spread and he would have to lose his voice.

A week before the operation he'd almost won a class alphabet game by spelling the words 'larynx', 'lymph nodes', and 'laryngectomy', although Mrs Fletcher made him sit down when he began describing the procedure with a red marker and a diagram of where the incisions would go. The day before, his mother had taken him and his sister to Wonderland where he screamed as loud as he could on every ride. And on the morning of the procedure, before a gas mask slid over his face, Sam's final words were, 'Batman, because he doesn't have any superpowers.'

Now, on the other side of it all, as his mother talked gently about how well everything had gone, as the machines around him huffed and groaned, he had a strange realisation: he wasn't breathing.

He felt his chest rising and falling. There was air getting to his lungs. But he wasn't breathing in and out. Not like usual. His mouth, his itchy nose, none of it was moving. There was no sensation of wind across his lips. The air wasn't passing through them.

It was his stoma—a word the surgeon had used that Sam had forgotten until that very moment. The stoma. The hole in his neck. A hole that he would breathe through now. Permanently cut into the bottom of his neck. That would never heal shut. That he'd once drawn for Miss Fletcher in red marker. A hole where his voice had once been.

Batman, because he doesn't have any superpowers.

That was the last thing he'd ever said.

5

His mother was still talking—Aunt Dettie would be by later, she was saying; the soccer coach sent his best wishes—and Katie, on the floor, was starting to stir, but all Sam could think about was his final line. *Batman*. He found himself repeating it over and over again in his mind. Staring at the wall, struck by the stupidity of it. What a dumb thing to mention—let alone be the last sentence he'd ever speak. The surgeon had warned him. He wouldn't have a voice anymore, he'd said. But somehow Sam hadn't actually realised it until that moment.

And all he wanted was to say something simple. To say, 'Mum', or 'Hi' to Katie, whose eyes were tracing fearfully along the tube that led from his throat to the machine helping him breathe.

He felt cocooned in plastic and crisp cotton. Even his mother's voice, soothingly familiar, became just a wordless hum. He closed his eyes, letting his nose itch, letting the drip in his wrist sting. The distant, smoky feeling in his head swept up and over him—through his shoulders, his head, his eyelids—and he slept.

He was woken by a doctor and nurse, and the slow whir of the electric bed raising him up. Once he was adjusted gently into place with pillows, the doctor looked him over, listening to his chest and scratching around on his chart, while the nurse busied herself plugging in some new instrument to the wall. Katie was gone—she was with Aunt Dettie, his mother explained—and the room seemed smaller than it had before, less filled with light and sound. The doctor went about his examination, talking to no one in particular about the discomfort Sam would feel in the next few weeks. Sam's mother sat on the edge of the same chair, twisting a clutch of tissues into a rope and nodding deeply, even though the doctor wasn't saying anything that needed a reply. Eventually, he slipped on a glove and began opening the bandages around Sam's neck.

At first there was only a peculiar, faraway sensation as the latex-covered hand moved near his skin, like the anticipation before a tickle, but the moment the breathing tube was peeled aside a whip of pain scored Sam's body. He jerked back, pinned in place, and failed to shout.

'Oops. Yep. That's all going to be sore for a while,' the doctor said. 'We'll have to get a little something more to help with that.' The nurse nodded and made her own note on a small piece of paper.

Something was hissing. Something close. Ragged and deep and hollow near Sam's ear.

'Now, we're going to clean this out a little,' the doctor continued, 'but we're going to be very gentle, okay?'

It was the stoma. The sound was his breath through the hole in his neck. A wet hiss, quivering at the sting. His mouth and his nose, still taped, weren't breathing at all, but his chest was heaving and the stoma was letting it out.

Sam stayed stiff as the nurse suctioned around his neck with a small tube. He felt his mother's hand clutching his arm, and closed his eyes until it was over. The pain was not so bad as it had been at first, and faded to an ache that flared only when they rewrapped his hose. More than the pain, though, it was the silence that had shocked him. Not a shout. Not even a moan. Just his snuffling, hollow hiss as he shrank from the touch. He had felt his entire body flash, but couldn't scream out.

The nurse unplugged the machine with the hose and wheeled it off into another room, leaving the doctor to go on talking to nobody. Eventually, he was saying, Sam could get an electrolarynx. Or he could try mouthing some words, if he really needed to. The process involved taking a mouthful of air and letting it out in a special way. Taking a breath, shaping the sounds; one at a time, and slowly. It might make him a little lightheaded at first, he said, but it would become natural. They could pass on the names of a few people who could help him learn.

'You'll have to plan out what you're going to say,' he said. 'But that, and a notepad, should see you through for a little while.'

The nurse returned, fished from the pocket of her scrubs a selection of pamphlets that she spread out on his dinner tray, and began administering an injection into the drain on his wrist. There was a brochure on the daily cleaning of his stoma, one on post-operative physiotherapy, and even one on learning sign language titled 'Your Voice, Your Choice'.

Sam looked down at the pamphlets, feeling the tender cold on his throat, hearing his oxygen tube hum. His mouth, he realised, was open. Unable to speak, unable to breathe, his jaw hung slack. Pointless. With all the drips and cords he wasn't even going to be using his mouth to eat for a while.

With an effort, his lips crackling, he eased it shut.

2

Dettie's operation had not gone as well as Sam's, and she told him so. The next day, as he lay still limp in bed, his head cloudy, a peculiar gnawing pain in his jaw radiating through the medication, Aunt Dettie sat on the edge of his mattress, one hand cupping his knee, while she told him the whole of her story. Or at least, everything she remembered. She spoke slowly, her voice warm and measured, as if reading a fairytale. From the first pinch in her chest, to the searing down her arm; from the thunder and sway of the ambulance; through the stench of ammonia in the operating room; until she woke on the other side of the anaesthesia, bruised and sliced and nauseous, a burning sensation still eating down into her heart. Sam remained pinned in place, trying to nod when it seemed like Dettie wanted him to, thinking he saw the faintest smile creep into the corner of her mouth.

She'd been lucky, she said. Blessed. She'd fought her way through. All the way back through the haze to that cold operating room slab. And so had he. And together, she said, they would both be stronger than they had been before. 'See, people break sometimes, Sammy,' she said. She shook her head. 'Like a toy, or a car, or a bone. Things come apart. But that's not the end of them. They can be put back together. Fixed up. And you know what? Afterwards, those things are stronger, always, in the broken places.'

Perhaps she was right, he thought. Perhaps he would heal stronger. But he certainly didn't feel stronger yet. What he felt instead was the tape tugging on the skin of his throat. He felt stitches underneath gauze pulling at his flesh. A hot, itchy throbbing. He could feel the other stitches that were still inside him, the ones that the doctor said would disappear over time. He already had the strange chalky taste of them dissolving at the back of his throat. That, and the taste of blood. And beneath all of it, beneath everything else, was a hollow he had never known before. The cold, empty ache of a place where his voice had once been.

Dettie told him her story again. And again. And once more. It became a ritual. Once every day for a week. She would stride through the doorway, kissing him the same way once when she arrived and again when she left. A loose wet smack on each side of his face, fingers sprawled behind his neck, her thumbs burrowing into his temples. In her handbag she would always have a new piece of cotton square to give him, cross-stitched, pulled tight and embedded with the scent of her tobacco. She had made them herself—rustic scenes, with Sam himself stitched into every square. A tiny rendition with overly-long arms and feet, stomping in bright country landscapes and yelling from the hills. Each time she pressed one into his hands she would tell him about the quilt she was going to sew them all into when he got home. In one design he was surrounded by birds and flying through the air, over clouds that Dettie had shaped to spell out his name.

But it was when his mother left them alone that she would inch closer, slightly hunched, stiff, clutching her handbag, to start telling her tale again. She would always begin with some new complaint about one of the other patients. Someone she felt wasn't handling things the way she and Sam had done.

'There's a teenager in the next room,' she whispered once. 'Just had his appendix out. But the way he's rolling around, making a fuss, you'd think he was shot through with a harpoon.'

Dettie seemed to regard Sam's silence not as a disability over which he had no choice, but rather a sign of stoic resolve. She could not abide fuss—or 'carry-on', as she called it. And there seemed to be a lot of it being indulged by the nurses as far as she was concerned. She'd huff and wave the thought away.

'Not like us,' she'd say, and start in again. With the spasm. With the stopped heart. With the complications that arose even once she'd made it to the 'safety' of hospital. Her nodding solemnly at every detail, Sam peering out into the hallway, unable to make a fuss even if he'd wanted to, wondering where in that cavernous building his own operation had occurred.

'And I didn't see any lights, or any tunnels leading off into the whatever,' she would say, shuffling even closer, petting his arm. 'There were no angel's choirs, or the face of Jesus staring out at me from an armchair. None of the things you're told to expect. All those things they tell you to believe in. That's not what's waiting.' She always paused. 'Instead, there's just the quiet. That's what I felt.' Her fingers would lace together, clenched tight. 'Can you imagine what that's like, Sammy? The quiet?

The silence? When that rhythm thumping away at the back of your ears just stops? And you're cold. Set adrift.'

Seven minutes later she lived again, two cracked ribs and a rope-shaped scar denting her chest where the doctors had massaged her back to life.

'You see, it's peaceful. Once you wander past all that fear and doubt and sadness. But that's why you have to fight against it, Sammy.' She would take his hand. 'If ever you feel like slipping away, you have to hold on. Have to cling to the noise and the feeling. Because God's out there, Sammy. He's waiting to scoop you up. But not until you give in to him.'

Dettie was God-fearing. That was the term she used. She talked about a creator who had forgiveness and grace, but her eyes flashed with excitement at his wrathful, old-testament ways. The God who punished to purify. Who lumped suffering on people to prove they were strong enough to survive. She never seemed to quote anything, though. Not like the school scripture teachers did. For Dettie it was all just a truth that you felt in your spirit, one that kept you prepared.

Whenever she left, Sam would sink down into his pillow, feeling the tape around the bandages tugging at his throat. The sutures in his skin and the unseen deeper stitches pulled tight in his flesh, and he was unable to imagine getting stronger when he felt held together with string.

3

Every day after school Sam's mother brought his sister to visit. Some days Katie would have Twistie crumbs colouring the corner of her mouth, others a stain of chocolate milk on her jumper. For Sam it seemed wholly unjust that his sister was being lavished with treats at the hospital canteen while he was the one suffering all the injections and checkups and daytime television of the children's ward. Sometimes he could barely bring himself to look at her as she chattered about what her friends at school were doing, or whatever class project she was working on.

His mother told him later that getting a snack was the only thing that helped calm Katie down before she saw him. The hospital terrified her. The thought of leaving Sam there overnight, even more so. Sam remembered that on the first day following his operation, once he was properly awake but unable to speak, his sister had sat on the edge of his bed, inconsolable, sobbing in a long, echoey howl. She bit strands of her hair into wet brown clumps. The freckles on her nose pinched in a terrified wince. He had only ever heard her make that sound once before—the time he'd had to read aloud to her the letter their father left behind when he moved to Perth.

That day, after the operation, once Katie had cried herself into a limp sleep and woken up quiet, their mother had given her a white handkerchief edged with blue embroidery. She was to use it whenever she felt sad. It was special, their mother said. It was especially made for tears. It would gather them up and hold them tight, and by the time the material was dry, she was guaranteed to be happy again.

Katie was sceptical and, still crying, hugged Sam's stomach extra tightly and altogether too long before she left for the night. From that day on, though, she kept the handkerchief tucked in the sleeve of her shirt, exactly as her mother had done.

4

At night, when his mother would head home to tuck Katie into bed, Sam could hear the hospital sigh as visiting hours ended. The hallways emptied, the guest-lounge television quietened, and once the kitchen ladies had finished clearing the remains of dinner from their trays, the sound of rubber wheels passing through the wards stilled to silence. Then Sam was alone with the sound of his own breathing, with the whistle in each suck and push of his lungs and the throb of his swollen jaw. The breathing tube was gone now to help the stoma heal, and in its place was a small plastic vent that he could feel shift in place when he moved. Beneath his bandages the inside of his throat was oddly itchy, and when he swallowed he thought he could feel scabs crinkling against his tongue.

He had a sick, churning feeling in his belly every day. In the daytime he could almost block it out—flick through the worn books brought to him from the patient lounge, watch the orderlies make their rounds, stare through the small television in the corner of the ward. But at night it was different. A swell of anger bubbled and frothed in his gut as he rehearsed the same bitter questions: Why *him*? Why *just* him? He was the only person he *knew* with cancer. What had he done differently? Was there something he shouldn't have eaten? Was Dettie right all those times she'd insisted that the microwave was radioactive? That it mutated your blood? Was there some way he could have noticed earlier what was growing inside of him?

In the nurses' station three goldfish circled in place, each of them opening its mouth wide, silent under the water. Sam curled tighter into himself, festering in his rage. He imagined himself lying in bed all those nights before his operation. Years and years of nights. His neck was so sore now; had it always been this sore? Had it always hurt just a little? Some tiny telltale ache that he ignored and didn't think worth mentioning? He wanted to go back. Back before now. Before this. He was suddenly furious that he couldn't. That this wasn't even an option. It didn't seem right that he was stuck in the after, when it was too late. When he'd had to give up so much. He wanted to go back to before, when he might have done something. Noticed something.

There was a hole inside him. An empty space he had never even known was once filled. He was supposed to sing the school song with everyone else at assemblies. His teacher had made him remember part of 'The Man from Snowy River' to recite at the yearly talent show. He'd just taught himself how to do an impression of Kermit the Frog. But all of that was gone now. It all seemed so enormous, and so silly, and so unfair, all at once.

He moved his lips as if willing the sounds—any sounds—to return. As if somehow, by some miracle, he could call them back into being. In his imagination he opened his mouth and a deeper, richer voice erupted. 'It's extraordinary,' he could almost hear his doctor saying. 'Never before in medical history have we seen someone's voice grow back! It's a miracle!'

There was a boy four beds over who had broken his ankles and dislocated his shoulder being thrown from a horse—Dettie had rolled her eyes at the big 'production' he put on when he needed to use the bathroom. Each day, he was taken to physiotherapy, where the nurses made him do exercises for his arm, strengthening his muscles, keeping them from wasting away. Eventually, once the casts came off, he would have to do the same for his feet. Sam sat dreaming up similar exercises for himself. Things he'd half understood from the pamphlets on his bedside table, and filled in the rest.

Think the word: *Banana*. Split it up. *Ba. Na. Na.* Mouth the sound. *Ba.* Move your lips. Breathe out.

Pah. Pah.

Mmmpah.

He wheezed and sputtered. His whole chest seethed. The hospital around him pressed in and his stomach turned. The fish kept circling, their mouths gaping, dead-eyed and mute. Sam collapsed back into his pillow and cried.

5

In the next bed there was a young girl who seemed to sleep most of the time. Thin and yellow and still, she lay surrounded by grey equipment and colourless tubes, all of which was circled by a thick plastic curtain. To Sam, the girl's skin seemed even waxier behind this shiny surface, and on the rare occasions she sat up to watch television or greet her family when they came to visit, he could see the slow way that she moved—her bony arms stiff and heavy. She was always cold, she said, and Sam wondered if it was because she was bald. He could see the bare skin beneath the knitted beanie she wore, and whenever she was awake he wanted to tell her that he knew how it felt, that he remembered the way it had been after each of his treatments, back before the operation: the strange tickling feeling of air across his scalp, the bruises, the vomiting, the dizziness. Sam wanted to tell her all this as they lay in the quiet, but he couldn't. And it didn't seem important enough to bother writing down.

Twice, when their dinner trays were being gathered before lights out, one of the kitchen ladies offered Sam the girl's untouched jelly. He didn't eat it though. Jelly felt good, cool and soft, as it slid down his throat, but it always seemed like the girl was watching. And anyway, after the bowl had been behind her curtain it reeked of antiseptic.

It was the quiet that made the hospital worse. Or rather, the beeps and hisses that filled the quiet. Sam could never sleep. The rough cotton of his pillowcase. The heat on his legs and the chill on his cheeks. The sizzle of fluorescent light from down at the nurses' station. The way the orderlies plodded along at such a hulking pace. The ward seemed hollow and ominous, the white walls pressing in on him, stark and cold; and whenever he closed his eyes he felt that he too was somehow going stale, stiffened and empty and sterile.

On the fourth night he was woken by the hiss of his curtain being pulled closed, but as he snapped awake there was no one by his bed. Instead, as he rolled over, he could see past his fabric curtain and through the girl's thick plastic one to where three figures surrounded her body. Two orderlies and a doctor were checking her monitors and talking in hushed tones. Sam watched them raise her slender arm, hold her wrist a moment, then set it back down. After a few minutes of the doctor thumbing through her chart, flashing a small light in her eyes, the orderlies kicked the brakes loose on her bed and wheeled her out from behind the plastic, over towards the hall. As they passed his bed, Sam propped himself up on his elbows. He could just make out the girl's face, still moving, her head rolling back and forth, one hand rising and falling.

One of the orderlies noticed Sam while he was pushing aside some detached cords with his foot.

'Shhh . . . It's okay,' he whispered, sliding the girl's thick curtain back against the wall. 'She's just getting her own room. That's all. Go back to sleep, little guy.'

But Sam watched the bed glide around the corner and out of sight, still trying to listen for the sound of the girl's breathing, wet and small.

He lay back down, and for the rest of the night stared into the dark, chewing on the corner of his pillowcase. For the first time, it seemed, he could hear a high-pitched ringing in his ears—faint, but everywhere. A ringing like he'd never heard before. Had it always been there? Had he simply never noticed? Had he never been quiet enough to make it out?

He closed his eyes. Nestled his face further under the covers.

It was still there—that ringing. It was only broken by the sound of his stiff sheets rustling as he moved. Or the occasional distant thud of a door being pushed through down the corridor. The buzz of a small fluorescent light near the nurses' bay.

Everything else was that ringing. All around him. Inside him. Through him. Him and this ring. The ring he'd never heard before, but suddenly felt he'd be hearing forever. Ringing and ringing and ringing. He chewed harder. The boy in the bed opposite stretched and gave a small moan in his sleep, rolling his face further into his pillow.

The ring in Sam's head settled deeper. Louder. Everywhere. He wanted to shout. To scream. To drown it out. He breathed instead—hearing that whistle, that suck of air, as something at least. Anything to fill the void.

The next morning two more orderlies came to push the remaining equipment out into another ward, and the cleaners arrived, chatting loudly, to mop the floor.

6

Dettie had a present for him in her handbag. It was his last night in hospital and she'd been promising him a special surprise for the past two days. He knew where she was hiding it, whatever it was, because she kept fiddling with her handbag, rubbing the leather and clutching the shoulder strap. Finally, when visiting hours were almost over, and Katie had asked her mother to take her to the toilets, Dettie eased down onto the chair beside Sam's bed and undid the clasp.

'You are a very lucky boy,' she said, her fingers picking through the contents of the bag, fixing on something. She held her hand poised there.

'Do you want to guess what it is?' she said. 'I *bet* you can guess.'

Sam stared at the back of her wrist. It couldn't just be another stitched square. He shrugged.

'What would you love more than anything else?' she asked.

She was smiling larger than Sam could ever remember seeing. It deepened the wrinkles around her eyes and made her

21

cheeks pull, pale and thin. He turned his head slightly, looking past her at the newly made bed sitting empty beside them.

'How about your daddy being here?' she said.

He jerked upright. She'd said it, and she was still smiling. Nodding. His eyes, now wide, flashed from the hallway door to the nurses' station and back. He felt a fluttering in his chest, and couldn't seem to breathe out. Was that where Katie and his mother were? Were they bringing his father in with them?

Dettie's grin remained wide, but she closed her lips. It made her face seem pinched and tight. She petted Sam's knee, humming, and lowered her gaze to her handbag, holding, waiting long enough for Sam to look back down at it too. Slowly, she drew out two rectangular cards and covered them with her palm.

'Now, you know how much he has wanted to come and see you,' she said.

He could already hear it in her voice. Sam's father wasn't there. But he still couldn't stop the tingling sensation circling his body, tickling him beneath his arms. He exhaled.

'And he really tried so hard to be here, Sammy. He was so cross when he couldn't make it.'

Fine. Not here.

The fluttering settled into a sick, heavy feeling in his belly. Sam already knew what was in Dettie's hand.

'He said to me: *You make sure my Sammy knows his daddy is thinking of him.* That's what he said.' Her eyes were watery. '*You tell him I'm proud of him.*' Her lips stretched white, like linen pinned across a washing line. She kept on nodding.

With her fingers still clinging tight to its edge, she held out one of the rectangles for Sam to see. It was a postcard. It had his father's name on it, his address in Perth, and the message read:

My darling son, Sam. I miss you and I am thinking of you always. I will see you soon. Love, your father.

It had been a long time since Sam had heard from his father, or read one of his letters out to Katie. He hadn't even sent something before the operation. The message sounded peculiar. Distant. Even his handwriting looked different now.

Sam's stare drifted off. His eyes followed the folds of bedsheet crumpled across his lap. The blanket Dettie had straightened at his feet as she sat down. He saw her handbag, which lay tipped over on its side. Saw the tightly creased tissues poking from its mouth. The corner of an unwrapped packet of cigarettes. The neat stitching of her cardigan. Finally, he was looking at her other hand, at the second card she was clutching. This was a photograph. It was a man holding a drink, a glass of beer, smiling. Sam could tell that it wasn't his father, but he had seen him before. The picture was of Dettie's dead husband, a photograph she'd always kept with her, old and crinkled and bound at the edges with sticky tape. Sam could almost remember him. Something about him and soup. A smell of soup.

'Isn't that good, Sammy?' Dettie was saying. 'To know how much your daddy loves you?' She turned over the postcard and started reading the words to herself.

On the front of the card, which Sam could now see for the first time, the image seemed odd: a kitten in a basket of flowers. It was fluffy and big-eyed, with long silver whiskers. He stared at it, tilting his head to get a better look, but it remained peculiar. There was nothing funny about it. No joke. It wasn't pulling a face or doing a dance. Whenever his father had sent a postcard

23

before it was usually a cartoon. A sheep wearing sunglasses or a crocodile with knives and forks saying, *Wish you were here!* This one was pink, with wide, watery eyes, embossed and glistening.

Perhaps his father had been really worried about him when he picked out the card. Maybe he was too scared Sam was in danger to try to be funny. Maybe he'd just lost his sense of humour altogether. It had been over a year now. Being in Perth might have changed him. Like the way Sam didn't think about soccer all the time anymore.

When his mother and Katie returned, the postcard was propped against the wall behind the lamp. Dettie didn't point it out, leaving it a surprise. But when his mother finally did notice, straightening his table as they prepared to leave for the night, she stared at it strangely, mouthing the words of the message to herself. As she finished, miming the words, *Your father*, she glared.

Obviously, no one had told her about it, and probably Sam's father had decided not to send the card to her in case she got upset. She never said anything out loud about it, though. She just smiled tightly, leaned over Sam's pillow and kissed him goodnight. On their way out into the hallway Sam could see her giving Dettie a long, curious look, but it didn't seem to be angry.

Only later, months later, would it occur to Sam that the card wasn't stamped. That it wasn't his father's handwriting at all.

7

The first afternoon Sam was home from hospital he secluded himself in his room and read comic books. His throat was still bandaged and the tape that secured the dressings to his skin itched horribly. Whenever he moved his head he could feel the stitches pulling, and he spent hours staring in the mirror trying to talk, as if he could somehow will his voice back. The inside of his throat felt tender, like a fresh bruise, and it hurt to swallow or breathe too deeply.

Katie had kept sticking her head into his room to smile and then run away. It bothered him to feel watched like that, so he shut the door and wedged his shoes beneath it. When his mother came to bring him lunch she had to knock with her foot and wait for him to open up. As she edged her way in, Sam turned and crept back under the covers.

She set the bowl on his bedside table and laid a spoon and a napkin on his knees. Steam drifted up from the soup and filled the room with the aroma of tomato. Sam grimaced and tried to roll away from the smell.

'What's wrong, honey? Don't you want something to eat? I can hear your stomach growling.'

Sam shrugged and pulled the blankets up over his shoulder.

'Come on, you love tomato soup.' She petted his hair. 'I made it especially. Honey?'

He curled up his legs and squinted until he could barely see. He wasn't going to cry until she left.

'That's fine, sweetie, you get some rest. Try to eat something. And if you need anything . . .' She trailed off. The silver bell she'd bought him was missing from his bedside table. Sam had thrown it across the room, and when she found it under a pile of his clothes, she nodded and left with it tucked inside her hand.

'We're here for you,' she whispered, and pulled the door to, but not shut.

With the lights off, Sam began to learn the creaks and clicks of the house. Soon he could make out the activity going on in the other rooms as he lay in bed. He heard the floorboards give in the lounge room as his mother moved about; the thump of Katie's door when the draft pulled it shut; the stomping whenever she ran down the hall. In the quiet, it was as though the house was breathing, and he wondered for a moment why this was something he had never noticed before.

Outside, he heard Dettie clatter through the back door and into the kitchen, jangling her keys and calling out a hello. The flyscreen swung closed and Sam could tell a bag of groceries was being spilled across the countertop. A few minutes later the kettle boiled, and for an hour or so the room went quiet while his mother and Dettie sat and talked.

Just as Sam had finished reading the same comic for the third time in a row, his door was elbowed open, and Dettie slid inside, the halo of her hair glowing above her silhouette like a match. She snapped on the light and Sam shielded himself from the glare.

'You'll ruin your eyes if you keep that up,' she said, and gently kicked her way through the toys on the floor. Easing down onto the bed, she tapped his foot. 'What are you reading?' She lifted the comic from his hands and flicked through the pages.

Sam scrunched his blankets into a knot. He shrugged.

'Hmm, looks exciting,' she said, unconvincingly. She flattened out its creases and placed it on the floor.

'So how are you feeling, Sammy?'

Motionless, he sat staring down at his empty lap.

'Yes, I know,' she said. 'It'll be sore for a while, but it'll keep getting better. Soon, you won't even feel it.'

Sam knew he was glaring, but he didn't care. He was grinding his teeth and he didn't mind that it pulled against the stitches.

'You're probably feeling like things are different now, aren't you? That you're not the same? That a piece of you is gone?' She shook her head, slowly. 'Maybe you feel like someone took something from you? Something that was yours.' She leaned in, and reaching over, flicked on his bedside lamp, turning it towards herself. 'And it's okay to feel like that, Sammy,' she said. 'They did take something from you. They had to.'

Dettie was undoing the top two buttons on her blouse as she spoke. Sam wriggled away, staring over at the closed curtains.

'See, I know how you feel,' she said, pulling open her collar so that he could see the top of the long scar left over from her heart operation. It was flushed pink and stretched down her chest like a strip of barbed wire.

27

'You might have a scar like this for the rest of your life too, but that doesn't mean that you've changed. You're still who you are. No matter what.' She was still holding her arms up. Her elbows started to tremble. 'You're not broken, Sammy,' she said. 'Remember what I said? People like us—we don't break. We get fixed, and we get stronger.'

Sam still didn't know what to say to that. And he remembered suddenly, almost disinterestedly, that he couldn't say anything anyway. He nodded.

Dettie nodded too, fixing up her blouse and pulling back his bedsheets. 'Now why don't you come out and sit with us in the lounge room?'

He wilted, but she took his arm and led him to the door.

Outside, his mother was putting away the shopping. 'Did you have a good talk to Aunty Dettie?' she smiled. 'Did she tell you about how impressed all the nurses were?'

Sam shook his head, but felt Dettie's hand squeeze him gently on the shoulder.

'Wonderful,' his mother said, smiling, and turned back to the pantry to shelve two more soup cans.

Sam shrugged, wandering over to sit on the floor by the couch.

8

His mother needed to get back to work as soon as Sam returned home. He was taking a couple of weeks off school to recuperate, but after the past year of tests and doctors' appointments and procedures she had no leave left, so Dettie offered to drop over each day from her apartment and watch him. Sam was meant to use the time to relearn his daily routine. How to bathe without getting water in his stoma. How to clean and strap his vent in place. He would dab the incision point with antiseptic, as the nurse had shown him, and clear it out with the suction squeezer. He'd rub ointment on the skin that was inflamed and blotchy red, and before re-wrapping it all, he would stare into his reflection, at his exposed neck. Into the hole. Without the vent in place. The hole open to the world. Dark and open and quiet. He would put his hand up to his neck and feel the warm air on his palm as he exhaled.

Mostly he stayed in bed. Dettie had given up trying to coax him out. He read comic books, listened to the radio. Katie brought him packages of homework from his teachers that he would skim through and leave unfinished on his bedside table. The few times he did sneak out of his room it was to use the bathroom or get a spoonful of ice cream from the freezer. Ice cream had become his primary pleasure. It was slick and cool on his tongue, dissolving against his teeth, all the sweeter for having been pilfered from behind Dettie's back while she sat on the couch humming whispery old tunes to herself, smoking and stitching colourful new scenes into ever more squares of cloth.

One afternoon, hunting through the laundry cupboard for batteries, Sam found a yellow cassette that looked strangely familiar. Back in his room he found that it was a recording of him and his father singing 'Mary Had a Little Lamb'. Sam must have been about two years old at the time. He was slurring a lot of the words and was wildly off-key. Between the drop-outs of the sound, and Sam continuously thumping on the microphone (his father kept breaking the melody to ask him to stop), it was difficult to listen to, even huddled close to the speaker so that Dettie couldn't hear. The voices seemed to belong to other people. Strangers, from another time and place. Sam's was garbled and alien, oddly nasal and squeaky, but even his father's seemed strange. Higher-pitched than he remembered. Somehow thinner and metallic. At one point he coughed and it sounded more like a small sneeze.

Sam stopped the tape, slipped it back in its case, and stuffed it under his bed.

'You had the sweetest little voice,' Dettie said that evening as they sat watching television.

Sam was balled on the couch under a blanket. She peered over at him with a gentle smile. He tried not to look up at her, feeling himself tense, pretending he was transfixed by the commercials. Was she talking about the tape? Had she heard? He'd hidden himself away. He'd only played it once. Barely above a whisper. How could she know?

'Like a little bird,' she said. 'Chattering all over the place. Gabbing away all day. But heavens, you'd shout the house down if you couldn't find your toys.' Dettie hummed happily. 'Oh, the noise. Remember that, Joanne?' she called out towards the kitchen.

There was no reply.

'Joanne?'

Sam's mother called out, 'What?'

'Remember when Sam was little? All that running about? The noise?'

Sam stayed transfixed by the flickering television screen. A pizza was twirling in a haze of steaming cheese. Katie, lying on the floor with colouring books, was rolling her head on the carpet, sighing.

'What, Dettie?' His mother appeared in the doorway. She was clutching a fan of papers and brochures. 'Pardon?'

Dettie chuckled. 'Just reminiscing about when Sammy was a toddler. Remember? All that shouting about—oh, what was it? Robot Boy?

His mother shook her head, blinking. 'Um, I don't—*Astro Boy?* Is that the one?'

'That's right! Yes! The funny little robot. Flying around everywhere. Remember that Christmas—you and Donald trying to find a toy with the robot on it?'

Sam's mother exhaled. Loudly.

'Sorry, Dettie,' she said, firmly. 'I'm just,' she waved the papers in her hand, 'I'm just a little busy trying to deal with some things in here.' She turned, digging her shoulder into the doorframe as she pivoted, and left the room.

Sam knew what she was busy doing. He'd seen the letters from his school, noticed the business cards for advisors and private tutors splayed on the table. Sam's school was arguing with his mother about whether they had the facilities to take him back. None of their teachers were trained to teach children with disabilities.

'He's not disabled!' he'd heard his mother shout into the phone at his principal. This was the day after he'd come home from hospital. His mother had called to give the school an update on his progress. 'He's not deaf! He can hear and see perfectly well.'

The principal had said something in reply, but whatever it was, Sam's mother was unimpressed.

'Well, that's not really *our* problem, is it? He can write and play and participate. He's smart. He can take care of himself. The only one who seems *incapable* of anything here is you.'

Somewhere more suitable seemed to be the common refrain, but eventually she had convinced them that it wouldn't be a problem. Sam would be allowed back to his same class in the same year, and she would arrange for a private tutor, at her expense, to help him regain some sort of speech.

Dettie seemed unfazed. 'Your father never did find that toy, did he, Sammy?'

Sam kept staring at the television, through the screen. He shrugged. He remembered the show, but not any toys. Not running about pretending to be flying.

Besides, he thought, Astro Boy was a robot. He could be rebuilt. Good as new.

9

The glass in the front door only looked dark brown from a distance. Up close, as the sunlight played across its rippled texture, streaks of yellow and swirls of orange lit up before dispersing back into a beer-bottle gloom. Sam could see no movement on the other side of the pane. It was quiet. A soft breeze nudged the leaves of the surrounding trees, and Dettie's car idled out on the road, where she and Katie sat watching him through their windows, waiting. He looked up again at the doorbell, shifting back and forth, more eddies of light bubbling forth and receding away. Around the button, painted onto the weatherboard of the house, a tangle of light green vines and pink roses had been shaped into a love heart. His palms were sweating.

Dettie honked.

The sound made him jump. As he turned to look, she pointed at her wrist and then the door. It was time.

Dettie had agreed to drive Sam to the appointment with his new speech therapist, but it was clear she wasn't enthusiastic about the arrangement. She had refused to get out of the car, not letting Katie, whom she'd just picked up from school, out of her seat either. She'd even kept the motor running. Perhaps, Sam thought, Dettie considered visiting someone to help with his voice a form of indulgent 'carry-on', and was only going to offer the minimum support.

Katie, oblivious to her aunt's impatience, smiled and waved at him.

He turned back and, holding his breath, pressed the doorbell. The electric chitter of 'Greensleeves' sounded behind the glass. For a moment longer the rumble of Dettie's engine promised escape, until a darker shadow of brown emerged from the murk and the door opened.

The woman who greeted him was one of the tallest people Sam had ever met. With long, tanned limbs and a puff of curly hair, she reminded him of a coconut tree. She smiled, warmly.

'Samuel?' she said, leaning over, eye-level, her hands on her knees, her floral dress pinned to her thighs.

He shrugged. Nodded.

She extended a hand. 'I'm Tracey,' she said. 'Your mother and I spoke on the phone.'

Sam lifted his arm and she took his hand, pumping it twice and smiling broadly again.

'Did you come all the way on your own?' She straightened up and noticed the car. She appeared to be about to manoeuvre around Sam and down to the footpath, until Dettie gave a curt nod and drove off.

Tracey watched her go and blinked. She started to say something, and smiled instead. 'Well, Samuel, why don't we go inside and get started?'

She gestured into the hallway.

Slouching, Sam stepped over the threshold and followed Tracey down a hall of polished floorboards, into a carpeted lounge room and onto a purple sofa. As he settled himself as far back on the cushion as he could, she sat in an armchair facing him, one leg crossed over the other. Somewhere, off in another part of the house, a television was playing. It sounded like sports. There were announcers and the occasional cheer.

'Now, Samuel,' she said. 'When your mummy and I spoke on the phone she said that she was too busy to come today, or for our first few appointments, but that she'll be coming later. But that's really good, actually. Because it will give *us* some time to get to know each other and to work through a few things on our own first. Won't it?'

Sam could feel her attention on him, so he stared at her foot, peeking out from under the hem of her dress. The sandal she was wearing was dangling off her heel.

'So why don't I introduce myself properly, and maybe explain the process, and what we're going to do today?'

He knew she was smiling again. Her eyes crinkled, head tilted sympathetically.

'So, again, my name is Tracey. I'm called a speech therapist,' she said. 'And that just means I'm trained in a number of different recuperative techniques for a variety of speech-related issues. Everything from stuttering—I have some people who need help with that—to people such as yourself, looking to regain their voice entirely, perhaps with the help of some voice prosthesis tools. And we can look at some of those options later.'

She gestured to a few devices laid out on the coffee table, but Sam left them in the corner of his eye.

'I also teach sign language,' she said. 'Your mummy mentioned that there might be some interest in the two of you learning that together. Which I think would be very nice. So we could do that.'

She hummed. She took a breath. The television in the other room crackled with a roar of applause.

'Can I tell you a secret?' she said. 'I don't know if *you're* feeling nervous.' Her voice remained soft, measured. 'But *I* am. Just a little.'

She was still smiling. He could tell from her voice. She moved in her seat and the sandal snapped on her foot.

'I usually work with older people,' she said. 'Not always, but mostly. So you're the youngest new friend that I've gotten to help. Which is exciting, isn't it?'

She seemed to be asking a lot of questions that didn't really need a reply. Sam waited, but nothing happened, so he offered a tiny nod.

A crowd, their voices thinned by the television speaker, cheered again.

'I'm sorry,' Tracey said. 'Could you just excuse me a moment?'

She stood and swept across the floor, opening a sliding door and stepping through. The television, which was in the very next room, was louder with the door ajar, and Sam could make out the rhythmic sway of a tennis match, the pock and grunt of a rally playing out, and the swell of spectators escalating with every returned shot. Tracey was talking to whoever was watching the set in a heightened whisper, far sterner than the smooth tenor she was keeping with Sam. He heard a man's voice in reply, also talking low, but clearly annoyed. Tracey said something about the 'appointment' and the man groaned.

sign

While she was gone Sam scanned his surroundings. It appeared to be a cross between a lounge room and an office. Several framed certificates adorned the wall beside a large bookcase. There were pamphlets and business cards on the mantle above a closed-off fireplace. Like the glass on the front door, the carpet, walls and ceiling were all shades of brown, but the space was busy with colour. A painting of a misty waterfall disgorging a rainbow hung by the window. Another, of a Native American man staring at the sunset, faced it on the corner wall. Multiple beaded dreamcatchers hung from the ceiling. There were small ornaments, of horses and dolphins, on every shelf, and a crystal unicorn sat in the centre of the coffee table.

Tracey's whisper rose to a hiss and the television quietened slightly. Sam could only hear the *thock* of balls on racquets if he strained to listen. She returned, smiling with her lips pressed tight together, and resettled in her chair, smoothing down the wrinkles in her dress.

She began talking him through the ways that people like himself could learn to speak again. She drew a diagram of his throat—a cross-section of his neck—and talked about the way it worked now. How *he* worked. Now.

She described the breathing technique that the doctor had mentioned. It was called 'oesophageal speech'.

'Did you and your friends ever burp out words?' she said. 'Swallow air and burp funny sounds?'

He didn't respond.

'Because it's a bit like that. Sort of,' she said. 'You swallow air into your oesophagus and shape your mouth and tongue and palate as you let the air out.'

37

She gave him a small demonstration of the process, just to get the idea. After sucking in through her nose she made a series of short grunting noises: *tah*, *pah*, *tie*, *kah*. It sounded peculiarly raspy, and Sam felt a quiver in his stomach.

'We do some exercises like that together,' she said, back to using her normal voice, 'and gradually we work up to saying full words, then sentences. Did you want to try a little now?'

He shook his head.

'Just a little go?'

He pressed back into the couch.

'That's okay. No hurry. Don't worry. We've got plenty of time.'

Next she showed him the handheld devices. She held one out to Sam, but he didn't take it. It was a black tube, about the size of a small flashlight. An electrolarynx.

'Nothing to it,' she said. 'It just creates the vibration that your voice box used to produce.' She raised it to her neck and pressed it against her throat. It made an angry humming, and when she opened her mouth, a sizzling noise came out. 'And it sounds just like this,' she said, her voice gnarled and robotic.

Sam felt lightheaded. The room seemed smaller all of a sudden. The dreamcatchers and dolphins pressed in on him. He was breathing faster.

'You just have to make sure that you're clean-shaven so that it has a tight surface connection. But that's not really a problem for me.' She looked up at Sam trembling in front of her. 'I guess that's not really—'

She adjusted herself in place, setting the devices out of sight on the floor. 'Why don't we—What if we learn a little sign language? A couple of things you can show your mummy?'

She demonstrated some words; ran through the alphabet. She spelled out *Samuel* with her finger and palms, and showed him very simple things like *Yes* and *No* and *Hello*.

'Hello, my name is Samuel,' she said, waving in a firm, practised way, and signing out the letters in a quick succession of gestures. He pretended to look while actually staring past at one of the flowers on her dress.

'Now you try.' She showed him her hands, palms out, and shaped the sentence again. 'Can you follow along?'

He tried. Sort of. His hands felt numb. The shapes he made were sloppy and backward. Eventually Tracey rose and crossed to the couch, sitting beside him and taking hold of his fingers. Shaping them.

He could smell cigarettes. She was a smoker. Like Dettie. He became distracted by the fuzziness of her hair. The tickle of it on his ear. In the other room the man watching television cleared his throat.

Up on the bookshelf, behind Tracey, Sam noticed a line of encyclopaedias. They were the exact encyclopaedias that he had at home. Funk & Wagnalls. Black and gold spines. All snug in place on their shelf. Something about the sight of them made him choke. He started huffing. He snatched his hands back. Suddenly he couldn't catch his breath.

Tracey eased away. 'That's okay, sweetie,' she said. 'I know this is difficult. It's a lot to take in. A lot all at once.' She touched his knee. 'Why don't we take a break? Let's have a hot drink of something.'

She left to make him a cup—a Milo for him and tea for her. She promised biscuits.

Sam sat alone, trying to slowly inhale. Exhale. Tucked behind Tracey's empty chair the electrolarynxes were waiting. On the table the diagram of his neck, sliced in half, tubes rearranged, stared up at him. In the next room commentators were enthusiastically reciting someone's statistics. Sam was shaking. His breathing was fast. Fierce. He couldn't stop. Couldn't catch his breath. The encyclopaedias that he had at home. That he used to research his school projects. They sat on the shelf. The man watching tennis coughed. Like his father on the tape. He coughed.

The room was too small. Cluttered. Choking him. Tiny dolphins. Horses. Horse pulling carriages. Tethered. He was sweating under the bandages. He stared at the unicorn. His head was getting light. One of its legs was raised. His breath. He couldn't. It hurt.

He was crying.

Gasping. Shaking. Sobbing. There was no way out. He was going to throw up. He tried to stop crying and cried harder. Silently. Wet, hot tears scalding his face. The waterfall painting and the dreamcatchers dissolved in a blur. His chest heaved. His neck whistled. Everything was getting dark.

At some point Tracey returned carrying a tray with two mugs and a plate of biscuits. 'Oh, no, sweetie, it's okay,' she said, setting them aside and easing down beside him again. 'It's okay. You're okay.'

He could barely hear her. He was doubled into himself. Eyes squeezed shut. Chest on fire. Trying to stop the sobbing. If he could just catch his breath. If he could just get control. What was going on? Was he dying? Was this what dying felt like? Dettie's dark beyond?

'It's perfectly all right,' Tracey was saying. 'Shhh . . .' She rubbed his back, but he couldn't feel it. 'We just need to get it out, don't we?'

But he didn't. He knew it. He couldn't get it out.

He hated her.

He hated her sign language. He hated her electric buzzing voice box. Her stupid burps. He hated her dreamcatchers and her ornaments and her husband watching tennis in the next room. He hated that she called him 'Samuel'. He hated her unicorn.

He hated Dettie for leaving him here. His mother for being at work. Katie for waving goodbye. The doctors. His school. Everyone. All of it. Everything.

He was alone with all his hate. Crushed under it. Lost in it. Choking his way deeper into it. Alone.

Eventually the sensation began to pass. Tracey got him to count out his breaths, and the choking steadily slowed to a shudder. Tears still welled in his eyes, streaked down his cheeks, but he could look around again. He could see the room and not feel so closed in. His stomach was sore, but the urge to vomit had passed.

Tracey spent the remaining time gently showing him again how to sign his name—all of the letters—but he barely took it in. He felt wrung out. His head was burnt clean. Light. Nothing he did mattered anyway, he realised, and there was nothing he could do. He let the Milo go cold.

When Dettie arrived to pick him up she honked from the street. Tracey led Sam back through the house, her hands on his shoulders, promising that everything would get easier with time and practice. He nodded because it seemed to make her happy to think that, and waved goodbye.

He decided he would never come back. No matter what. He would fake stomach-aches, postpone dates, convince his mother he was fine without it. Anything. But he would never come back again.

As he climbed back into the car it seemed like days since he'd seen his sister and aunt. While Katie told him about the park down the road he laid his head on the back of his seat and watched the door of Tracey's house close. If she noticed, Dettie didn't ask him why his face was puffy and his eyes were red, and he decided that he wouldn't tell her anyway. He'd never experienced anything like that before, and the thought of it made him feel ashamed. He would leave it there. Behind Tracey's door, its glass now dull and brown again in the distance.

10

The third Monday Sam was at home Dettie couldn't babysit. She'd gone on a weekend church trip to the Blue Mountains and the bus had broken down before they'd started for home. The whole group had to stay a second night. Dettie was livid, calling from the hotel, raging at the disorganisation, saying she didn't know why she got involved with such things anymore. She offered to take a train back in, to be there by morning, but Sam's mother told her not to worry. Sam could come with her to work for the day.

Sam was excited. His mother's bank had always been one of his favourite places to visit. He liked seeing his mother at work. At home she always seemed slightly harried and breathless, but at work she seemed to glide. She smelt of hairspray and wore pantyhose. The things on her desk were always neatly aligned and her chair rolled on wheels across a plastic mat. She had a leather shoulder bag loaded with complicated documents that she seemed to be able to fill out with barely a thought. The way her co-workers said her name, 'Joanne', sounded different to the way Dettie said it, more playful, less pointed, and they would always bring her cups of coffee and ask her advice because she'd been there the longest.

Two years earlier, the day after he had broken his wrist, he had spent most of the afternoon at the bank. It was before they knew anything about the cancer. Before the radiation had given him weeks of nausea and hair loss. Before the battery of tests. Back then he was just some kid who'd crashed his bicycle doing wheelies and busted up his arm.

He remembered being shown to a conference room that no one was using, and being told it was his for the day. He got to spread out his books and pencils. People brought him snacks from the vending machine. The receptionist—an attractive woman with long earrings and heavy eyebrows who smelt of vanilla—gave him a bowl overflowing with Minties. There was a television set up in one corner where he watched daytime game shows and a knock-off Canadian version of *Lassie* while he folded Minties wrappers into little houses and cars and arranged them across the table. After lunch one of his mother's co-workers even brought him a video of *The Jungle Book*, and at one point he stretched himself out under a few chairs and took a nap.

In a weird way, he even remembered the injury fondly. There had been a dull, constant ache, and when he tried to twist his arm beneath the cast the pain was blinding, but there was always a feeling that he was steadily getting through it. 'On the mend,' his mother said. As he thought back on it now, feeling the hollow bite of his stitches and the discomfort of the vent pressed into his neck, he remembered scratching beneath the plaster with a ruler, or trying to carve some extra wiggle room for his thumb, and it all seemed so silly. A mere irritation, something chafing and sweaty they eventually sliced off into three discoloured, reeking shards and threw in the rubbish bin. Pain. What a joke pain had become.

This time, when his mother led him through the bank's foyer, behind the teller windows, and out to the back offices, the tone was immediately different. He remembered the whole place bustling previously, with people wandering past to offer a happy welcome, to laugh and ask how he'd 'banged' himself up. To chuckle and shake their heads as his mother recounted the story, telling her 'boys will be boys' and shooting Sam a wink.

This time, everyone was oddly quiet. When they smiled, it was with a short, firm nod, before they quickly turned back to count money, add sums or make phone calls. At first he thought it was just a busy day, but he heard more than one playful conversation stop as he drew near, only to restart with a whisper as soon as he had passed. Near the break room he thought he recognised someone—a red-haired man in a suit who, last time, had drawn a Smurf on Sam's cast with blue biro—but the man didn't seem to register him. Perhaps it was someone else, Sam thought. Maybe.

The receptionist with the Minties had been replaced by an older, heavier-set woman with thin, drawn-on lips. She gave him a tiny wave, but stayed firmly on her side of her desk. When she spoke, it was in a loud, slow voice: 'Hello, Sam. Good. To. Have. You. Here. Today.'

Sam's mother let out a quiet sigh and ushered him quickly on. It was only later, thinking back on the moment, that he wondered if the receptionist had assumed that he was deaf too.

The same conference room had been set aside, but now it seemed smaller, darker and more tucked away. The only people who passed by seemed to be on their way to the bathroom, meandering along, unaware that he was in there. When they did look up to see him, his neck bandaged, peering out at them through the unfrosted portions of glass, they ducked their heads and quickened their steps. The man with the sandwich cart who sold Sam's mother their lunch merely stuck his head and arm through the door wordlessly, sliding Sam's plate onto the table, before backing out again. This time no one gave him fizzy drinks or lollies. The only film in the video player was an instructional video on mortgages.

As the day wore on Sam started to feel, in a strange way, like the girl behind the curtain at hospital. Locked away behind her plastic screen. Under the fluorescent lights his skin even looked pallid and yellow like hers. And it didn't help that everyone seemed to be acting as though they thought he might infect them—nervously recoiling whenever he emerged to use the toilet, stepping out of his way as though they thought he might bite.

The only person who actually spoke to him—like he was a human being, and not some lifeless ghoul haunting the back room—was Roger. He was his mother's new friend—at least, that was how she introduced him. They dropped by for their lunch break, Roger eating a salad from a styrofoam container, his mother a sandwich and slice of carrot cake. Sam had lukewarm soup and yoghurt. Roger was tall and broad-shouldered, with dark skin, a beard and long legs. He seemed nervous, but not like everyone else. Rather than ignoring Sam, or smiling while avoiding his eyes, he asked him lots of questions. What was his favourite subject at school? English? Maths? Science? He nodded at history. What sports did he play? He nodded at soccer, shrugged a little at cricket. What TV shows did he like?

sign

He wrote *Star Trek* on his mother's brown paper bag. And Roger would always reply. He was horrible with history; his memory was terrible. He used to play soccer too, when he was younger; he was goalie. And even though he hadn't watched *Star Trek*, he liked the first movie—the one Sam found boring. After a while, it almost seemed like Roger was trying to impress him. And when he and Sam's mother gathered up their rubbish and left to head back to work, Roger said he hoped to catch up again soon.

Having not brought his homework with him, Sam spent much of the afternoon reading through the new *Choose Your Own Adventure* book his mother had bought him. It was a tale about searching for an underground kingdom, and as he scanned its pages, reading ahead while keeping his fingers threaded into the decision points he had left behind, he eventually followed each narrative to its often grisly end. Most times the main character—the *you*—seemed to die in some spectacular fashion: frozen to death, killed in raging rapids, thrown into lava, shot into space, choked on poison gas, sucked into a black hole, lost on an icy tundra . . . There appeared to be almost no way out, and even the 'good' endings frequently involved giving up, or getting stranded under the earth's surface forever.

The only other thing he had to look at was a booklet on learning sign language. It was one of the information pamphlets Tracey had given him, alongside the phone numbers for some local support groups. For most of the day he avoided looking at it, but after reading about himself getting eaten by mysterious spider creatures for the third time, he fished it from his bag and started flicking through.

There were squares showing how to perform simple words and letters, with cartoons of grey-skinned figures standing stiff and expressionless. In some drawings their fingers seemed to be hooked into claws, in others flattened or balled into fists. They were often surrounded by lines that denoted movement in vague, confusing ways.

The alphabet in particular was a jumbled mess. Not even faces, just diagrams of fingers interlocked, crisscrossed or layered over one another, seemingly at random. There were circular shapes, and pointing at certain spots, and one looked like calling for a timeout. Even the letters he had practised with Tracey didn't look right. The letter 'P' at least resembled a 'P'— sort of—but he was pretty sure he was using the wrong hands, or doing it the wrong way around, as he stared at his reflection in the switched-off television, stretched in its convex screen.

He felt his breath start to quicken again.

He gave up. Shoved it aside. He stared down at his hands, two fists that had slackened into red clumps, prickled with sweat. It was impossible. He'd never remember it all.

He'd fail.

Already exhausted, sore, and with the stitches in his throat tasting even more like old yoghurt and chalk, Sam tried to sleep under the table for a couple of hours. The churning of the office just beyond the wall kept him awake; its chatter and laughter and footsteps were giving him a headache. Eventually he turned the television on and switched it to a channel of pure static, hating himself for liking the way it filled his head with a soothing nothingness.

11

His first day back at school, Sam was moved to the front of the classroom. His new desk, a large wooden side table that used to hold a fish tank, was twice as big as anyone else's. It was decided that he needed special facilities, and so the computer that usually sat at the back of the room, the machine everyone took turns playing *Where in the World Is Carmen Sandiego?* on at recess, was moved beside him. Its fat green face buzzed ceaselessly in the corner of his vision, cursor blinking, expectant, waiting for him to type something worthy to be seen. Sam tried to keep away from its keyboard as much as he could, because every time his fingers neared the keys his teacher would gravitate towards him, eyebrows raised expectantly.

At least sitting up the front meant that people weren't constantly staring at his neck. The bandages were mostly gone, but he still wore a patch around the incision, and a velcro strap held his vent in place. In particular, his friend Paul, who used to sit next to him at the back of the room, and with whom Sam played Battleship in the blank pages of their workbooks, seemed unable to stop staring. At recess Paul kept asking him if it hurt when he ate. During lunch, Susan Pally asked him if he had to drink through the hole now, while her gaggle of friends looked on, curious. In the bathroom, where Sam waited in a stall for the bell for class to ring, he heard a couple of fourth-graders talking about the kid who had come back to school after having his throat hacked open with a butcher's knife.

The next day Sam wore a loose skivvy under his school uniform, letting his neck heat up with every exhale into its material.

As the weeks wore on, the novelty of his situation faded. Although his classmates remained reluctant to be partnered with him for group activities, they scrutinised him less, and seemed more perplexed by the new vice-principal, who had only one arm. Paul went back to drawing little stick-figure action scenes with him in their notebooks at the library, and they would still play handball and share soggy meat pies with too much sauce at lunch. Still, Sam still felt lonelier than he could ever remember being, surrounded by a room full of noise with only the clatter of his keyboard to pronounce himself over the din.

12

At the beginning of spring Sam's mother revealed she was dating. Her boyfriend was Roger, the friendly man who had eaten lunch with Sam and his mother at the bank, but it was a few months before either Katie met him or Sam saw him in person again. For the longest time he was just the man with the beard they would watch through the lounge-room window, driving off in his silver car as their mother waved goodbye from the footpath. One day their mother had a new necklace— from Roger, she said. Most evenings she'd spend half an hour on the phone, laughing. Twice he sent flowers to the house.

Dettie hated him.

'The ink,' she said one night while babysitting, 'is not even dry on those divorce papers she sent your daddy, and there she is, out gallivanting around.'

Dettie was washing up as she said it, and the shudder that shook through her arms with each word was so ferocious, Sam worried she might smash the dishes on the drip tray.

'I mean—what would *he* think?'

As he stood beside her, wiping mugs dry with his tea towel, he watched her reflection in the kitchen window.

'One day,' she said, 'you kids are going to go to Perth to be with your father again. And all this nonsense—dating strange men, children getting confused, unfaithfulness—will be put to an end. Once and for all. You mark my words.'

Dettie had never remarried, and as Sam stared up at her image, paled in the glass, watching her take each slow, deep breath, he thought of the photo she kept of her husband—crumpled and sticky-taped around the edges—tucked in the bottom of her handbag.

Seething for the rest of the night, Dettie sat in the kitchen, hunched over endless cups of tea, asking Sam and Katie to keep the television down in the next room. When the sound of their mother's keys finally jangled on the other side of the door, Dettie forced a tight smile, woke Katie, who had fallen asleep on the couch, and led the children into the hall to greet her.

'How was your night, Joanne?' Dettie asked, tightening her fingers on Sam's shoulder.

'Oh, Lord!' His mother was startled. Clicking the door shut quietly behind her, she entered, setting her handbag down by the phone.

'It's so late,' she whispered, kneeling down to kiss Sam and Katie each on the cheek. 'What are you two still doing up?'

'They wanted to see their mother,' Dettie said, pulling them both firmly against her belly.

Unfastening a clip in her hair, their mother sighed and brushed past them into the kitchen. 'Well, they've seen me now, Dettie. Thank you.' She dropped her keys in the fruit bowl and ran herself a glass of water. 'But come on, you two. It's late.

And you both look exhausted. Run on to bed. I'll be there in a minute.'

Katie had barely opened her eyes the whole time. She turned robotically and clumped off towards her room. As Sam wandered into the hall, he saw Dettie, still glaring at his mother as she sipped her water. He saw her lean over to ask in a hushed tone, 'Joanne, have you been drinking?'

'Dettie.' Sam's mother's voice hardened. '*Enough*. For heaven's sake.'

As he passed his mother's bedroom Sam could just make out, lit softly by the streetlight through the window, an old photograph of his father still hanging on the wall. His father's face looked down over his mother's dressing table. He grinned at the camera, head tilted, holding up a newborn Katie in his arms to show her off. Sam wondered what indeed his father *would* think. Then he wondered where he even *was*. Or whether he thought about them at all. His father, frozen in time, stretched his crooked smile.

13

His shorts were sticking to the sweat on the backs of his legs. As he peeled the material away with one hand, Sam used the other to flap the bottom of his shirt, trying to waft some air up onto his chest. There was no breeze at all, and the sun felt moist and heavy on his skin. Flies crawled on his shoulders, getting in his eyes, and they kept settling back on his hair whenever he swiped them away. He was out on the wing. He hadn't played wing in a long time. Before his voice had gone, the coach usually put him in the centre, on the attack, leading the ball up to the goal; but now he stood waiting, watching the ball being passed in the distance.

The trees lining the soccer field were drooping and still, and he could see Katie, his mother and Dettie all standing together in the shade. Roger was there too, wearing a wide-brimmed hat and sandals with long socks. He seemed flabbier than Sam remembered, his polo shirt pulling tight across his chest and around his belly. When he wasn't clapping he would rest his hands in the little valley above his belly. This was Roger's first outing with the whole family.

sign

Roger had arrived early to attend the welcome-back speech the coach delivered to Sam before the game. He was even planning to stay after the match for the celebratory sponge cake and lollies that were softening on a fold-out card table near the car park. When the coach called Sam 'brave' and insisted everyone shake his hand, Roger had clapped louder than anyone else. Now he and Katie were laughing about something together over on the sideline, and Sam couldn't tell if it was his sister's smile, or Roger's arm on their mother's shoulder that was making Dettie so mad. She was standing back from their conversation, shaking her head, sipping sharply from a briskly of water.

For most of the first half of the game, kids on both teams had been nervous whenever Sam was near them. If the ball came in his direction the players would peel away, keeping their distance. Once, when he'd actually gotten his foot on the ball, the opposition's defender just let him take it. He'd stopped chasing, pretending to kneel and adjust his skin guard under his sock while Sam kicked the ball on to a teammate who wasn't even asking for the pass. In the second half, people were starting to relax, even if he still felt them slowing their pace around him, tentative, as though he were breakable.

There was shouting, and a low thump sounded in the distance. Suddenly, the ball was on its way back up the field. A loose kick had sent it tumbling and leaping across the turf. Two of the other team's players were following it, trying to match its pace, but Sam was closer. It was coming towards him, unguarded, crossing most of the field. Both teams were facing his way. Unlike before, this time someone was yelling at him, telling him to go for it.

He ran, startling the flies crawling on his cheeks. At first he could hear his mother's cheering through the air rushing in his ears, but soon it was just the sound of his feet thudding on the grass, the suck and wheeze of his stoma. He was already puffed. Ahead, the ball had slowed, crawling to a stop, and somehow the other two players had drawn closer. He held his breath and tried to push harder, but the taller of the two was there already, hooking his foot around the ball and flicking it back down the ground.

Sam eased off—they were gone already. He let his legs slacken to a heavy jog. He was wheezing, feeling the pound of his heart in his neck. His belly was tight. He stood, gasping, trying not to appear too winded while everyone watched.

His calves hadn't sprung the way he remembered. Instead it seemed like he was landing harder on his ankles, heavier than before. With all the radiation, the medicine, the trips to the hospital, it had been months—almost a year—since he'd played a real game, and now his body felt completely different. Not his own. He was actually thinner than before, but his speed was gone. Now everything felt like lead.

On the sideline, his mother was still clapping, bobbing up and down on her tiptoes. She'd been so excited when Sam had agreed to rejoin the team that he'd found her ironing his uniform in the middle of the lounge room a week before the game. She'd even pressed his long socks and scrubbed the dried dirt from the edges of his cleats. Now she was yelling out encouragement, even though everyone else was watching the ball being passed around the goal at the other end of the field. Roger was nodding, giving him a thumbs up, but the pitying expression behind his smile made Sam look back down at the grass.

sign

Soccer had become another of the many things that felt unnatural now. Like watching Katie sing along to the radio, or the way he heard someone else's voice in his head when he read to himself. Or how at school his teacher would only ask him to answer questions once she'd knelt beside him, blinking patiently while he typed his answer onto the computer screen. He could picture her face perfectly, nodding, wide-eyed, staring at him, just like Roger was now, over by his mother. Trying to be friendly. Smiling. He was tired of everyone smiling. Simpering. He was tired of feeling clumsy and out of place in his own skin.

There was another shout down the field, and again the pounding of feet. One of the players on Sam's team, the captain, had broken away with the ball and was heading in his direction. Everyone else was following, shouting. Sam was completely in the open. He waved, but the captain pretended not to see, dipping his head and pushing on. Behind him was a shorter kid with a flat nose whom Sam had seen at the speech before the game. Then, he'd been clearing his throat loudly, continually spitting into the dirt; now he was gaining, stretching out one leg as he ran, prodding at the ball. Sam waved harder, jumping slightly as he jogged into a better line. From his angle the goal was open. The goalkeeper hadn't been paying much attention to him the whole game. Sam could feel the muscles in his throat tighten, wanting to call out. He could see the short kid nudging closer to the ball.

With a swift flick, the ball was clipped out of the captain's control and the short kid spun around to meet it. Glancing over his shoulder, he smirked quickly at Sam, sizing him up as no threat, then turned back towards the rest of the players. Sam felt his face flush. He sprinted forward, following. He ignored the ache in his chest, pumping his burning legs until he caught up with the short kid, drawing level beside him. He seemed to need two steps for the other kid's one, and he tasted the sweat beading off his face, but he blocked it all out. All he could think about was the short kid's smug little grin. For a moment, all the other people on the field, everyone else's tender half-smiles, all their polite but sad nodding, all their pity, faded away. He was fired up, focused on that cocky smirk, and he ran.

The ball leapt between the kid's ankles as he and Sam wove side by side through the other players. Every time the ball tumbled just beyond the kid's reach, Sam's heart leapt until he saw him catch up to it again. Sam was inching closer. Stretching out his leg. Trying to get his shoe onto the ball. The short kid's elbows were digging at his ribs. Their shins whipped close together. Sam could hear the kid's grunting as he sucked at the air. The kid was tiring. He was slowing.

Suddenly, something was tugging on Sam's neck. Pulling. It was his collar. The kid had grabbed his shirt, twisting it in his fist, yanking it downward. And just as Sam felt himself pitching forward, aware he was still running but feeling everything tipping over in slow motion, the short kid with the flat nose hooked his foot in front of Sam's, and took his legs out from underneath him.

Sam tripped, tumbling forward into the dirt, his arms collapsing limply underneath him, his legs twisting. On the way down someone's knee had clipped his back. As he tried to curl into the fall, he managed to twist his ankle against his other calf. Stunned and winded, he lay for a moment with his ear pressed into the ground, hearing the clump of feet passing by, clearer through the earth. A whistle blew.

Katie was shouting in the distance. There was laughter. The short kid had run on, tried for a goal and missed.

Sam couldn't feel the sting of anything yet. His body was numb, but there was an ache creeping slowly into his bones. Sitting up, he checked himself over. His face had dug into the grass, collecting a mouthful of soil. His chin was scraped and his elbows were bleeding and stained green. The collar of his shirt was torn. His vent, miraculously, was still in place—even if his neck burned with pain. Players from both teams milled around, keeping their distance, but peering down at him. Somewhere, Sam's coach was yelling for a penalty.

The referee jogged over, holding his hat in one hand as he wiped his forehead. He parted the players, taking the ball from one of them, and knelt down by Sam's side.

'How are you doing, mate? You all right?'

Sam nodded, wheezing. His head throbbed behind his eyes, but beneath the grimace he was smiling.

The kid had just smashed him down. He'd fouled Sam like he would have anyone else. Dirty and unfair. He wasn't afraid he'd break him or knock his windpipe out. He'd just grabbed and thrown him over. Sam ached, but the thrill of it coursed through his whole body. He felt great. Finally he was just like everyone else again. They didn't have to be so timid around him anymore.

The referee nodded, slipping his hand under his arm to help him up. 'Did you trip?' he said. 'Did you slip over?'

Sam shook his head. He pointed down at his legs, and tugged on his collar to show the rip.

'Fair enough. Just be careful where you're going, mate. Don't overdo it. We don't have an ambulance here.'

Gesturing at the upturned dirt, Sam tried miming the fall, but the referee just smiled at him sympathetically, petting his shoulder, then jogged away, tossing the ball to the opposing team's captain.

The other players broke apart too and ran back to their positions. No one was arguing. Nobody had seen what happened. Even the kids on his team were either shaking their heads at him or shooting awkward, reassuring looks as if to say they didn't blame him. Sam's arms were heavy and tired. His chin was starting to hurt. The excitement of being fouled faded away. He spat dirt from between his teeth.

Sam looked over at his mother on the sideline. She was wiping tears from her eyes while Roger stood beside her, still pumping his thumbs in the air. A strange sensation crept over him. It was probably the numbness slowly fading from his body, or the slick feeling of sweat cooling his skin, but suddenly it felt as if his body wasn't his, like it was some kind of shell. Beneath layers of grime and already crusting mud, in a uniform that hung baggier on his body than it ever had before, he felt, he realised, as if he were wearing a mask. Or that he was trapped behind one. There was the Sam that everyone around him apparently saw: the one in the hospital gown, meek and tender, still attached to tubes and hobbling silently in place. The Sam who belonged on that soccer field—the goal attack who used to fit into his loose guernsey; who could scamper around the opposition with the ball—that Sam seemed to be gone. Either hidden under the layers of whoever he was now, gone from the field entirely.

The only things that seemed to be his now were the ache in his lungs and the burning at the base of his neck. Those, he knew, were his alone.

Somewhere, a whistle blew.

14

That night Roger came over for dinner. It was the first time he had ever been inside the house. Every room had already been thoroughly tidied, but even so, as they sat together on the lounges, their mother frequently leapt up from her seat to nervously adjust a picture or flatten a rug or straighten the magazines on the coffee table. Roger didn't seem to mind the interruptions. He just smiled at her as she circled the room, still talking, lightly petting her knee whenever she sat back down. Sam wondered, watching his mother fidget with her dress, if it was Roger's touch that kept making her stand back up.

Dettie was still in the kitchen. She had decided she wanted to cook, and had spent most of the day getting everything ready. Katie had asked to help, and together they had set out all the tableware, folded each cloth napkin, and arranged flowers in a vase in the centre of the table. There was a pie still baking in the oven, and Katie had gathered the apples to make it from the tree in the backyard. She'd carried them inside suspended in the front of her skirt, like a hammock, and Dettie had let her wash and peel them over the sink while she was rolling out the pie crust. The two of them had spent the whole afternoon weaving around each other as if they were dancing, portioning out handfuls of chopped apple, getting covered in flour and giggling.

Dettie had made spaghetti, and Sam had watched her assembling the meatballs, rolling each slimy mass between her fingers, shaping them into perfect spheres and measuring out the spaces between them on the oven tray with her thumb. And as he looked in at her now, still fussing at the stove, the meatballs bubbling and spitting in their pan of tomato sauce, he suddenly remembered that spaghetti and meatballs had always been his father's favourite meal. They would have it on special occasions. A clear image of his father surfaced in his mind. He was sitting at the head of the table, his elbows propped on the wood, shaving portions of cheese over his plate. Grinding pepper. Sam went on trying to remember more, but his concentration was broken when Roger laughed at something Katie had said. In the kitchen Dettie kept stirring her pasta around in its pot.

No one else seemed to recall this about Sam's father, or at least nobody mentioned it, as they all took their places at the table to eat. Sam's mother even leant extravagantly over her plate to breathe in the aroma.

'Mmm, this is wonderful, Dettie,' she said, but there was something in the look she flashed across the table. 'It smells delicious.' She turned to touch Roger's arm as he was adjusting himself on his seat. 'Didn't I tell you she was marvellous?'

Roger sat up slightly, nodding across the table at Dettie. 'Absolutely fantastic,' he said.

'Well, don't forget our little Katie.' Dettie put her arm around her. 'She's been my helper today.'

When everyone turned to give their congratulations, Katie stretched so high she was almost standing in her seat.

'My, yes. We are getting special treatment,' their mother said. 'Sam and Roger and I will have to do this more often.'

Dettie's face pulled tight. She waved across the food and told everyone to start in before it got cold.

Sam took a large gulp of his juice, liking the way the sugar tightened his throat a little as it went down. Katie, meanwhile, had already eaten half a bread roll and was mashing her largest meatball apart with her fork. No one else was moving. Dettie, motionless, was staring across the table, watching their mother, who now sat with both her hands clenched together above her plate. Her eyes were closed, and beside her, Roger's head was bowed. He seemed to be saying grace, mouthing the words to himself, and their mother, though her lips were still, was obviously doing the same. Dettie didn't seem sure how to take the sight. She glanced between the two of them, her palm lying flat across her cutlery, still waiting to pick it up. Sam watched the cheese sweating slowly on his food, collapsing into the sauce.

A moment later Roger whispered, 'Amen,' and exhaled, flapping open his napkin and smoothing it across his lap. When their mother opened her eyes she breathed in and unclasped her hands, straightening her table setting. Dettie kept watch, tapping her fingers softly on the tablecloth.

Roger was glancing around at the food as if seeing it, finally, for the first time. He pulled his plate closer and began cutting a meatball, lifting half of it into his mouth and humming loudly as he chewed. 'Oh. This really is delicious, Dettie.' He chewed with a serious expression, humming again, and wiping the sauce from his lips.

Sam's mother smiled. 'We're lucky to have her around, I say.'

Dettie dropped her gaze to her chest, the knife and fork now tinkling between her fingertips. Slowly, she unfolded her napkin and began grinding pepper across her meal. Katie, who had been watching Dettie since their mother started praying, saw this movement as a signal to go on chewing.

Sam turned his fork around in his spaghetti, watching as each strand slid together, knotting, until it was its own little planet whirling in the middle of his plate, the cheese surrounding it stretched and glistening. Everyone else was concentrating on their food. It was quiet, with only the clinks and scratches of dinnerware.

'I like your skin,' Katie said.

Dettie dropped her knife and fork onto her plate with a clank, huffing loudly. Their mother looked to Roger, biting a grin and offering a tiny shrug. 'Sweetie—' she said, taking Katie's hand. Roger—whom Katie had been talking to—just seemed amused.

'What?' Katie looked around.

'Heavens, girl.' Dettie's posture stiffened even further in her chair.

'It's all right.' Roger leant forward, smiling. 'Thank you very much. I like it too,' he said. 'And I think you have very pretty hair.'

Katie beamed, then, suddenly shy, huddled back down to her food.

Sam, like Katie, wasn't sure what all the fuss had been about. Roger did have nice skin. A smooth, warm cinnamon. When he smiled his whole face seemed to light up, wide and welcoming. Bright teeth beneath his dark, trimmed beard. Soft hair flecked with silver. His high cheekbones shining. He reminded him of the vice-principal, Mr Pauls, who was part-Aboriginal, and always ran the annual Dreamtime festival at school. Perhaps Roger was Aboriginal too. Sam wished he could ask, but suspected that even if he could, the question would probably be met with a similar jolt of surprise.

Everyone was eating again, and Sam heard his mother murmuring something about putting music on. He went back to enjoying the slick sound of his pasta as it twirled and slurped on his fork.

'Hmmm. Now, Dettie. *Dettie*. That's quite an unusual name, isn't it?' Roger said at last, taking another large bite.

Dettie looked up again. 'Do you find it unusual, Roger?' She seemed almost amused, smiling slightly the way she did whenever she caught one of the children in a lie.

'No. No, not unusual,' he said. 'I've just not heard it before. Does it—' He swallowed. 'Does it stand for anything?'

'*Stand* for?'

'Is it short for anything?'

'Bernadette,' their mother said, wiping her mouth. 'Her name is actually Bernadette. But we've always known her as Dettie, haven't we kids?'

Roger was nodding, clutching his cutlery tight. To Sam, no one appeared to be saying anything all that interesting, but Roger's eyebrows were knotted, his forehead creased heavily as though this were all somehow very important.

'Bernadette,' he said. 'That's one of those classic names you don't hear too often anymore. It's nice.'

He smiled at Dettie with food in his mouth, but she was looking away, concentrating on slicing apart her spaghetti. For a moment everything turned quiet again. Katie was finishing her third piece of garlic bread, sucking the salt from her fingers and kicking her legs beneath her chair. Sam was taking bites from his ball of pasta, feeling the strands disentangle and drop down his chin. As he ate, he realised his mother was shooting Dettie long looks across the table. Finally, Dettie sighed.

'So,' she said, slowly. 'Roger.' She nudged the food around on her plate. 'You're religious?'

Roger was taken a little by surprise. He had just cut another rather large mouthful, and took a moment, raising his finger slightly while he chewed.

'Sorry.' He swallowed. 'Um, raised Anglican,' he said, and smiled. 'Joanne says you're very involved in the church yourself?'

'She told you that, did she? Hm.' Dettie's eyes swept the table before she turned back to her food. 'Yes. My husband and I were very active. Very committed.'

Sam thought he heard her voice tighten on the word *husband*.

'So you work at Joanne's bank?' she said.

'For now, yes. I'm an underwriter mostly. Mortgages. Business loans.'

'Hm.'

Roger took a sip of beer. 'I'm hoping to get back into law eventually.'

'So you're a lawyer?' Dettie seemed to chew a little on that sentence.

'I was. For a time. Before I moved. Before the bank. Contract law. Negotiations. Things like that. Very boring to anyone who's not me, I'm sure.'

'Negotiations? What—like divorces?' Her eyes narrowed.

'No. Not really that kind of—' Sam noticed the way Roger's

beard rippled a little whenever he licked the insides of his mouth. 'You know when a business has a lease agreement with the people who own their building?' he said. 'Or when a manager has a contract with the company he works for?'

Dettie was nodding. 'You wrote up contracts, did you?'

'No,' he said. 'Well, I *could*. I did sometimes. But mostly— well, say that the person who'd written the contract, say they wanted to get out of it. They were sick of it. My job was usually to help them do that. To help them find a way.'

Dettie's voice lowered. 'To help them *out* of the contract?'

'Yes.'

'Help them *break* it?'

'Well, not break it, exactly. Find a fault in it. Find a way out. So they didn't have to be stuck in an arrangement that was bad for their business.'

At that, Dettie became oddly quiet. Her lips were pursed and she pushed her plate away untouched, setting her knife and fork aside. As she sat silently, taking little sips from her water, she stared straight down at the tablecloth, ever so slightly shaking her head.

After a few minutes, their mother excused herself and rose from the table, slipping behind Roger into the next room. Everyone sat motionless for a moment, waiting. Sam and Katie looked at each other, confused, until they heard the stereo begin playing the one classical music record they owned. As she squeezed back into the room their mother touched Roger gently on his shoulder.

'You know, you two don't look like each other at all,' he said, as she sat back down. After the quiet, his voice seemed rather loud.

Dettie straightened. 'Pardon?'

'For sisters,' Roger said.

'What on earth?!' Dettie snapped.

Their mother laughed, quickly, like a cough. 'No. No, we're not sisters.'

Dettie refolded her napkin, tightly, and cleared her throat. 'I'm *Donald's* sister,' she said.

Katie looked up at the sound of her father's name. Dettie seemed rather pleased with herself.

'Really?' Roger gestured between the children's mother and aunt. 'Because you seem much closer.'

Their mother swallowed. 'Well, when the children's father—' She stopped and took a breath before she continued. 'When that ended. When he *left* us. Dettie was here. Lucky for us. She was priceless. She helped out. She got the kids to school while I was working. She was there if I needed to talk, or if the children wanted for anything.'

Roger nodded enthusiastically. He sipped from his water and raised his glass to them both. 'Good for you,' he said. 'What a blessing.'

'Well, my own husband had passed on,' Dettie said. 'So I was only too happy to pitch in where I could.'

Their mother looked at her sister-in-law strangely, her mouth slightly ajar, but Dettie stared straight ahead at Roger with a sad smile.

'See, that's wonderful,' he said. 'Nothing's more important than family.'

Dettie raised her hand. 'From your mouth to God's ears.'

Sam wasn't sure what that meant, but it seemed to stop the conversation entirely.

15

When Roger got ready to leave at the end of the night, he stood for a moment beside the front door, his jacket draped over one wrist and his other arm extended to shake Sam's hand. As the evening wore on, Sam had realised that he didn't really like the sound of Roger's voice. It was deep and thick, and he always spoke slowly, as though he were trying to explain something very complicated to people unable to understand. It was a tone Sam had noticed most adults using when speaking to him since the operation—although Roger seemed to do it to everyone. But as Sam felt his hand being surrounded by Roger's palm, and as he heard that loud, low voice calling him the 'man of the house', saying it was a pleasure to see him again, he felt larger all of a sudden. Older. There was a warm sensation in his chest, and for the first time since leaving the hospital he didn't see pity in his mother's eyes as she smiled down at him.

The front porch light spilled out onto the road. As his mother walked Roger to his car, their bodies were yellowed beneath the glare. Katie had fallen asleep on the couch, and Dettie woke her gently, ushering the children to their rooms to get ready for bed. Katie slipped straight under her covers, not bothering to change out of her clothes, but as Sam washed his face in the bathroom and began brushing his teeth, he could hear through the window the murmur of voices echoing up the driveway. Finally, the sound of an engine starting filled the empty street, and when the noise had faded away the front door eased open again and pulled shut.

'So you've said your goodbyes?' Dettie was whispering, but her voice carried up the hall.

'Yes. Both got early mornings tomorrow. He said to say thanks again.' Sam could tell by the way his mother's voice trailed off that there was something else she wanted to say. 'Are the children in bed?' she asked.

Dettie grunted. 'Just settling down now. Too much excitement for one day.'

Their voices rose as they walked through to the dining room. Sam went on brushing slowly so that he could still hear, spitting quietly into the sink.

'I think that went rather well,' his mother was saying. There was a soft clatter of dishes and cutlery as they began clearing the table. 'Roger loved the children. Obviously. And I think they took a liking to him.'

Dettie cleared her throat. She was quiet.

'Everyone—I think everyone got on quite well.' Over the tinkle of empty glasses, Sam could hear that same tone in his mother's voice—she was getting ready to say something. 'Everyone was comfortable. They enjoyed themselves, I think.' She was in the kitchen now, and it was only because the house was so quiet, the street outside so empty, that Sam could still listen in. 'It got us talking,' she said. 'Roger and I. We started thinking that—well, since it went so nicely—in a week or so we might take the next step.'

'Next step? *What* next step?' Dettie's voice sharpened.

'Well, we just thought . . .' Sam's mother took a breath. 'We thought it might be good for the children if we spend some time over there. At Roger's house.' There was a clunk that sounded like pots being stacked. 'So we can all get more comfortable. All together. Next Friday, we were thinking.'

By now Sam was standing by the bathroom door, peering out, toothpaste dribbling from his mouth onto his hand. He could see shadows from the kitchen cast against the hallway wall, but they were still.

He heard his aunt exhale. 'I don't want to go over to his house, Joanne,' she said. 'I don't want to, and I won't.'

'That's fine. That's—that's actually okay. We were thinking it might be a good idea if the children and I went by ourselves. We thought we'd give them some real one-on-one time.'

Sam's mouth was filled with paste and saliva. He wanted to spit again, but was afraid it would break the silence. He knew he was eavesdropping—that he shouldn't be doing it—but lately it seemed he was always overhearing things. Suddenly, he had a faint recollection of listening in on his mother and aunt like this once before. Was it before his operation? What was it they'd been talking about? His father? Soup?

'The children? Over to Roger—' Dettie stammered. 'What, alone?'

'Not *alone*. I'm going to be there.'

'But—why? What purpose—' Even from the next room Sam could make out her indignant panting. He could picture her wringing her hands. 'Does he not want to come here anymore?

Is that it? Is this not good enough? Because this is where you *live*. Where the children—' She was talking faster now. Almost hiccoughing. 'Why do the children have to go there? To him? All that unnecessary hassle. Fuss. Why not have him come here? This is *their* place. Where they feel comfortable.'

'It's really not a big thing, Dettie. Really. We just want everyone to relax. To get used to one another.'

Dettie didn't respond. There was a quick tapping, a fingernail on a table, but as Sam looked on, the two shadows stayed motionless on the wall. No one was speaking. From the next room he thought he heard the squeak of Katie turning in bed. Eventually, Dettie cleared her throat and there was a tinkle of glasses. The shadows moved. They slipped apart, and somebody started the kitchen tap running.

Taking advantage of the noise, Sam turned on the bathroom faucet softly, rinsed his mouth and spat.

'I mean, it's perfectly natural,' he heard his mother saying. 'Would it be so bad if—'

'So *this* is who you've been spending your time with? Who you've been having your *children* spend time with?' Dettie said.

'What? Roger? What's wrong with Roger? Everyone had a lovely night.'

'A lawyer, is he?'

His mother took a moment to reply. 'Yes,' she said. 'He was a lawyer. What's your point?'

'And all the drinking. All night. The bottle never left his hand.'

'He had *two beers*, Dettie. What are you on about?'

'You know what they're like.'

The word *they* hung in the air a moment. When his mother next spoke her voice was firm. Slow.

'Know what *who* is like?' she said. 'Lawyers?'

'Don't be so naive. You know full well what he is. Black as the ace of—'

A stack of plates slammed down on the table.

'No! You are unbelievable. How dare you.'

'Oh, don't get all—I'm just saying, there are certain realities, Joanne. *Cultural* differences. Sensitivities.'

'No. That is appalling. *No*, Dettie.'

'It's being realistic. When I was a girl my father had a farmhand—'

'Shut. Your. Mouth. You are not poisoning my children's minds with that kind of disgusting, ignorant—'

'I've called Donald.'

Dettie had lowered her voice, but it was as if she had shouted for quiet. The house was suddenly still. As soon as Sam had heard his father's name he'd leapt back over to the door. For a moment, as he pressed his ear closer, wiping his mouth on his wrist, there was nothing. He could feel the silence stretch out, picture his mother's face, her mouth ajar.

'You what? You—when?' she said. He saw a shadow shift. 'What in God's name—why, Dettie? *Why* would you do that?'

'I called yesterday. I think he has a right to know who his children are spending their time with, Joanne.'

'No. No, he *doesn't*, Dettie.' His mother's voice was fierce. 'He *doesn't* have the right.'

Sam heard his aunt sniff. She was rattling a handful of cutlery. 'Well, he's not very impressed.'

'Do you think I give a damn what that man—'

'He's your husband, Joanne. He's your children's—'

'It's none of his business! It's none of *your* business! You are so far out of—'

'When I lost my Ted—'

'Oh, don't start with all that.'

Dettie exhaled. Sam heard water swishing. 'Call Donald, Joanne. Call your husband. Talk to him.'

'That is enough!' There was a crash as plates and pans scattered, something rattled against glass. In the quiet of the house, the sudden noise sounded like a roar. 'I am *not* having this conversation again.' His mother was talking slowly. 'Your behaviour.' She sighed. Loudly. 'I don't even know where to begin.'

'I'm just—'

'*Goodnight*, Dettie. Go home.'

There was a moment's silence before a clatter of dishes echoed in the sink and his mother's shadow swept down the hallway, through to her room, and slammed the door.

16

The following morning the windows of the house were propped open, and the summer breeze that slipped through the kitchen was so moist it left a faint chill in its wake. The radio was on but turned down to a metallic patter. Dettie had not gone home and was finishing up breakfast with the children, refilling their juice glasses. Sam's mother walked in from the hallway, fixing her hair. As she passed him the comics section of the newspaper she touched both him and his sister on their shoulders and squeezed. Sam noticed the way she kept glancing at Dettie, and he could tell that his aunt was intentionally avoiding her gaze.

'Good morning.' His mother crossed to the refrigerator and grabbed a tub of yoghurt. 'How did everyone sleep?'

Katie nodded and slurped up another spoonful of milk from her bowl. Sam shrugged.

'Very well, thank you,' Dettie said, scraping a sliver of margarine over her toast. Sam knew she was lying. Her eyes were puffy and she had been massaging a crick in her neck since she'd sat down to eat. She was still wearing the same clothes as the night before, her brown skirt and grey blouse both crumpled, and when Sam had emerged from his room there'd been a blanket and her knitted cardigan folded on the arm of the couch.

Their mother checked the water in the kettle, and measured a scoop of instant coffee into her travel mug. 'Sam, Katie, I was very proud of you both last night,' she said. 'You were really well behaved. Roger said he'd never met two nicer children.'

Dettie rolled her eyes, her lips pursed, pushing her plate aside until it clicked against her teacup.

When the kettle boiled, their mother poured hot water into her mug, stirring it in. 'Which reminds me,' she said, sucking her spoon clean. 'Did I ever tell you kids about Roger's house?' She tucked the coffee jar back on its shelf. 'He has a pool. His own pool. He said you kids are welcome to try it out some time. And Katie, did Roger mention last night that he has two cats?'

Katie's eyes widened.

Their mother smiled, screwing the lid onto her mug. 'Well, if you like the sound of that,' she said, 'after work, I've got a big surprise for you.'

Dettie exhaled loudly. She took a bite from a triangle of Vegemite toast and examined the marks left by her teeth, turning it in her thin fingers.

'Honestly, I don't understand you, Dettie,' their mother said, setting down her drink on the counter. 'I would have thought you'd be happy about all this. If everything works well, we won't have to go out so much. See? I won't have to lump the kids on you all the time.'

Dettie rose, crossed the floor and dropped the rest of her breakfast in the plastic bag hanging under the sink. Turning, she dusted off her hands and adjusted her wedding ring. 'It seems to me you've already made up your mind, Joanne,' she said. 'You've been seeing this fellow for months now. He's sat at your table. Does it really matter what any of us think?'

Sam let the same bite of crust sit in his mouth. Katie wiggled her toes so that her slippers slapped on her heels. Dettie's breath shook.

Their mother was blinking heavily. 'Of course it—' She took a breath. 'I am trying—'

'Oh, I know what you're trying to do,' Dettie turned her back to her and started clattering dirty dishes into the sink, twisting the tap on. 'If you really want my opinion, you should call your husband,' she muttered.

The pipes squalled in the walls and water blasted over the cutlery.

Their mother gathered up her purse, her mug, and her keys from the fruit bowl, and threw a Chapstick into her handbag. 'Oh, I'll call him,' she said. 'Don't you worry. I'll be talking to him today.'

On her way to the door she kissed both Sam and Katie on the forehead. 'Mummy's going to be a little late,' she said. 'Be good. Listen to Dettie. And don't dawdle on your way to school.'

When the front door had closed and their mother was gone, the radio went on chattering, louder in the quiet, and the apple tree in the backyard rustled against the flyscreen.

ROAD

17

There was an hour until school, so Sam helped Katie brush her hair into a ponytail while they watched cartoons together in the lounge room. On the screen, colourful bears shot rainbows out of their bellies, and Katie wiggled excitedly on her cushion. Dettie, meanwhile, fumed. She stood up from her armchair. She sat down. She rose again, looked out the window, then settled back into her seat. She lit a cigarette—something their mother never allowed in the house—and smoked it all the way down, ashing it in her empty teacup. She stared straight ahead, breathing heavily. Sharp, shallow, fast breaths. Sam watched her as he fixed Katie's hair tie in place, remembering his own breathing attack at Tracey's house, wondering what was going on in her mind. Dettie was nodding. She seemed to be working herself up to do something. She smoked a second cigarette. Then a third. Sitting and nodding. Finally she blinked, and the tight expression on her face went slack.

'I've got to make a phone call,' she said, raising herself up again. 'You both wait here until I call you.'

'Can I have a chocolate?' Katie asked.

'Just wait here!' Dettie snapped. She stuffed her cigarettes into her handbag and stomped out into the hallway.

For a moment it was quiet—someone in Katie's cartoon was learning a lesson about forgiveness or something—until Sam heard the thudding of the push-button phone being dialled.

'Hello! Yes! Hello, Joanne!' Dettie called out. 'Now, Joanne, I want to talk about this morning. I was very upset.' She was talking loudly, her voice carrying down the hall as she paced the length of the phone's cord. 'You wanted to talk too? Very good. I'm glad.'

Katie leant closer to the television, trying to hear over what, from Dettie, was almost shouting.

'Oh, you called Donald, did you?'

Both Sam and Katie turned at the sound of their father's name.

'That's wonderful news! I can't wait to tell the children!' Dettie leant into the room, holding the receiver away from her ear, to give them both a big wink. When she saw the children's gaping expressions her face lit up with a smile. She disappeared back into the hall. 'Yes, Joanne, that's *fabulous!* I *knew* you two would work it out!'

Sam's heart was beating fast. Katie was clutching her shoes and socks in front of her, motionless.

Their father?

Their mother and father had talked?

But they never talked.

'Go *now?!*' Dettie was saying. 'Of course! How exciting! What a wonderful idea!'

Sam was tingling with sweat. He stood, but couldn't bring

himself to walk out to Dettie in the hallway. Instead, he watched her shadow shifting on the wall.

'Yes, of course we can go now! All right. That sounds good. See you soon. Bye!'

She slapped the handset down with a clang. The tone of the bell inside the phone reverberated around them all.

'Change of plans,' Dettie said, returning to the room. 'We've got to get moving. We're going on a very exciting trip.'

She ushered them both into their bedrooms to get changed out of their school uniforms and stuff another set of clothes each into plastic bags. Their mother had just called their father, she explained. She'd gotten to work and phoned him up, and once the two of them had spoken for a little while, they realised what a big mistake they had made when they split up. They said right then and there that they wanted to be back together. They wanted the *whole family* back together. As soon as could possibly be.

So everyone was going to Perth.

That was what their mother had just told her. In all the excitement Dettie misspoke, saying that it was their mother who had phoned home, when, of course, Sam knew it was Dettie who had called her, but in any case, it was all being arranged.

'Where's Perth?' Katie asked.

'You'll love it,' Dettie said. 'And we'll be there in no time at all.'

Dettie, Katie and Sam were to leave immediately, in Dettie's car, to get a head start. Their mother would stay behind to fix up a few things—the house, her job, bank accounts—and would be along in a day or two with the moving van.

'Can't we wait for Mummy?'

'Oh, no, dear,' Dettie said. Their mother would be far too busy getting everything done. If they stayed behind it would just delay everything, and their father was desperate to see them both again as soon as possible. He missed them terribly.

His father's face flashed into Sam's mind suddenly, more vivid than it had ever seemed to be. He was going to see him again? He wanted to be with them all? The photograph of him holding Katie, the tape recording of him and Sam singing 'Mary Had a Little Lamb', their mother's wedding ring, which hung on a hook at the front of her jewellery box. It all merged together. Maybe he'd never *really* left. Not forever. Maybe it was just a strange pause while he went to get settled in Perth. That was probably why he hadn't visited or called. He was too busy setting things up. Hoping they would join him.

He knew that Dettie spoke to his father—she said they often phoned each other. They must have been hoping for this the entire time. And now that his mother and father had made up, it was all going to happen. The question of Roger flashed, momentarily, into his mind, but was forgotten in the rush.

Sam barely noticed what he had gathered together—a T-shirt, a change of shorts, a spare vent and the cleaning supplies for his stoma.

'Hurry, hurry, hurry!' Dettie sped through the house clapping her hands. 'We've got to get going! Fast as you can!'

They left the dishes, unwashed, in the sink, stepped over their schoolbags, still packed with books, in the hallway, hastily snatched some snacks from the cupboards, and in minutes they were in the car, snapping their seatbelts on as Dettie frantically searched the rear-vision mirrors, reversing down the driveway. With a quick stop at Dettie's apartment to grab her chequebook and medications, and an even faster visit to the bank, where Sam and Katie waited in the car, they were soon passing through the thinned-out morning traffic, watching commuters in suits and dresses sing along to their radios. After two or three suburbs Sam stopped recognising places he knew, and started wondering, vaguely, if they would ever be back again.

When they turned onto the highway Dettie let out a loud sigh she had apparently been holding for some time. They settled into the overtaking lane and began passing long trucks with rattling mudflaps and cars with pokey caravans attached. The shape of the city faded away behind them. The posted signs began listing towns hundreds of kilometres away. Sun nuzzled on their necks and the road stretched west.

18

As they met a patch of cracked asphalt on the highway, the lolly wrappers rustled on the floor. Sam had been steadily growing nauseous the more the car shuddered over potholes and swept around bends. Outside, crushed foxes and dead kangaroos lay on the side of the road. Katie was watching out the window whenever one slipped by, boosting herself up on her arms.

'Just kick the back of my seat if you get too hot back there, Sammy. I'll open up another air vent,' Dettie said, peering back at him through the rear-vision mirror.

Sam nodded with his mouth open and his forehead rattling on the window. His thumbs were hooked in his shorts, trying to relieve the bloated feeling in his stomach.

'You want me to switch the radio on?'

He didn't respond, so Dettie skimmed through the stations. There were snatches of conversation and squeals of static until finally the car throbbed with a wail of pipe organs and drums. Dettie's foot tapped a beat on the pedal, and the car surged along with the percussion.

sign

They'd been driving for hours now, and as the sun had risen higher in the sky the air had dried out, until the wind blasting through the vents simply pushed the heat around. Dettie's driving was much looser than his mother's, sweeping over rises in the road and gliding heavily around curves. Katie, in the front seat, was fine, but in the back it made Sam's stomach churn.

Katie was still staring outside. 'Why are there bags on the road?'

Dettie tried to hum the melody but didn't know the tune.

'Aunt Dettie?'

A car flashed by, and Dettie complained about people crowding the road.

Katie turned to Sam. 'Why are there bags?'

Even if he hadn't felt so ill, Sam wasn't sure how to convey to her what they were. What they had been when they were alive. He shook his head.

From his position slumped down in his seat, the sky was bigger than Sam had ever seen it. Thin clouds hung like silky scars on the horizon, and birds lapped across it in wide, heavy arcs. The horizon seemed so low—unblocked by buildings or trees—that the undulating hills looked like a great green ocean frozen in place. Sweat dampened his skin, and he tried to position his face beside Dettie's seat to catch the breeze from her vent. Her breath smelt of smoke and the liquorice allsorts she'd been snacking on, and the scent of it, blown back over him, churned in his belly.

A roar of air drowned out the radio as Katie started winding down her window.

'Katie, I told you to leave the window alone,' Dettie snapped, leaning over and clicking her fingers. 'Now put it up. Quick smart.'

'But I'm hot.' Katie waited, still holding on to the handle.

'Look, I'll turn up the fans a bit if you'd like.'

'I want the window down.' Katie's voice was sleepy in the heat. Sam felt the wind whip on the back of his head, cool beneath the sweat in his hair.

'Katie, I said put it up.'

'Why?'

'Do you know how many impurities are in the air out there?' Dettie covered her nose with her wrist. 'How much pollen and car fumes? The insecticides these farmers use? And us travelling at this speed? You could breathe in a bug, or goodness knows what else.' She let out a couple of little coughs, frowning. 'Now I'm tired of explaining myself, just put it up.'

Katie rolled her eyes and puffed out her flushed cheeks. 'It's too hot,' she said, winding up the window slowly, letting the air hiss through a small gap at its top for a few seconds longer. When their aunt glared at her she turned it shut.

Sam's hair fell flat again. He felt wet and queasy. The velcro strap for his vent was already soaked with sweat. Something seemed to be swirling in his chest.

Katie leant towards the air vent, opening her mouth and sucking deeply in and out. She waggled her jaw, watching Dettie from the corner of her eye.

'Will you stop being silly and settle down?'

Katie turned her attention back to the road, stretching up in her seat. 'Aunt Dettie, what are the bags on the side of the road for?'

'Nothing. Never mind.'

'Are they blankets? They look like bags.'

'Don't worry about them.'

sign

'But why?'

'It doesn't matter.'

They rumbled on, passing several fields dotted with grazing cattle, a vineyard and a couple of dams so low they looked like craters dotted with chocolate milk. The occasional house, nestled beneath the shade of spreading gum trees, vibrated by.

'How long is it to Perth?' Katie sat up on her hands, scanning the road ahead, her face knotted with concentration.

It was as though Dettie had not heard her. She pursed her lips and pushed a little harder on the accelerator.

Katie pointed to another brown lump approaching them along the road.

'That one looks like—' She leant forward, pressing her face to the glass. 'What are they?' He voice quivered slightly. 'Are they blankets?' she said again, already clearly certain that they were not.

Dettie exhaled. 'They're not blankets,' she said, and lowered the volume of the radio.

19

The engine ticked as it cooled. Cars swept by along the road. Sam's legs were heavy and his shoes scraped in the dust and loose gravel. Waves of heat rippled from the ground. He shuffled closer to his aunt and sister. They were already standing over the lump of matted fur, looking down at it, and Katie shook, weeping. The sight of the animal, its brown mass, was too much for Sam to take in all at once. His mind seemed to break it apart into pieces.

Dettie was waving flies away from her face. She bowed her head, took both children by the shoulder, and hugged them to her hips. 'This, Sammy, is what I was always talking about. You remember? What lies on the other side of that fight to survive. When you give up.'

Flies were squabbling in its baked blood.

Katie choked, wiping her nose on her sleeve.

'Oh, now don't be upset, little one,' Dettie said. 'This is just what happens out here. Out in the wild.'

Spikes of matted fur were encrusted with dirt.

'It's dangerous. That's why we all have to stick together. Keep each other safe.'

Strips of skin, like carpet, hung back from its pearly muscle.

'Aw. Don't feel bad. See how peaceful he is? So still? You'd almost think he was sleeping.'

Her thumb was burrowed into his shoulder, but Sam was only vaguely aware of it. He wondered what his aunt was even talking about. Peaceful? Giving up? It had obviously been hit by a car. Its chest was crushed and bloodied by the impact. Its front paws were twisted. It didn't look at peace. It hadn't just laid down on the road and *decided* to die. A tingling feeling was crawling up his skin. The animal's mouth was torn up in a ragged sneer.

'But that's not us,' Dettie was saying. 'We've got a long trip, and we've got each other, and we're not going to let anything stop us. Are we?'

An exposed pupil bulged through its rubbery eyelid. Light-headed, Sam leant his face against his aunt's blouse and inhaled her thick scent of smoke. Blotchy ripples drifted across his vision. A fly crept across the animal's eyeball.

Katie howled.

Dettie's voice was fading to a murmur. 'We can all pray for him if it'll make you feel better.'

Ants, swarms of them, rippled beneath it on the gravel. At first Sam thought it was a shadow, but they surged, dark and liquid. He could feel them. It was as though they were covering his own body, crawling, swirling. The twisted head. Its rigid, bent arms. The long motionless tail. The stench. All of it swarmed over him at once. It was roadkill—or that's what it was now. Before, it had been a kangaroo. Now it wasn't. Now he was staring down at it, rotting on the side of the road.

The spit in Sam's mouth went slack. His sight blackened and the oxygen drained from his head.

20

Standing bare-chested in the women's toilet, Sam watched the door as Dettie scrubbed cold water into his T-shirt. He could smell old urine, his own vomit, and the wet lemon towelette she'd used to wipe his lips. Dettie's hands knifed through the water, wringing out the material so hard that the neckline stretched. A sliver of yellow soap was smeared in her palm, excreting feeble bubbles. 'How are you feeling now, Sammy? A little better?'

He flinched as a gust of wind entered from the open ice freezer outside.

'You let me know if you feel sick again. There's an ice-cream container in the car if you need it.'

Each breath was cold, straight through his neck into his belly. His hands shook.

'This doesn't look like it's coming out. I might—'As she spoke the tap gouged her ring finger, spitting red into the porcelain bowl and over his T-shirt. 'Blast it!' she yelped, and sucked the cut, taking soapsuds into her mouth.

Snatching his T-shirt from the sink, she led Sam back through the door and out to the car, leaving behind a trail of dribbling water. 'We may as well get you something else to wear,' she said, and tossed it over the bonnet.

Dettie popped the boot and fished through their spare clothing.

'Oh, blast!' she said again.

One of the juice boxes they had packed had been crushed and leaked all through the plastic bags. It had left a sticky, pulpy purple mess, its sweet aroma soured by the heat.

Katie rolled down her window. 'We should have packed more,' she said.

Dettie dropped the bag onto the ground and pulled out a first-aid kit from beside the spare tyre. 'Katie, I said that your mother is going to be bringing all your clothes with her when she comes.'

'When can we see Mummy?'

'When we get there.' Dettie picked through bandages and ointment. 'We've discussed all this. We're going on ahead. She's going to meet us.'

'How long is it to Perth?'

'Katie, will you stop holding me up?' Dettie's thumb was pressed to the cut to stop the bleeding. 'I have to get your brother a new shirt or he's going to burn to a crisp. Is that what you want?'

She elbowed the boot closed, a bandaid curled in her fingers, and led Sam inside to the petrol-station counter. The news on the radio was warning of a strict fire ban. The man at the register hadn't shaved. His black stubble was flecked with silver. His hair was white. Sam noticed his bloodshot eye as he punched in their bill. 'That'll be seventeen forty-eight, darlin'.'

He smiled at the top of Dettie's head as she fished in her purse for change. When he noticed Sam behind her, he nodded.

Suddenly, Sam realised he wasn't wearing a shirt and crossed his arms over his chest. The muscles in his legs tightened up. There were goosepimples standing out on his skin, bubbled and hard under his fingertips.

The shopkeeper's eyes flickered to Sam's neck. The smile drained from his face. It was a gesture that Sam had become familiar with: the whip of a stranger's face from curiosity to alarm. Each time, at first, people thought his vent was some kind of strange necklace; only then would the shock register. The shopkeeper dipped his head as Dettie counted coins into his palm. The radio trumpeted out of its news report and into the weather.

Newly self-conscious, Sam wandered out of view to the magazines. Most had women in bathing suits arched over motorbikes or kneeling stiffly on rugs. On the shelf behind them were the comic books. He fanned them out and flicked through the covers. There were dog-eared copies of *Richie Rich* and several different faded *Phantoms*. There was a *Mad* magazine, some *Archies* and a digest of reprinted newspaper strips—but no copies of *Batman*. No *Justice League*.

There was one comic that caught his eye. It was called *Tales of Fear*. On the cover a horde of zombies was tearing open a car, exposing the terrified passengers within. He slid it from the rack.

Dettie and the man behind the counter was listening to the weather report sign off. In its place a syrupy country song unsettled the store with a nasal twang.

'Fires are a worry,' the shopkeeper was saying. He dug his thumb in his one red eye and rubbed. 'You heard about all that?

They reckon it's kids. Bloody hooligans. Should round 'em up to be shot.'

Dettie hummed and snapped shut her purse, still sucking on her finger. 'Do you sell any clothes?' she asked, gesturing towards Sam.

The shopkeeper ambled across to a rotating display of souvenirs tilted in the corner. Dettie followed him over and began spinning the rack past key rings and hats and stuffed koala toys. None had price tags.

'How much for a singlet?' she said.

'Oh, let's see what we can do, darl.' He clicked his tongue and drummed one hand on his thigh. 'How about a fiver?'

The zombies pulled at a woman's yellow hair and bit into her face. She was kicking at them, screeching. The word *Heeelllp!!!* spilled out of the panel, inflated and shuddering. Sam turned the page. Another zombie, in a tattered business suit, had torn a mouthful of flesh from the woman's neck. It swung from his teeth like shreds of torn fabric. It reminded Sam of the dead kangaroo. But drawn like this, colourful and exaggerated, it wasn't scary so much as exciting. The damaged flesh didn't look dry or leathery. Here, even with blood spraying everywhere, the wound was pink and clean. He lifted the comic closer until the colour separated into tiny red dots. He traced each line around the woman's ripped neck, her wide mouth, the dark hollow of the cavity in her throat.

Back outside, Sam pulled on the new singlet and tucked it into his shorts. It was yellow across the shoulders and green on the chest where *Australia* was spelt out in thick white letters. It was snug around his stomach, and he wished it were something with a collar.

sign

Dettie stopped sucking the cut on her finger and wrapped a bandaid around it. Telling the children to wait, in the car, she ducked back into the toilet to rinse the juice out of their clothing, and returned, laying each article on the floor of the boot to dry. She tucked the first-aid kit away in the back of the car, slid into her seat, fastened her seatbelt, and paused with her hand above the ignition. In the phone booth, near the shop, a teenage girl was giggling into the receiver and scribbling on the wall with a pen. Dettie looked at the dashboard. She was staring at the small St Christopher magnet standing on top. The glue beneath his feet was stretched. He was leaning back awkwardly, held up by the windscreen and faded by the sun. Her shoulders tensed, clutching the keys. Waiting. Staring at his lopsided, placid face. Finally, with a huff, she let out the breath she had been holding and turned the ignition.

'We're off!' she said, and the engine kicked to life.

21

Over by the register a fat golden cat sat winking. One beckoning paw swung back and forth in a small robotic motion. It was inched up to the very edge of the countertop alongside a large bowl of complimentary fortune cookies, each wrapped in glittering plastic. Its painted face smiled. Smiled and winked and waved. Sam wondered if it was supposed to be waving goodbye. Back turned to the customers who came in from the street, it instead looked into the restaurant, peering out, one-eyed, over the room, taking in the red decor and the golden trim, the line drawings of mountain villages and yellowed photographs of koi fish. Looking in at the families gathered in circles around their steaming plates, watching over it all. Winking and waving.

Somewhere near the door to the kitchen a tape of Chinese pop songs was playing. The sound was cheery and bright, even if Sam couldn't make out what any of it meant, and every time the waiter entered with new dishes to deliver it was muffled, until the door swung shut.

'Sammy, you've barely touched your dinner there.' Dettie gestured with her knife.

He poked his fork back into his plate of oyster beef, weighing up which bit of curled onion or withered green leaf to try next. He'd actually wanted honey chicken, but Dettie had misinterpreted what he was pointing at on the menu, and he hadn't realised until the meals were delivered and it was too late to correct. Katie had ordered sweet and sour pork, and was now chasing bright pink pieces of carrot around on her plate with a spoon.

Dettie, who seemed wary of anything too unusual, had ordered an omelette, and spent much of her time slicing out anything suspicious before lifting each bite to her mouth.

'Eat up. We've had a long day, but it's going to be even longer tomorrow.'

She sipped from her cup of black tea.

'In fact, that's what I want to talk to you children about,' she said. 'We need to get straight what's going to happen. Okay? Because it's a long way to Perth. A very, very long way. *Days* even.'

'Days?' Katie set down her spoon. Her jaw hung open, her lips stained red.

'Yes. *Days*, Katie. It's going to be very tiring for us all. So we'll all have to be on our best behaviour. We don't want any attitude. No complaining. No getting upset. It's just the three of us, travelling together for days, and if we don't help each other out it's not going to be much fun at all.'

Katie harrumphed and sagged in her chair.

'I'm going to need all your help. But at the end of it we'll be back with your daddy again. Won't that be nice?'

'When's Daddy going to meet us?'

'At Perth, silly. He's got a whole house set up for us. Bedrooms for both you kids. A big backyard. Bigger than your little place in Sydney. My goodness. Houses in Perth? You've never seen anything like it.'

'Is that why he moved there?'

Dettie prodded a piece of grey meat off her fork and into a pile on her serviette. She was shaking her head.

'Well, he got his job, didn't he, sweetie? So he could take care of you. It just took your mummy a little while to see that, that's all.'

'See what?'

'Katie, this really isn't our business. That's Mummy and Daddy's concern. All we need to know is that they've sorted it out—thank goodness. And now it's just like the old days.'

While Dettie was talking it struck Sam, all at once, that his father hadn't seen him since he lost his voice. When they met again, he wouldn't even be able to say hello.

At the next table, a pretty girl, around twelve, in a green tartan dress, sat eating dinner with her family. She and her family were Chinese, and Sam was struck by her beautiful thick black hair, cut straight and framing her face; she was like something from a magazine. She was partly the reason Sam hadn't corrected the mistake with his order. Although her family were all sharing their dishes, the girl had given herself a large portion of something that looked very similar to what he was eating, and she seemed to be enjoying it. He watched her from the corner of his eye, blushing.

She was quiet too, but unlike Sam, who felt like he was twisting inside, she appeared to be very relaxed. She took small portions of food and chewed them up, wiping her lips neatly.

When her parents and grandparents spoke to her she smiled, but rarely replied. He was nervous about his stoma, and tried to hide the vent with his napkin. But when she finally looked over and noticed him, she smiled.

It felt wonderful. Even in his dorky singlet. Even with the faint aroma of vomit still in his nostrils. She smiled at him and he felt his cheeks glow.

Katie was asking about Roger—what was going to happen with him and their mother?

Dettie reacted as though she had swallowed something vile. 'That was nothing,' she said. 'Don't worry about all that. Roger and your mother were just friends. I'm sure he's happy for them both.'

Katie was turning the lazy Susan, watching the soy sauce bottle spin in place. 'Mummy said she liked him.'

Dettie waved the comment away with her knife. 'I'm sure they got on very well,' she said. 'He seemed like a nice fellow. But these sorts of relationships don't work out.'

'What sorts?'

Dettie swallowed her mouthful of omelette. 'You'll realise this when you're older, kids, but people are attracted to what's familiar. Roger might have been lovely—who knows?—but he comes from a very different background. Different from us. Now I'm not saying *bad*—but different. Different values.'

Sam remembered overhearing what his mother had said to that. The disgust in her voice. He was sure it wasn't true. His mother had broken up with Roger because of their father—not because he was Aboriginal. People could be attracted to things that were different.

The girl with the lush hair scooped more white rice onto her plate. He watched Dettie eating the rest of her omelette, dissected until it was just boring old eggs, then looked down at his own meal. The meat and vegetables were a mural of colour and texture beneath the brown sauce. Carrots cut into little stars. Red and green strips of capsicum. And even though his meal had cooled, he relished loading up his fork and filling his mouth. For his mother, for the way the pretty girl at the next table made him feel in his belly, he savoured its salty tang.

'Your mother and father have a *history*. That's what it is.' Dettie adjusted herself in her chair. 'Did I mention she told me on the phone that it was just like old times? Her and your father. Just like old times, she said.'

The black-haired girl's family rose from their table and gathered their things. They made their way to the door, her father speaking warmly with the restaurant staff as he settled the bill. When the woman at the cash register offered, the girl reached up to take a fortune cookie from jar. Her shoes, a black patent leather, glistened as she stretched. She unwrapped her cookie and snapped it open, unfolding the slip of paper. As she read her future she moved her hair out of her eyes, tucking it behind her ear and revealing the cream plastic of a large hearing aid. It was so thick that it actually pushed her ear forward slightly as it wrapped around the lobe.

Was that why she was so friendly towards him? Had she only smiled because she saw that he had a handicap too? Was Dettie right? Were people only attracted to what was familiar?

He heard his aunt scratching through her purse beside him, preparing to pay for the meal, and was vaguely surprised by the wad of cash she withdrew from a zipped compartment. It was more money than Sam had ever seen in one place before, but he didn't think much of it; instead he watched the girl's family file out into the street, each squinting at the last of the sunset bathing the footpath a ruddy orange. As the girl left, she smiled at him one final time—perfect teeth, straight and white—and stepped beyond the glass. He waved, but she was already gone.

Only the fat golden cat remained, waving back at him. Silent and winking.

■

It was almost midnight when they pulled into a rest stop off the highway. When he opened his eyes, Sam was surprised by the darkness. His arm felt fuzzy where it had been pressed against the doorhandle. His mouth was dry and he still felt the heat of the day on his skin. Katie had curled her legs up and squashed the side of her face into the back of her seat. Hair stuck to her lips. She'd drooled all down her seatbelt.

The car drifted to a stop beneath a tree, its engine rattling slightly before it sighed into silence. Dettie pulled on the parking brake and flicked off the headlights. Sam heard her scratching in the glove box before the ceiling light came on. Dettie's face was lit orange as she leant over her seat, stretching, to tug the cushions out from under the back window.

'Oh, are you awake, Sammy?' she whispered. She passed him a pillow and hunted beneath Katie's seat for a blanket.

Sam nodded and closed his eyes. The pillow cooled his cheek. He heard the sound of material being tugged free, and Dettie's grunting. Dust tickled his tongue as he felt the blanket fall across his body, up over his shoulders.

Another car hummed by on the highway. Through the glass Sam heard leaves being stirred by the wind. They seemed papery and distant in the back of his ears, hushing him back to sleep.

■

Still night. Breeze. Smoke. Feet stretched against the door. A buckle digging into his back. Sam opened his eyes. The ceiling light was off and a strand from the blanket tickled the inside of his ear. Dettie's door was open. She sat with her legs out of the car, thumbing a cigarette. There was moonlight tangled in her hair. She was whispering something—a prayer? a song?—her mouth barely moving as she stared into the dark and let the smoke peel from her lips. A whistle started in Katie's nose. It sounded far away to Sam, echoing, like a squeal coming over the hills.

All afternoon he had been reading about zombies. Every time he finished his comic book, he would immediately turn back to the first page to start over. Even though reading it in the car had made him feel nauseous again, he would drink in a few panels of each page before looking up at the scenery until the queasiness passed. And now, in the middle of the night, Katie's nose shrieking softly, zombies were all he could think about. Brightly coloured zombies that crawled out from the bushes and ripped apart cars. He could still picture each image of the undead, now stretching their rotting fingers towards him. Breaking through glass, through upholstery. Punching metal. Snarling. Tearing skin from silky white bone and snapping at his throat. He could almost feel his old stitches—long healed now—pulling against his flesh.

Sam tucked his feet under the blanket and wondered when the sun was going to come up. The darkness made it hard to read his watch. He held it to his eyes and strained to make out the digits. The clock face had been scratched the week before he'd gone to hospital. Carrying a bowl of tomato soup out onto the veranda, Sam had tripped on one of Katie's shoes and it had scraped on the concrete. Dettie and his mother had been outside talking, and when he fell they hurried over to gather him up. The bowl was smashed, and at first he hadn't noticed his watch for the pain in his knees. He remembered his mother later spraying the soup away with a hose.

He tilted his watch towards the window. The scratch across its face glistened in the light, but beneath it the numbers were an indistinguishable black.

Sam closed his eyes, nuzzled down on the seat. No more cars passed on the highway. It was still and quiet. A strange, familiar quiet. The scent of cigarette smoke crept in through the window. Dettie went on puffing quietly, muttering into her hands. Trying to banish the ravenous zombie hordes from his mind, Sam thought about his mother and couldn't sleep. How far behind them was she? And what had his father said to convince her to come back?

22

The lounge room had seemed emptier somehow, as though there was furniture missing or rearranged. He remembered the walls felt more exposed, barren—although actually only a couple of his father's jackets and a pair of shoes had disappeared from beside the phone stand. The curtains were closed and the sun behind them washed the room a thick red. From his position on the couch, resting through his latest migraine, Sam had heard a patter of laughter from out on the street, and a familiar exchange of dogs barking three houses down. In the kitchen his mother and Dettie were sitting opposite one another at the table, staring into two cups of untouched tea.

'What—what did he say *exactly*, Joanne?' Dettie's voice had jerked and cracked.

Sam's mother was rubbing her forehead. 'It doesn't matter, Dettie. He said nothing. Nothing. We just talked. He said what he felt. Everything that he felt. That's it.'

'But it might not be—I mean, he might—'

'No. That's it. It's done. He was perfectly clear. Horribly.'

His mother fiddled with the handle of her cup. 'And anyway, I couldn't.'

'And he just—' Dettie clapped her hands together and held them out open in front of her, empty.

Sam's mother watched the ribbon of steam lifting from her cup. She turned the handle absently and nodded.

'It's just—it's despicable,' Dettie shook her head, scratching in her handbag. 'To just come home from work—To drop a bombshell—'

'It's been coming for a long time.' Sam remembered that his mother had sounded tired. She'd seemed unable to stop staring at things with a surprised expression, her eyebrows raised, frozen on her face. 'I knew,' she said. 'We both—I think we *both* saw it coming. The bickering and the brooding. Snapping at each other all the time. Every little thing. When they offered him the job . . . Well, there was nothing . . . He thought there was nothing—' Her voice had sounded tighter, and she paused a moment, breathing. 'It was time,' she said.

Dettie had dabbed a tissue to her nose. She turned in her chair, glancing back at Sam—who scrunched his eyes shut, burying his head.

'Well, *you* can tell yourself that, Joanne,' she said, 'but I don't believe it. For him to just skulk off—pack his bags and flee. Like some *criminal*. To not tell me. His sister. His *children* even! I mean, to not even wait for them to get home? To give them some idea of what it's all about?'

His mother shook her head quickly, blinking her eyes. 'He left them a letter.'

'A letter?' Dettie squeaked. 'Oh, how very *managerial* of him.'

'He said he couldn't stand it. Couldn't bear to see their faces.'

'Oh, what a load of rot. "Couldn't stand it"? Too ashamed of himself, more like.' She was sputtering. 'No. I don't care *what* he could stand, Joanne. There are children involved. In his entire life he has never—not once—'

'I know. I know, Dettie. And I agree. And I'll be angry. I will. I'm just—I'm just not there yet. For now I can't even . . .' Her voice quavered, rising. She picked at her coaster. 'Look, what he's done,' she said, *'how* he's done it, it's awful. It's wrong. God help me, there would have been better ways. But it's for the best.'

Dettie had straightened in her chair as if to speak, shaking her head, but she didn't. Instead, she watched the way his mother ran her fingers through her hair and sighed.

'You'll be all right, Joanne.' She leant over to his mother, touching her arm. 'I know it doesn't seem like it now, but you will. I'm here. The kids are safe. Everyone's healthy. Maybe we all just need some time to calm down. To rethink. Us. Donald. Nothing's set in stone.'

'I'm just breathing, Dettie.'

'You know I'll help. If I can. In any way I can. I'm only a phone call away. Since Ted passed on I've got all this free time. And another set of hands. In fact, if you need to go and lie down . . .'

His mother had laughed like a hiccough as Dettie spoke. She sighed. 'I'll be fine,' she said. 'I just need to breathe.'

And so they sat, breathing softly, until his mother's tea was cold and Dettie had drained the last of hers from her cup.

23

The sunburn on Sam's arms and neck had just started to blister. Beneath his singlet he felt the weight of the sun pressing on his flesh. Flickers of shadow cooled his skin like sprinkles of water whenever a tree passed overhead. The fabric was itchy and clung to the aloe vera Dettie had rubbed over him. It made him sweat even more and he had to peel it away from his body whenever he moved. Katie stared out the window. The radio was off and she had stopped asking why. Dettie chewed on a straw, biting it flat and dragging it between her teeth. She had opened the air vents as far as they would go.

Sam had read his comic through so many times he almost knew each page by heart: when Pamela and Tim hide in the rest stop cabin; where Tim goes outside to restart the generator; the glint of the zombie's eyes from out of the tree line. Sam wasn't sure why it filled him with such a peculiar thrill. All that anger. All the violence. The zombies revolted him, but there was something exciting about them too. Something primal. Hunger and aggression. And no fear. No nervousness, no awkwardness. No jobs or school or family.

No voices.

He knew what they reminded him of. Angry. Silent. Changed from what they were. As he sat there picturing their rotting flesh—his own skin stinging, bubbled and red—it made him feel sick, but that twisted nausea in his belly was somehow better than what he'd been feeling for months. Less hollow. Less unfamiliar and lost. The zombies, rotting and shredded as they were, had taken all that rage and loss and self-loathing and run with it. Used it to tear up whatever got in the way. It made them strong. Something to fear, not something afraid.

'Did you see that flock of birds back there?' Dettie called over the noise of the fan.

Sam's eyes were heavy. She was looking at him, so he nodded, his neck feeling thin and rubbery.

'Katie, did you see them? That big flock of cockatoos?'

Katie crossed her arms. She closed her eyes as warm air blew in her face.

Sam looked out at fields of dry grass passing by. Sheep ambled slowly towards a shrunken dam. His skin throbbed.

'Did you know that most times, Sammy,' Dettie called, 'in a flock of cockatoos, they have galahs travelling with them too? Two of them.'

Way off in the distance he thought he could see birds, two grey figures in a patch of speckled white, but his vision was blurred and it could have been dust on the window.

'I don't know why they do,' she said. 'But they're pretty easy to spot because they stick together. Have you kids spotted any?'

Katie still didn't answer. Sam was tired and pressed back in his seat. He let the motion of the car shake his head.

'I want my other clothes,' Katie said.

Dettie took a breath. 'Katie, we've talked about this. There wasn't time—'

'Sam got a new singlet.'

'Sam *needed* a new one because his T-shirt was ruined.'

Katie tugged at the juice stain on her dress. 'This one smells like petrol.'

'Well, if you want new clothes maybe you should stop sulking and start behaving like a member of this family.'

Katie thumped her body against the door. 'I want to go with Mum.'

'Oh, for heaven's sake, girl.' Dettie stepped on the accelerator and the car roared. 'You don't hear your brother complaining, do you?'

'Yeah, but Sam . . .'

She stopped. The car faded back to a hum. Katie kept staring out the window with her arms crossed, but slowly she let go and laid her hands by her legs. Sam tasted a bead of sweat as it rolled down his lips. Angry. Silent. Outside, two birds, grey with a spot of pink on their bellies, bobbed in a hazy sea of white.

24

It was an old department store, lined with cream wallpaper that had faded brown in places, but still glittering with gaudy, drooping chandeliers. They passed glass cabinets filled with bottles of perfume and jewellery that glowed yellow. The countertops were trimmed with strips of gold.

'Keep up, come on,' Dettie said. 'We don't have all day.'

She found the children's section—girls and boys—and began snatching up a few items. Shirts, shorts, some packets of children's underwear. Katie ran over to a stand of bright skirts and flicked through them, the sound of each plastic hanger snapping against the next as she went.

Before long the two of them were bickering over a pair of shorts, so Sam sat down on a cushioned vinyl bench beside the fitting rooms, holding whatever new clothes Dettie handed to him, feeling his skin pulse. Around him stiff pink mannequins stared dead-eyed beneath coarse black wigs, and he joined them, peering straight ahead at the maroon carpet, hearing soft electronic piano music drift from somewhere, and realising,

sign

with a curiously detached calm, that he had absolutely no idea what town he was in.

Half an hour later a bubbly young shop assistant was ringing up their purchases, folding them into a plastic bag as she chewed a piece of bright green gum in the corner of her smile. The summer dress printed with flowers that Katie and Dettie had finally agreed upon. The ugly skateboarding T-shirt Dettie had picked for Sam that he was too sore and exhausted to argue against. Socks, underwear, thongs. The register sputtered out a receipt.

'And will you be paying by cheque or—?'

'Cash,' Dettie said swiftly, drawing a note from the thick bundle in her purse and pressing it into the woman's hand, waving away a receipt.

25

Near the seesaw and the roundabout children ran squealing. They played tag and tossed pieces of bark at one another. It looked sweaty and dusty and free. It reminded Sam of the prickling sensation he used to feel across his skin whenever he ran on the soccer field, his fingers dirty, his knees scuffed. He could imagine the itch of the grass in their hair and the metallic smell on their hands from the chains of the swing. He was sitting under the tallest tree in the park, bathed in shadow. Dettie had him swaddled in a blanket, hidden beneath her large pair of sunglasses and a straw hat. Watching the children, he was heavy and hot, and as he tugged handfuls of grass from the ground he rubbed the coarse sensation of each blade into his palm, enjoyed the lush stain it left on his fingertips.

Katie picked at her potato and gravy with a fork. Her shoes and socks lay beside her and she stretched her toes out in the sun. Dettie shooed the flies away from their plates and wrapped the last of the roast chicken back into its bag.

'Are you kids done with this?' she asked, standing up with the rubbish.

Katie nodded slowly. Sam was full and still had the taste of salad vinegar around his mouth.

Dettie crossed the park to the bins. She stretched and dusted the crumbs off herself. When Katie and Sam were looking in her direction she waved and pointed to the toilets.

Katie watched her go, and when Dettie was out of sight she exhaled and put her plate aside. 'Is Aunty Dettie angry with me?'

Sam shook his head, shrugged and picked again at the ground.

'She keeps yelling at me,' Katie said. 'All the time.'

The sounds of the other children playing swam in the air.

'I wish we could have gone with Mummy.' Katie's eyes watered. There was a wobble in her voice. She whispered, 'I don't want to go to Perth.'

Sam wanted to agree. He wanted to say, *Me neither.* So he squeezed her arm and nodded.

He was surprised Katie hadn't yet mentioned all the friends she was leaving behind. The girl in their street she would always go with to the swimming pool. The two blonde girls from her gymnastics class. Or her schoolfriend Sarah who had the same birthday. Sam hadn't had as many close friends since he was diagnosed, but even he wondered when, or if, he would see his friend Paul again. He wouldn't be able to call him on the phone, but he could write a letter saying goodbye when they got to Perth. In all the shock of the move, with the speed at which it was happening, the reality didn't seem to have hit Katie yet.

The last two days had certainly been a rush, which had made it hard to think of much beyond the journey ahead. Between the giddy surprise of their mother's phone call, and the flurry to get packed into the car; with the thought of their father, longing to see them after a year away, and the mysterious promise of Perth waiting on the horizon, there'd been little room for anything else. Sam had barely given a thought to how much work their mother must have to do back at home, packing everything up. Indeed, he realised suddenly, they had been in such a rush that he wasn't even sure if they'd locked the back door of the house when they left. But now, finally on motionless ground, the chatter and squawk of other children scrambling over each other in the fresh air, the enormity of the move started to press in.

They were in Mildura now, as the nearby railway station informed him. According to a sign advertising the local Lions and Apex clubs, the play area was called Jaycee Park. In one direction, lime green trees puffed up like towering mushrooms, in the other, willows almost kissed the grass, and in the midst of both, children, squealing with joy, were climbing all over a black steam engine, now inert on a block of concrete.

There was a whip of laughter. Somebody called out, 'Jump!' There was a squeal, then a soft thud emptied the air of noise. Sam turned to look across the lawn. Children were gathered by the biggest wheel of the train. A choked moan sounded from somewhere in the group, and two girls who'd been standing back watching started to scream.

Katie stood and wiped her eyes. 'What happened?'

Sam took Dettie's sunglasses off and sat up.

The crowd was milling around, pushing in tighter. They only parted when Dettie ran over, pushing through, to kneel at the edge of the concrete. Sam hadn't noticed her returning from the bins, but as the group moved in closer he unwrapped himself from the blanket, pushed their things into a pile, and together he and Katie ran over.

The other children were gathered around a thin boy with freckles. He was bleeding from a gash over his top lip and Dettie was cradling him, rocking his body, with a handkerchief in her hand. She hushed him and stroked his red hair.

'You're okay. Shhh . . . You're being very brave.'

The boy hiccoughed and rolled around in her arms. Dettie held him and caught his hands so he wouldn't touch his mouth. She noticed Katie and Sam standing quietly behind the others, staring.

'Katie, darling, can you do me a favour?' she said. 'Can you be a big strong girl and run to the car? On the floor in the back there's a little red box. A first-aid kit. Could you go and get that for me?'

Katie nodded, and when Dettie smiled at her, she ran off.

'And Sammy?' Dettie said. 'Can you go get a cup and pour some water into it from the tap? Then bring it over here for us, please.'

The blood was shiny as it slid down the boy's chin, a rich, wet red with tiny bubbles winking at the corner of his lips. It wasn't like in the comic; it wasn't spurting. And it hadn't yet dried into the dark brown colour that had stained the kangaroo.

'Sammy?' Dettie called.

He nodded and hurried back over to their plates, holding the hat to his head. He pulled a plastic cup from a bag and filled it under the tap. When he returned, the injured boy was clutching Dettie's hand close to his chest. His lip had swollen, and Sam could see through the blood that his two front teeth were chipped, one almost a triangle.

Dettie saw Sam and waved him closer. Thanking him, she dipped her handkerchief in the water.

'Now, honey,' she whispered in the boy's ear, 'I know you're hurt, but I'm just going to clean you up. I promise I'll be very careful.'

The boy whined and twisted away, but as she held him closer she touched the cloth so lightly to his face that he settled down. The blood was almost cleaned from his chin by the time Katie returned with the kit, and children had started pushing closer to see his broken teeth. They whispered to each other as Dettie disinfected the wound and dried the cut.

When the boy's parents finally appeared, a parcel of fish and chips tucked under the father's arm, they crouched beside her, leaving their son in Dettie's lap and thanking her again and again. While she spoke to them, calming down the boy's mother who had started to cry, Dettie sent Sam and Katie to clean up the rest of the food and wait by the car. They nodded, and wandered back to the tree, Sam rolling up their blanket, and Katie throwing the plastic plates and spoons into the bin.

Beside the car Katie sat down and pulled her socks on slowly. She was staring through the crowd to where Dettie was still rocking the boy and comforting his parents. Slowly, the other children were gathered up by their families and led away, and eventually Dettie helped carry the boy to his family's van. He held on to her hand, scarcely breaking eye contact until the door slid shut. The boy's mother kept pushing her hair nervously from her face as she talked, and leant over to give Dettie a hug. It was impossible to hear what they said, but the woman smiled and Dettie nodded, and as they drove off, she waved them all goodbye.

sign

'How are we, kids? Are you all right?' Dettie asked when she returned to the car. Adjusting the bandaid on her ring finger, she reached into the glove box and pulled out a cigarette.

Katie rocked on her feet. 'How is the boy?'

'Oh, he's fine, sweetie.' Dettie sparked the lighter. 'Thank you for your help.'

Katie rubbed the hem of her new floral dress.

Dettie blew smoke straight up in the air and checked her watch. 'I'm going to wash off,' she said. 'You kids be ready to go when I get back.'

26

Tiny dots of sun glowed through the weave in Sam's straw hat. When he moved his head they rippled and sparked. He forgot the burns on his arms for a moment and enjoyed the swirl of reds and yellows across his eyes. His chest felt warm. It felt puffed out and spongy, like the muffins Dettie would usually make for them on weekends. They always tasted chalky and never had enough sugar, but Sam liked to hold them to his nose when they were still hot from the oven and breathe in the smell. And his chest felt like that now, he thought. Baked all through.

Dettie had been gone a long while and he needed to use the toilet. He knocked on the car window and gestured to Katie. She was hunting through the first-aid kit and reading what she could of the labels.

There were toilet blocks over in the park, just beyond the play equipment, but Dettie had headed in the direction of the train station, so Sam crossed the car park and found the doorway into its darkened men's toilet. The only light came through holes cut into the bricks around the ceiling, and there was a musty funk of wet concrete and stale pee. He used the urinal, washed his hands, and because there were no towels or fans, wiped them dry on his singlet.

On the way back to the door a hollow chirping sound near the stalls surprised him. He stopped. When he listened it seemed to be coming from beneath him, underground. When he bent over, his elbows on his knees, he could make out the soft echo of wings fluttering on dirt. It was a bird, but it wasn't singing. It sounded like it was caught on something, injured, squawking and twisting in place. He followed the chirping noise down to a drain by the sink, but after a minute of peering through the rusted grate into the darkness, he decided there was nothing to see. If the bird was in there it was too far back. He tried to round his lips and whistle, but, of course, that was not how his throat worked anymore. He puffed, and made popping sounds with his cheeks, tried sucking in air and burping, but he'd never learnt to make the sound come out properly. He felt light-headed, and the bird, if it was even trapped at all, had already gone quiet.

27

Outside, Sam spotted Dettie standing at an open phone box near the train tracks. He walked towards her, still trying to squeeze some kind of whistle from his mouth, wondering if she was talking to his mother. Her back was turned and she was crushing a cigarette under her toe.

'No. No, *you* listen.' Her voice sounded strained. 'I'm not the one flying off the handle—' She was hunched over the handpiece, hissing. '*Yes*, of course I realise how far it is. That's not the issue—'

If it was his mother, that meant that Dettie had called to check on her. To see how she was going with the movers. Which meant she hadn't left home yet. And Dettie seemed oddly tense, shifting her weight on her feet.

'Oh, they're *not* terrified,' she said. Sam stopped. Dettie's back was still turned, and she stammered, 'Don't be so melodramatic.' The voice on the other end of the line was obviously yelling.

'No. No, I'm *not* telling you. Not until you calm down,' Dettie said, pressing her fingers to her temples. 'You sound crazy, Donald, honestly.'

sign

It was his father. She was talking to his father. Sam's body went stiff. His first thought was to run back to the car and get Katie, but as he stood in place, watching Dettie's stilted movements, her little puffs and starts, it was obvious his father was shouting. He was shouting at Dettie.

Was there a change of plans?

Their parents had spoken to one another. They'd patched things up. Dettie had spoken to them both. Everything was fine. When Dettie called their mother at work it was like old times, Dettie had said. She'd said, 'Old times.' They were all going to live together in Perth. They were already on their way. Two days in. If they had to turn around now . . .

Sam had tried to be wary about it all at first. It had all happened so fast. So very fast. He'd wondered about Roger. He'd wondered about his mother's job. And school. But he'd put it from his mind. They were on the road. Heading to Perth. It was happening.

Except now he found himself standing beside a railway-station toilet, frozen, feeling suddenly exposed. Had it been too much to hope for? It was just like being back in his bedroom, reading Katie their father's farewell letter again. Or in his hospital bed, staring at the card Dettie had delivered from his father wishing him well, but apologising that he couldn't come to visit. Was this all just another promise he was stupid enough to let himself believe? Were they going to have to turn back?

He knelt out of sight behind a bin and strained to listen.

'How?' Dettie was saying. '*How*, Donald? Your children were petrified. This family was being ripped apart. *Strangers* were coming into their house. Their mother is—' Dettie's voice was rising as she poked the air. 'No, this is *happening*, Donald, so *your* children don't grow up not knowing who their father is.'

The sun was lying on his back, but Sam was shivering. He wanted to run to the phone and yell into it. To tell them not to fight. That it was all okay. He wanted to tell his father that they were sorry—whatever was wrong. That *he* was sorry. That he and Katie missed him. That they couldn't wait to see him. That Perth would be *great*. But he couldn't. He wasn't even sure what was happening. Why they were both upset. Just like the bird in the drain. He couldn't tell what was going on. Useless. His mouth hung open and dumb. His throat tightened on his vent. He felt tears in his eyes.

'I don't appreciate that, Donald. I really don't. I would not touch a hair—' She was squeezing her lighter, tapping it on the glass.

Sam tried to look back at the car, but saw only the wall of the concrete toilet block.

'Oh, don't be foolish. You want these kids thinking— Donald. Donald, calm down. That *language*. I thought you might want to know we're on our way, that's all. I could just as easily turn around.'

Sam's stomach lurched. So they were still on their way! But she was threatening to head home? Why would she do that?

There seemed to be more shouting, and Dettie shushed into the receiver. She started to turn towards the garbage bin Sam was crouched behind and he tensed. He needed to run. To grab the phone. Every muscle felt it. His whole body was clenched. But then what? What if he made it worse? The feeling went on, chewing him up. It was as if just running itself—running nowhere, even—might be enough to soothe the ache in his belly.

'Well, fine. If that's the way you feel—'

He thought of Katie alone in the car. Should he run to her? And do what? He felt his breath quickening. Sweat prickled on his skin. His head buzzed. A familiar darkness began closing in.

'We'll see you soon. Yes, I *will*, Donald. And you'd better be a bit more rational. I'm warning you.'

So they were still going? The trip was still on?

'Honestly, I thought you'd be a bit more mature.'

Sam crept out and inched slowly over the dirt. The further he got away from her, the more bent and fierce Dettie seemed to become, pacing around the phone, snarling. When he had passed the toilets, he turned and sprinted.

The car doors were hanging open. Katie was cupping her hands around her lips, blowing raspberries through them. Spittle sparkled on her chin. He was out of breath, and his sunburn throbbed.

'Did you hear my elephant call?' Katie smiled.

He stood still, stalled by the sight of her playing happily. He wondered what to say. He wondered how to say it. And if he did tell her something, what then? Their father was waiting. Or he wasn't. Either way, there was nothing for them to do. Their father was in Perth. Their mother was on the way. They were stuck. But they had Dettie. Like she had the boy with the broken teeth, she would take care of them. Keep them safe until their parents—one, or hopefully both of them—arrived.

The sun faded and the sound of the park sprinklers slapped the air. Sam looked up into the shadow of the tree. Its branches shook.

28

The last house on the outskirts of Mildura disappeared behind them. A vineyard, with rows of grapevines covered in plastic. Sam watched in the side mirror as the road swallowed it up. The car lurched around curves and over hills. Dettie didn't slow down, and she hadn't spoken since they'd put their seatbelts on. Sam was tugged from side to side and Katie bounced on the back seat, singing. His blanket had been kicked onto the floor and he had the straw hat on his lap, covering his arms.

'Do you think they can put the teeth back in?' Katie leant forward to ask.

The car rattled over a line of potholes and Dettie jerked it back towards the middle of the road.

'You know, the boy?' Katie asked. 'I heard at school if they find the tooth they can stick it in again. Except for if you swallow it. Then it's gone.'

'He's fine,' Dettie said, not glancing away from the road. The tight sound—the sound from the telephone call—was still in her voice.

Katie played with her kneecaps, thinking. She sat forward. 'Wasn't I fast to get the first-aid kit, Aunty Dettie?' she asked. 'I ran really fast.'

Dettie nodded, staring at the back of the ute ahead of them.

'Sam was fast too. But I had to run all the way to the car and back.'

'Hmm . . . You were both fast.'

'And he was just getting water, but I had to look everywhere. Even under the seats.'

Dettie hummed quickly.

'And then, when I lifted up the pillow—'

'Katie!' Dettie snapped. 'I'm trying to concentrate on the road.'

The car veered around a corner and the hat shook off Sam's knees. Katie's mouth hung open. Her eyes darted from Dettie to Sam to the first-aid kit beside her. She was going to say something, then slumped down in her seat and chewed her lip.

Dettie cleared her throat, blinking. 'I was very proud of you both,' she said, and loosened her grip on the steering wheel.

The shaking eased off as they swept around each bend. The air vents hissed.

In the glove box, under the car manual and scrunched receipts, Sam fished out a faded map and a pen that worked. He folded the map so its blank side was exposed and wrote as legibly as he could manage, *Are we still going to Perth?* He held it up to Dettie.

At first she didn't look, but he kept holding it. Eventually, she glanced down at it, twice. She raised an eyebrow, and smiled. 'Yes. Yes, of course, honey. How silly. Don't you see the signs? You watch next time one comes along.'

White road markers shot past on the road. There were no signs, or none that he'd seen that said *Perth*. But he knew that Perth was west, and they were driving towards the sunset.

He scrawled again on the paper, *Does Dad want us to come?*

This made Dettie look at him strangely, steadily, like she was weighing up something in her head. She re-read the message. 'Now that is a very silly question,' she said slowly. 'Your daddy's waiting for all of us. In Perth. Waiting for us to get there.'

He ducked a moment, writing, and lifted the map. *Where's Mum?*

'Yes, your mother too.' Dettie exhaled a hiss. 'She's waiting.'

'Mummy?' Katie sat up. 'Is Mummy there already?'

'Yes, yes. She's with your daddy. They're setting everything up. Now settle down.'

Sam started on a question, but Katie was faster, 'How did Mummy get there so fast?'

Dettie checked her side mirror. 'Hmm?'

'To Perth. How did she beat us?' Katie stretched forward.

'Well, she's—she's not there yet. But soon. She'll get there before we do. And she'll be waiting.'

'How did she get in front of us?'

'It doesn't matter.'

'But how?'

'She just did!' Dettie snapped. 'Now both of you stop bothering me. I need to drive.' The car jerked.

Sam scratched out what he'd written. The look of the words sitting there, exposed on the page, bothered him somehow.

Katie moaned and flapped her arms. 'I'm hot.'

Dettie jabbed the fan's setting as high as it would go. '*There.* Is that enough?'

'Can we open a window?' Katie whined.

'Katie, I don't want bugs—'

'There's no bugs. I'm *hot . . .*'

'Katie, so help me—'

'I want to wind the window down.' She had her fingers on the handle.

'Katie!' Dettie barked. She had turned, looking back, taking one hand off the wheel. 'Do you want me to pull this car over?'

'Mummy lets us wind the window down. All the way down.'

'Well, your mother isn't here.'

'Where is she?'

'Honestly, Katie, if you don't settle down—'

'I'm sick of this!' Katie yelled, kicking the back of Sam's seat. 'I want to go home!'

Dettie slammed on the brakes. The car skidded and wobbled. It veered to the left. Katie screamed. The belt pulled the wind out of Sam's chest and the motor sputtered. When the vehicle had stopped they were nosed into the dirt at the side of the road. Dettie's buckle snapped open and she leapt out.

'Quick! Get out! Come on!'

Sam fumbled with the doorhandle. His hat was crushed under his feet. Whimpering, Katie scrambled out and stood in a patch of grass, looking back at the car. She grabbed Sam's elbow tightly, afraid, twisting his sunburn.

Ahead of them, Dettie was wringing her hands. 'You want to go home?' she called out. 'Back to that? Back to a house that—' She squeezed the bridge of her nose, covering her eyes.

Katie stared at the engine. Sam's legs shook. Dust was settling around the wheels. Suddenly, he wanted to run again. The feeling tightened his legs. Katie's fingers gripped harder.

'Look where we are,' Dettie said. 'Both of you. We're nowhere.'

In every direction all Sam could see were browning fields and long stalks of straw. A corrugated tank tilted like a giant sleeping head in the paddock closest to them, and further along, a barbed wire fence was bent under a fallen branch.

'We don't *have* a home anymore,' Dettie said, swiping at the flies. 'This is us now. Our home.'

Katie was bent over. She was crying.

'Remember that kangaroo? Remember? On the side of the road?' Dettie was pointing off behind them, pacing on the spot. 'Because that's what happens in the wild,' she said. 'Out here. And that's us now. Wild. So if you want to end up like that, then fine.'

Sam felt sick. Tears stung his eyes.

'Out here,' Dettie said, pressing a hand to her neck, 'there's no giving up. We have to hold on to each other and not let go, or we're lost.'

Waves of heat lifted from the bitumen. Their shoes were sinking into the tar.

'I want to go home,' Katie whispered.

Dettie smiled, and the cold look in her eyes started to fade. 'There is no home back there, sweetie. It's gone. There's just Perth now. Where you belong. With your daddy. And your mummy.' She lowered her arms, her shoulders going slack. 'And with mean old Aunty Dettie who has to drive you there.' She peered down at them with a sad smile, tilting her head.

Katie's grip on Sam's elbow loosened. A soft breeze pushed the grass around. An ant crawled up Sam's ankle and he shuddered, recalling the way the kangaroo had rippled with insects. He hurriedly kicked his leg, bending to brush it from his flesh.

Shaking her wristwatch until it faced upward, Dettie checked the time. 'Now let's all get back in the car, shall we? Let's stop messing about. We've got to go and put our family back together. Quick smart.'

Sam and Katie were still trembling, but they followed her, slowly. As they climbed back in Dettie noticed Katie was wiping her eyes with a handkerchief.

'Where'd you get that?' she asked.

Katie jerked, surprised. 'Mummy gave it to me!' she yelled, and stuffed it into her sleeve.

29

Flocks of birds speckled the fields. As they landed they would fold away their long white wings and dip their beaks to the earth. Some hopped about, raising their heads as the car went past. Sam tried to imagine the squawking among them all, bickering over a seed or a nut—he wasn't sure what cockatoos ate. What if one was in charge? He'd seen TV shows about dogs. How they were pack animals. One was always in charge, and it would bite at the others to make them stay in line. Pack leader. He searched for the two galahs Dettie had told them about. The ones that travelled in every family. Sometimes they were in the furthest corners of the group, other times surrounded by the swarm. But she was right. They were always together.

Since the ant had crawled up his ankle a prickling sensation had been irritating his leg. He tried to scratch it slowly, rubbing the base of his palm along his skin.

Katie lay on the back seat with her pillow over her head.

Dettie had let her cry until she was quiet, but she kept looking over her shoulder to check on her. 'Let's all play a game,

shall we?' she said suddenly. 'Let's all try to remember a fun
memory about your father. Do you want to do that?'

Their mother's handkerchief was twisted around Katie's
finger, and before she had buried herself beneath the pillow,
Dettie seemed distracted by the way Katie was cradling it,
stroking the cotton.

'That sounds good.' Dettie grinned, her yellow teeth
clenched. 'I'll start. Let's see,' she hummed, tapping her nails on
the steering wheel. 'All right. Here's one.' She sat up in her seat.
'When your father and I were little, we had chores to do around
the farm. And my job, you see, was to bring in the eggs from the
hen house. So one morning I go out, as usual, and all the eggs
have just disappeared. Couldn't find one.'

She hunted in the rear-view mirror for Katie's reaction.

'I didn't think much of it until the next morning when
the same thing happened,' she said. 'Then the morning after
that. And the one after that. Two weeks and not a single egg.
Eventually, I woke up extra early and snuck out with a cricket
bat, thinking maybe there was a fox—but I looked, and there
were the eggs, still under the chooks. So I hid and waited to
see what was happening. Soon enough, here comes something
sneaking in through the door. And what do you think it was?'

Sam was glad he couldn't speak, because Dettie didn't
bother turning to him with the same look of expectation that
she trained on his sister. Katie didn't move.

'My brother,' Dettie said. '*Your* father. With a filthy big grin
on his face.' She was smiling at the thought of it, shaking her
head. 'So I wrestled him to the ground, telling him what a dirty
stinker I thought he was, and he fought and screamed and
punched. We ended up waking the whole house, and that was

that. Your grandpa pulled us apart with his big hands. He said we were thick as thieves, and gave us such a hiding I couldn't sit for a week.'

Dettie chuckled and laid her hands at the bottom of the wheel. 'Turns out your father had been stealing them for weeks. He was taking them to school. Selling them to his friends. Throwing them at other kids on the way home. I tell you, he was the dickens back then,' she wheezed.

It was hard to imagine Dettie that young. With her tense jerking gestures and the tight sound in her voice, she had always seemed old to Sam. Even the photo of her as a child that hung in her apartment had always looked peculiar, as though it was somebody else's face shining out from it, smiling carelessly over the tricycle's handlebars.

'Does anyone else have a story?' She flashed hopeful glances at them both. 'Sammy, I bet you'd remember your daddy getting you ready for the swimming carnival,' she said, drumming her thumbs. 'How he took you down to the pool with him in the mornings. The two of you sneaking out of the house with your towels.'

Sam remembered the swims, but not fondly. He turned back to the window.

'He'd hold you up in the water. Your little legs kicking. The sun still creeping over the city.' Dettie hummed. 'How I wish I could have been there to see it.' The corner of her mouth turned up.

What Sam recalled was very different. His father, off on his own, running long, steady strokes, face down, unspeaking, in the water. Sam thrashing through a sloppy lap or two before waiting around in the shallow end, hungry for breakfast, tracing circles

with his feet on the concrete base of the pool and ducking his
shoulders below the surface of the water to avoid the morning
breeze.

The itch on Sam's leg began to sting. His skin was pink from
scratching, so he pinched either side of the most irritated area
and squeezed. The flesh dimpled white beneath his fingers.

Sam preferred the beach. The warmth of the sand. Feeling
his body held aloft by the chill salt water. Tumbling about in
the foamy wash of the waves. But now, since the operation, he
wasn't allowed to submerge his neck in water at all. Just having
a shower was problematic. So even if he wanted to go swimming
with his father now, he couldn't.

'What about you, Katie? Can you think of anything?'

Katie's elbows flapped as she pushed the pillows harder onto
her face.

'Your father, dear?' Dettie turned. 'You must have stories.
Birthdays? Holidays?'

There was no answer from the back seat.

'Come on. Sammy had one,' Dettie sang. 'There must be
plenty of things to talk about. I know. Do you remember, there
was a time at one of Sam's soccer games—'

Katie squealed and threw a pillow against the opposite
window. She lay rigid across the back seat, glaring at the ceiling.
'I don't remember,' she said. Her voice sounded strange. Deeper.
'I don't care.'

The pillow had startled Dettie. She blinked and wiped her
mouth. 'Oh, settle down,' she scolded, then turned back to the
road and stopped talking.

135

30

First things first. The two of you are the most important part of my life. You always will be. His father had typed the letter for them at work. *So I don't want you to think that you did anything wrong, or that any of this is your fault.* He'd printed it on office paper with the company letterhead. Sam had to read it five times before the words began to sink in.

Your mum and I have come to a decision that it would be for the best if I lived somewhere else. Because sometimes, even when people love each other very much, it's still not enough reason for them to stay together.

Katie had sobbed, asking Sam what each sentence meant, asking him to stop and read each part over again.

Other things can get in the way. Sometimes it's big things. Sometimes lots and lots of little things. But your mum and I still love each other and we always will. We just want to be fair . . .

But Sam couldn't remember the next part. *We just want to be fair . . . Your mum and I still love . . . We just want to be fair . . .*

Fair to ourselves?

sign

Fair to you?

Once, he could have recited the whole thing. Now, he squeezed his eyes shut and tried to block out Dettie's whistling. She was scratching through her box of cassette tapes. There were rattles and squeaks of plastic. *Plenty of people live apart, but that doesn't mean that they're not still a family.*

The itch on his leg was stinging . . . *watching you grow up* . . . The familiar throb of sunburn . . . *knowing it's the right thing for us all* . . .

The rest slipped out of his memory.

Your eyes . . . I saw your eyes among the shadows of my dreams . . . The blonde woman had said it as the zombie leader crawled across her car. The zombie's teeth were red triangles.

His father's letter. He tried to picture the words, to trace over the lines of them in his head. *Dear Sam and Katie, I love you both.* The company logo was a charging bull.

The radio squealed as Dettie gave up on the tapes and skimmed the local stations. Sam tried to block his ear with his shoulder. *Other things can get in the way. Sometimes it's big things.* No, he knew that part.

My boyfriend. Tim! You killed him! You and your unholy horde . . . Yellow, bulging eyes, and those teeth.

A sputter, and the twang of a country guitar filled the car. Sam squirmed further away from the noise. Dettie was tapping again on the steering wheel.

'Oh, I'm sorry, Sammy, did you want to get some sleep?' she asked.

He kept his eyes closed, and in a moment the music was lowered.

Sometimes lots and lots of little things.

Its fingernails were tearing into the metal.

Suddenly, for some reason, vividly, the memory of his watch being scratched resurfaced in his mind. He'd been walking through the house. Balancing something. Was it soup? Then something happened. Then the scratch. He remembered rubbing his watch face afterwards, failing to get the mark off, while Dettie cleaned his grazed knee.

He tried to concentrate on the memory of the letter again, but it was too late. He could almost smell the tomato soup; feel the warm bowl slipping through his fingers, the burn. Katie's shoe beneath his foot. He had been walking out to them. Dettie and his mother. They were out on the veranda. The washing line was full and tipped slightly in the breeze.

It was a week until the operation. He had been yelling at Katie for using his favourite spoon. She'd sulked off to her room. Slammed the door. The whispering from outside was getting clearer. Soup lapped at the rim of the bowl. He'd gotten used to everyone whispering around him. About him. He could hear his mother's voice. She was holding a handful of hospital papers.

'He's going through something terrible, Dettie. Maybe he needs you to talk to him.'

Why would Dettie need to talk to him? And why was his mother being so negative? Usually when she talked about the operation she would get sad, her voice would tremble, but she would smile and promise him that everything was going to be all right in the end.

Dettie had been clutching the handrail, clicking her ring on the metal. 'I wouldn't even know how to talk to him,' she said, and sniffed.

sign

The hospital forms rustled. 'You're acting like he's dead or something.'

Sam's ankle bent over Katie's shoe.

'He may as well be dead,' Dettie hissed.

The bowl left his fingers. There was concrete. Soup.

A newsreader had come on the radio. Her thin, nasal voice hummed past Sam, almost lost in the vibration of the car, '. . . speculating that the fires may have been deliberately lit. Residents of the Koolyanobbing and Bullfinch regions are being warned that a westerly change may be set to draw the fires in their direction in the coming hours.'

Dettie's fingers were poised above the volume control. Sam watched her long nails quivering above the knob from the corner of his eye. He thought about what she'd said. *He may as well be dead.* Her neck was stretched, one ear tilted towards the speakers.

'. . . his appreciation from the West Australian Premier.' The newsreader cleared her throat. 'In other news, police are on the lookout—'

Dettie snapped off the radio and fussed with the rear-vision mirror. 'Sammy, are you still awake?' she said. 'Katie? Do you want to stretch your legs a minute?'

Through his eyelashes, Sam could see a small service station approaching. Dettie slowed the car, turned off, and parked not by the pumps, but in front of a fruit stand in the car park. The doors creaked open and the sand everywhere glowed white on the ground.

In the shade of the building, the fruit stand was little more than a makeshift roadside stall—a card table loaded with stone fruits spilling out of the back of an old station wagon discoloured with rust. The elderly man watching over it sat slumped in a foldaway canvas chair, fanning himself with a racing form. The blue heeler at his feet lay sleeping on its paws, opening its eyes occasionally to follow passers-by with a hazy indifference. Katie, at first drawn by the sight of the dog, was soon nosing at the fruit, wondering aloud what a mango was and excitedly running her hand across each fat pastel globe.

Watching Katie's face intently, Dettie insisted that they try some. She loaded up a plastic bag with several, along with a few slightly withered apricots. The salesman rose from his chair and kept smiling at Dettie, holding her gaze too long, and leaning in to show off particular fruits he said were 'ripe for the eating'. As she paid, he kept slicking back the side of his hair with one hand and counting out her change with the other, knocking off a couple of dollars because he 'liked her face' and popping in a nectarine for free. He kept running his eyes up and down her. Wandering over to a clearing of yellowed grass, Dettie stopped beside a tilted corrugated rubbish bin and tossed the nectarine in with a thud.

They folded up some blankets from the car to cover the weeds. Dettie and Katie sat, both leaning back against a couple of short wooden posts that marked out the edge of the car park. Dettie lit a cigarette and let it hang on her lips as she began fishing through the contents of the plastic bag, sharing it out. The worst of the burns on Sam's skin had faded slightly and were gradually bronzing over, but he still felt the sting of the sun gnawing away at him. The day was wearing into the afternoon, so he stood back, trying to position as much of himself as he could in the pool of shade being cast by the petrol station sign.

Dettie was looking down at the mango in her hands. Her wrinkled fingers encircled its firm, blushed flesh, her cigarette seething away at its side. 'Katie—sweetie, you've got happy memories of your father, don't you?'

Katie's legs were stretched out in front of her across the blanket. She shrugged.

Somewhere nearby, overhead, a bird shook out a long, guttural caw. Like the old man's dog, it seemed too stupefied to put much effort in.

'Aren't there any special things that you and your daddy used to do that you remember?' Dettie's voice was softer now, tentative. She swayed a little as she spoke. 'Sammy remembers going to watch football with your dad. You must have had something just the two of you used to do as well.'

Sam didn't actually remember going to the football with his father—but the point seemed irrelevant. He just chewed a bite of apricot around in his mouth, enjoying the flavour. A little dry, perhaps, but tasty.

'Did you play any sports together?'

Katie was turning her mango over in her hands, trying to discern how best to start in on it. 'No,' she said. 'Soccer was Sam's thing.'

'What about your school plays? Your gymnastics?'

Katie picked at the stem. She sniffed the fruit deeply and shrugged again.

'He took you to the pool too, didn't he? Taught you to swim?' Dettie waggled her cigarette thoughtfully, the smoke leaving a feather of white punctuation in the air. 'You and he and Sam?'

Katie was trying to bite through the mango's skin, gnawing at it with the side of her mouth, spittle glistening on its surface. 'That was just Sam,' she said, not really paying attention. She held it up, rubbing her teeth with her tongue. 'Do you have to peel it?'

Something in Dettie collapsed a little. Her arms slumped, her chest deflated. Her forehead was knotted in thought. 'Did you—did you go to the zoo?' she said, more quietly this time. Almost to herself.

Katie was digging into the fruit with no success, using all her fingers. Crushing the flesh but still making no incision. 'We went to the Show one time.'

Sam knew. Even before she went on, he already knew—

'The Easter Show?' Dettie said, perking up again.

'Yeah.' Finally, clawing at it with her fingertips, Katie broke through, exposing the fierce orange beneath. Juice ran down her wrists. 'We got showbags,' she said. 'Two showbags each. We watched the animal parade.' She sucked and lapped at the run-off. 'And he took me on the Octopus. Even though I wasn't supposed to be big enough for the Octopus.'

'Oh, that's lovely,' Dettie said, and sighed. She sat back, happily resettling the hem of her dress over her ankles. 'The two of you. Out and about. Thick as thieves.' She was staring off somewhere. Imagining. 'Oh, and Sammy too,' she said quickly, and offered him a smile. Sam could already tell what was coming, though, and he tried to look like he wasn't listening, focusing instead on the last of his apricot. 'I bet you were exhausted after a long day like that,' she said.

Katie was busy slurping, trying to chew through the wreckage in her hands, determined. Her face was soaked, her chin speckled with juice and pulp. For a moment, while he hoped Dettie would get off the topic, Sam watched his sister savouring her snack, licking her lips and ducking back in for another bite. It reminded him of the image of the comic-book zombie, gnawing at the doomed boyfriend Tim's brain. Hunched over, slurping and growling. Its face a mottled green, spattered red. The thought was so idiotic, and such a weird contrast to the sunny, yellow sight of his sister before him, that he almost tried to laugh.

Dettie ran her thumbnail along the side of the mango she was cradling, drawing a divot down its length, likewise struggling to rupture the skin. 'Might need a knife for this.'

'No,' Katie said, looking up, and Sam flinched. He *knew*. 'No, that was Uncle Brian. I forgot. Daddy wasn't there. Uncle Brian took us.'

Uncle Brian. Their mother's brother. Who had taken them to the Show twice, two years in a row, when he was visiting. Who loved the taste of corn dogs and tomato sauce, and who, for some reason, always insisted that they look through all of the arts and craft exhibitions—even the boring landscape paintings.

Dettie hummed. She gave up trying to cut into the fruit and tapped her fingers on its base. 'Brian,' she said, her eyes lowered. She was staring at the ground ahead of them. At the wilted blades of grass, tipped over in the sun, the lawn pockmarked with patches of cracked earth. At the ants scuttling around beneath the rubbish bin. She glared, her lower jaw rising and falling rhythmically, as though she were sucking on something sour. Her cigarette smouldered between her knuckles, a trail of ash that eventually petered out. She flicked the butt into the distance.

Minutes passed. Sam rolled the dry apricot kernel around in his hand, shaking it like a die. Katie went on eating until, eventually, what she held in her hands was a soggy, gnarled mess. Strips of skin and chewed fuzz, matted to a centre that, to Sam, still looked too large to be a seed. She turned it, looking for more purchase, when it slipped, rolled from her hands and plopped in the dirt. Like in his comic. Like a wet, fluorescent heart.

'For goodness sake, girl!' Dettie snapped. 'Be careful! Don't be so wasteful.'

Katie had been smiling, her grin slick with juice, but now she was frozen, her hands still extended, flinching.

Dettie looked her over. 'What in the blazes?' she said, scowling. 'Just look at you! Look at the *state* of you! What a mess!'

Wide-eyed, Katie moved to regather what she had dropped.

'No, don't touch it!' Dettie waved her away. 'You're already bad enough.' She exhaled loudly. Shaking her head, she dropped her own uneaten mango back in the plastic bag and spun it shut. 'All right. That's it! That's the last of that. No more.'

'No—' Katie said quietly. She slumped back against the post.

'Don't give me that rot. You're completely filthy. Just look. You've been eating like an animal and now your clothes, your face, *all of you*—in total disarray.' Dettie groaned and levered herself up, taking the bag with her. Glaring, she waved her finger. 'We've got to get back on the road, and there is no way you can travel like that.'

Katie, still sitting in place, was focused on the remains of her mango, staring at where it lay, rolled in a crust of filth. Sam moved over to help her up, his back to his aunt. As he gathered their blankets and shook them out, he tried to offer his sister a sly smile, to catch her eye—to show her, somehow, that it didn't matter. That Dettie was being ridiculous. That he was there for her. But Katie was quiet, downcast. She looked baffled more than anything. Her hands were upturned, still sticky with juice.

Muttering to herself, Dettie sent them both off to wash up while she drove the car the short distance to the pumps, filled it with petrol, and paid. Katie took longer than Sam in the bathroom, so while he waited he filled their water bottles at a tap beside a stand of motor oils. When the toilet door finally swung open, its rusted hinges wailing like a baby, Katie was clean, her dress dampened with water, her eyes reddened and puffy. She stomped past him, out over to the road, to stand peering at where it snaked around a bend in the distance and disappeared.

Sam watched her, slowly screwing on each bottle lid, until Dettie stepped back out into the sun, shoving a book of crosswords and what looked like a screwdriver into her handbag. She dropped her bag into the car, tied back her hair, and found a squeegee by the pump to wash the dust from the windscreen. When she'd finished, she lifted a watering can from beside the pump and called them back to her.

'Come on, come on,' she said, flapping a hand at them both. A dribble of water trailed from the nozzle bobbing at her hip.

Sam ambled over. When he was close enough she grabbed his shoulder and squeezed, pulling him closer. He wilted, staring at her shoes. Katie was tossing rocks at a give-way sign. She waited until Dettie called again, threw a final stone, and finally strolled over, taking her time to read the advertisements for ice and cola, kicking the dirt.

'All right now. All right. Stop being silly,' Dettie said when Katie was finally slouching in front of her. 'I know we're all hot and tired and cranky. So far it's been a long trip.' She exhaled heavily. 'A lousy trip. And I'm sorry I got cross.' The water inside the watering can slopped around. 'But we've still got a long way to go, and a long time before we get there. So if we're going to be stuck together, maybe we should all agree to start afresh. Can we do that?'

Katie rolled her eyes back in her head. Sam pushed a rock around with his shoe. When no one spoke, he nodded.

'Good. That's good.' Dettie smiled. 'Because I know we've all said things we wish we hadn't. And we're all sorry about the way we've behaved. Aren't we, Katie?'

That bird, cawing again, seemed to flood the air with a sad rattle.

Dettie splashed water on her hand and wiped it over her face, sighing.

'Anyway, I thought some water might get rid of this sticky feeling. Cool off all our heads a little,' she said, flicking her fingers dry. The bandaid beside her ring was loose, and its end had curled. 'Sammy, do you want to go first?'

He was going to shake his head, but she'd already tipped the watering can. A lukewarm stream slapped over his face and gushed into his singlet. His lips weren't closed and a trickle slipped around his vent, into his stoma.

He doubled over, hacking.

'You all right, Sammy?' Dettie said, as he coughed and sputtered.

He tried to indicate that he was choking, but she had moved on.

When he finally had his breath back, his neck still wheezing, his face flushed, Katie was already soaked too and was using the handkerchief to dry herself.

'So all's forgiven then?' Dettie asked, replacing the can by the pumps.

sign

Sam spat some gritty water onto the ground. The scent of plastic and petrol was faint on his skin. His chest ached. Over in the dirt lay the mango. A fluorescent heart, still wet, already troubled by the flies.

31

The sky was clear and spilling over with stars. Sam thought about all the times at home he had looked up at them, trying to block out the streetlights, seeing nothing but the occasional glitter, muffled through the grey. Here, the Southern Cross was perched above them, vivid among an expanse of crisp, cool blue, and in the darker spaces, miniscule specks clustered together like fine mounds of shimmering sand. Katie was lying in the front with her seat rolled back, and just as Sam was about to fall asleep too, Dettie began easing off the accelerator. The shell of a rusted car, abandoned on the highway, slipped by the window as Dettie turned into an emergency stopping bay and shut the engine off.

Dettie was toying with something in her lap, whispering to herself, but with the grumble of the motor finally quiet, Sam's eyes were heavy. He heard a door pop open and the ceiling light came on, but then the door was quietly pressed shut and all was dark again. Dettie must have stepped out for a cigarette, he thought, and rolled over onto his back to check his watch.

sign

The moon, circled with a faint glow, shone on him through the back window. The road was quiet. Sam's head was swimming, a weightless, drifting fog pressing in. The chill outside. The soft light. The scent of antiseptic from the first-aid kit. He remembered, suddenly, the children's ward. Lying in the hard bed, listening for the sound of footsteps down the corridor. And with that he was awake. In the grass beside the road crickets chattered like tiny heart monitors. Even Katie's steady breathing reminded him of the girl lying behind the thick plastic curtain. He tried to recall his mother visiting after work, Katie with chocolate milk spilt on her shirt, the sun buttery on his arms as he sat by the windows in the patients' lounge—but his mind was filled with the metal bed frame, the squeak of the nurse's sneakers, and the girl. He felt he could almost picture the girl's hollow eyes following him as she walked—or was wheeled—from the room. But of course, she hadn't looked at him as they'd rolled her bed away. She'd barely seemed aware of anything in the room anymore.

Sam looked at his watch again. Dettie had been gone for almost an hour. He sat up and looked around. She wasn't anywhere near the car and when he wound the window down a fraction there was no scent of smoke. The horizon stretched out in the distance, flat, dark and empty. An alien landscape under an unfamiliar sky, and he and his sleeping sister were all alone in it. For another quarter of an hour he waited, his eyes searching the gloom—the tangled tree line, the dull road—trying not to blink. Dettie's keys still dangled in the ignition, but her handbag was gone.

Had she left them? Sam flopped against the door. Had she waited until they were asleep and deserted them on an empty

149

road, miles from anywhere? Alone? He tried to remember the name of the last town they'd passed by. Rosington? Roseworthy? At the time he'd been distracted by the sheep truck in front of them. One of the sheep had its leg caught between the bars and was kicking, a helpless, frantic little spasm. They were in South Australia. He knew that. They'd gone through the border. He'd been awake then. He was starting to feel tight in the chest. There would be traffic in the morning, wouldn't there? Someone to wave down? His eyes were aching.

Katie's head rolled away from him as she slept. First his father had left, then his mother was gone, and now Dettie. Everyone peeling away. Recoiling from him. The hollow sensation that accompanied that thought seemed to reverberate in his mind, colouring everything. Even the girl at the hospital. Somehow, it was as though she'd abandoned him too, glaring at him as she left. Her yellowed lips sneering. Her brow creased in contempt. His fingernails were cutting into his palms. He squeezed harder.

It was his fault. Dettie had driven them for days. She was taking him and Katie all the way to their parents and they hadn't even said thank you. And she'd wanted to start fresh. She'd snapped at them, sure, but she was tired, and stressed, and struggling to remember something good about their father. Desperate to connect with both of them amid all the rush of the move. And they'd resented her. Fought her. She must have known Sam was angry. That since the phone call in the park, he wouldn't look at her. He'd offended her. Broken her heart. She'd waited until he was asleep and left. Just like everyone else.

Now they were alone.

Suddenly he heard rustling from outside—a crackle, as though something were shuffling softly over sticks and gravel.

sign

Sam whipped around to peer through the window, out at the silvery shimmer of the road. The nearest tree branch swayed slightly, but there was no breeze. Sam held his breath, listening for footsteps. Even the crickets were silent. And as he was staring into the darkness, straining to separate the shapes of the bushes from the roadside posts, a shadow moved.

He ducked, feeling his face flush. Something was outside, lurching towards them, hunched over. Gradually, the sounds of broken twigs and a quiet scraping of tin drew closer. He could hear it clearly—too clearly—as if he were standing outside himself, or as if the door were open. Or the window. Panicked, he looked. The window *was* open. He'd left it down a few centimetres when he checked for Dettie's smoke.

An image of zombies flooded his head. No longer cartoons. No longer thrilling. He pictured hands, clawed and rotting, tearing through steel.

You killed him! You and your unholy horde . . .

Slowly, listening for any movement, Sam inched across his seat, stretching out his fingers into the darkness for the window handle. Just as he felt metal, something clattered on the tar outside. There was a scuffle, and something moaned.

Decayed heads, faces collapsing in on themselves, sniffed at the air, drawn to the scent of flesh.

Your eyes . . . I saw your eyes among the shadows of my dreams . . .

He found the handle and quickly wound it shut. The noise muffled and he was alone with Katie's soft snoring. He wheezed, curling into a ball and squeezing his eyes shut. For a time he lay still, his forehead pressed into the upholstery, his vision a swirl of blue washes and orange sparkles behind his eyelids. There was blood and teeth and torn muscle in his mind. He waited for the sound of shattering glass.

Instead, when he had calmed slightly, he noticed a faint sound—a tapping. When he listened carefully he could make out a rusty squeaking, coming from behind him, vibrating through the frame of the car. He opened his eyes and, forcing himself, turned over to kneel on the seat. Staring up at the stars, he listened until the squeaks wore down to silence. His legs were locked together, but he took a deep breath and pulled himself up to peer through the back window. When his eyes focused, he hiccoughed.

There was something there.

Something was hunched at the back of the car. Scratching at the bumper. Its rounded shoulders, grey in the light of the moon, hiding its head from view. But it was pulling, clawing at the car. Trying to tear it open. Huffing.

What do you want with us? What foul misdeed will sate your bloodlust?

There was nothing left in Sam's mind of the colourful comic-book zombies that had delighted him. All that remained was this twisted, grey bulk. This physical thing only a metre away from him through thin, transparent glass. He saw rotting triangular teeth in his mind. He saw blood. He saw himself and Katie, left like that mangled kangaroo by the side of the road.

If Dettie was there she could have driven off. Her keys glistened beside the steering wheel. His thoughts raced. What if she hadn't left them? What if she'd just gone for a cigarette? Stepped out into the dark to find the zombie waiting for her? No melodramatic dialogue. No pleading. No peaceful giving up. Just the stench of decay and an animal savagery from the shadows.

sign

Sam heard a snap. The car jolted, and something came loose in the zombie's hand. It grunted, and dropped a metal chunk of the car into the dirt.

He scrambled to check that all the doors were locked. Dettie's wasn't, so he snapped it down and buried himself under the blanket, trying to tuck himself onto the floor behind the front seat. The noises paused, as though the shadow outside was listening. The silence became too much and he squashed his face in his hands, praying for the sunrise.

A tingling ran down his legs to the soles of his feet, but he stayed hidden. The comic-book zombie's mouthful of flesh; the kangaroo's rubbery eye; the girl's bony hands, draping from her hospital bed; the boy in Dettie's arms, twisting in pain, rivulets of blood down his face—everything swam in Sam's mind all at once, all bound together somehow by the empty feeling in his chest, and the pale grey shape outside, pressing on the car, trying to chew through. Slowly, the clicking and scratching moved around to the front, near the engine, closer to Katie. He gasped, waiting for the sound of breaking glass and shrieking.

Eventually, though, it was quiet. A silence even more ominous when he realised again that he couldn't call out to it, even if he'd wanted to. When he finally dared to glance outside, the road was empty. The creature, whatever it was, was gone. The car was still intact, he was alive, and Katie hadn't woken. And as he lay down, staring up at the stars, Sam felt desperately tired. He had seen something. Grey, and bent, and groaning. He'd heard it. He'd felt the car move. Wondering what time it was, he tilted his watch face towards the light. It was after two in the morning. As he lowered his wrist, he saw outside the window a shrunken grey face staring in.

Sam opened his mouth to cry out, but couldn't make a sound.

The face smiled and a knuckle rapped lightly on the window. He stopped kicking and looked again. It was Dettie, her small features colourless in the dark, and she was pointing at the lock.

She was back. She was fine.

Sam jumped to open the door for her and she slid back inside, fussing with her handbag.

'That was silly of me,' she whispered. 'I went and locked myself out. Of all the stupid things.'

Sam leaned over and locked the door behind her.

'Thank you, sweetie.' Dettie was puffing, and as she turned to check on Katie, Sam could make out the whites of her eyes, bulging through the shadows. She smelt of sweat and nicotine.

Sam pointed out the window and mouthed the word *zombie*.

Dettie rolled her seat back, and squinted. 'I can't believe you're still awake, Sammy.' She petted his arm. 'You must be exhausted.'

He shook his head and gestured at her with his fingers bent like claws.

'Sammy, I'm sorry. I don't know what you're trying to say,' she said. 'It's too dark.'

She lay down and pulled a cardigan over herself, closing her eyes. 'And you need to get some sleep.'

Sam stayed perched at the edge of his seat, shivering, until both Katie and Dettie were snoring softly in front of him. He wasn't tired, and each rustle of the trees outside shook him alert again. Eventually, he rolled up his blanket and laid his head on top, watching out of half-closed eyes and listening in case Dettie's door creaked open again.

32

Later that morning they showered in the white bathroom cubicles of a caravan park. Dettie had bought them thongs so that they wouldn't have to walk on the tiled floor—which she insisted was probably swimming with disease. Sam let the stream of water hit his back and kept his entire neck dry as much as he could. While he waited for Katie to emerge he returned to his comic.

After seeing something real—whatever it was—the comic seemed a little silly now. All the characters' faces were rubbery and distorted. The dialogue read like something from a daggy old black and white film. He didn't find it thrilling anymore, and it certainly wasn't scary. For some reason, as he scanned the pages, it just made him sad. The humans gawped and fled in the face of the undead horrors that stalked them, which was fun, but the zombies themselves . . .

Once, they had looked fearsome and furious. They had reminded him of himself, silent—but unleashed. It excited him to see that abandon running wild. Snarling and vicious. Unstoppable. Now they all seemed to be miserable. Eyes squinched and weepy. Mouths not snarling so much as slack. Hands stretched out, not to threaten, but to plead. Fingers gesturing desperately, shaping themselves to be understood. They growled simple words. '*Braaaaains* . . .' '*Hunger* . . .' And as he read them over again he realised it was Tracey's voice he was hearing in his head. Her weird burping speech. Raspy and grunting. '*Bah. Rai. Ns.*'

Then he knew why it made him sad. It was *him*, peering up from the page. Discoloured skin. Neck slashed. Hands grasping. Grunting. Wordless and gesturing. When Dettie and Katie returned, Sam wiped the tears from his eyes and stashed the comic under the car seat.

They headed off to find a roadside diner for breakfast. Sam could hear an unusual rattle shuddering in the car's engine whenever Dettie sped up. As they parked, though, the noise disappeared, and while Dettie stood by the diner doorway having a cigarette, Katie scuffed her thongs in the dirt and then lifted her feet, watching the grey sand pour from between her toes.

They ordered three hot meals, and when their food arrived, Dettie slid the trays across the table towards them. 'Long way to go today,' she said. The undersides of her fingernails, Sam noticed, were stained black.

He ate a bacon sandwich and had another two pieces of toast smothered in strawberry jam. Katie mashed up the eggs on her plate and drank half her orange juice. They were sitting in the corner of the restaurant beside the kitchen, their backs to the other tables.

Sam's eyes were blurry from lack of sleep and the urge to cry. He kept rubbing them, peeling his lids apart when they felt sticky.

sign

'Are you right, Sammy? What's wrong with your eyes?' Dettie asked, peering over her coffee at him.

Sam shook his head and looked away behind her. On the wall was a framed road map of Australia. As he stifled a yawn he strained to read the names of each of the towns.

'Well, don't keep rubbing them, they'll get red.'

They were now in a place called Gawler. Since Dettie had wandered off during the night, he'd made sure to look for the town's welcome sign when they drove in. He'd even written it on one of the advertisement pages of his comic while Dettie was busy adjusting her side mirror. Chewing his toast, he repeated it to himself in his head, spelling it out.

Gawler.

Whenever the door to the kitchen opened they heard hissing water and the clatter of dishes being stacked. Sam was watching the shadows on Dettie's cream blouse dim to yellow in the fluorescent lights. She was fidgety, twirling her lighter in her hands, and he noticed she seemed to be shooting nervous glances at the other customers.

A waitress with a pot of coffee and a tray full of saltshakers squeezed past their table. As she filled Dettie's cup she smiled down at Katie and Sam. The waitress smelt of vanilla, and as she swept away Dettie arched her neck to watch her go. Her gaze followed the waitress all the way across the room to where she set down her trays by the payphones.

'You kids almost done?' Dettie asked. 'Katie? Have you had enough?'

Katie had her chin on the table, tapping a fork on her plate.

Sam blinked the cloud from his eyes and concentrated back on the map, looking for Gawler.

The waitress had started wiping down a booth, sweeping loose pepper and used sugar packets into her palm. Dettie was still watching her, eyes narrowed. She lifted her coffee to her lips, sipped it too fast and burnt herself.

'Blast!'

Katie sat up. The coffee had spilt over Dettie's fingers, and she wiped it off hurriedly with serviettes. By the time the mess was soaked up and she'd turned back to watch the phones, the waitress had moved out of sight.

'I'd better go wash off,' she said, fanning her hands dry. The bandaid on her finger had stained brown. 'You kids finish up and get ready to go. Katie, you'd better hurry. Your food will get cold.'

When she'd wandered away, clutching the strap of her handbag, Sam walked closer to the map and searched for Gawler along the lines of the roads. It was tucked away at the bottom of the country, inland, above Adelaide, beside a crack in the coastline. He hunted around until he found Perth, in capital letters, all the way over on the left of the map. Sydney was on the opposite side, and when he traced his finger along the roads from Sydney to Gawler he kept getting lost along the way. If he pressed his palm flat to the glass he could fit his hand five times in the space between Sydney and Gawler. The boy had fallen off the train in Mildura, which fell under his right index finger. The zombie must have appeared behind his third finger and pinkie. Between here and Perth they still had over seven hands to go, and the road looked straight and empty across the yellow-coloured section of the map.

Katie was folding serviettes into floppy shapes of swans and playing with them. She made soft cooing sounds and floated them about, dipping their beaks in her orange juice.

'Sam, don't leave fingerprints all over the place,' Dettie said, pushing her chair back under the table.

Sam lifted his hands off the glass, and wandered back over.

'Oh, aren't those *lovely*, Katie,' Dettie said. 'How'd you learn to make those?'

Katie stood up and crushed the serviettes into balls. She turned, silently, and walked towards the door, leaving them mangled to soak up the remains of egg yolk smeared on her plate.

33

'Did you get enough to eat, Katie?' Dettie was watching the other motorists in the car park, studying their expressions as she unlocked the car. Her voice had a tiny squeak.

Katie crawled into the back seat. She tossed the colouring books and box of crayons Dettie had just bought her onto the floor. She clipped together her seatbelt and went back to folding another drooping swan from her mother's handkerchief.

She had been quiet for hours now, and Sam couldn't actually remember the last time she'd said anything. Even when their father had left she'd yelled and stormed around the house, and cut the hair off all her dolls. But now she was still all the time, and wouldn't smile. He had tried playing Tic-Tac-Toe with her earlier in the car. Offered to fix her ponytail. But whenever he looked at his sister, her eyes would just drift down his face as she turned away.

'I bet you feel better after that nice hot shower this morning,' Dettie said, turning the key in the ignition. The strange new

160

noise in the engine started again almost immediately, rattling somewhere behind the steering wheel.

Katie lifted her head to look out the window at a family unloading an esky from their station wagon.

Dettie coughed. 'You know, Katie, it's very frustrating talking to a brick wall all the time,' she said, and peered over her shoulder to reverse out of their parking space. 'You and I—we have a very important role in this car.' She popped the car into gear and steered it around the service station. 'We provide conversation. Poor Sammy can't do it, can you, love?' She flashed Sam a tight smile and went back to talking into the rear-vision mirror. 'So we can't afford to keep ignoring each other, can we?'

Katie turned towards the front of the car and peered at the approaching intersection emerging from the heat.

'I thought we'd all forgiven one another,' Dettie sighed. 'Put all this silliness behind us. Were moving on.'

Katie sat up. 'Help me.'

'What?' Dettie turned. 'What was that, sweetie?'

Katie leant forward and pointed through the windscreen. 'Help me,' she said, louder.

When he followed her gaze, over towards the upcoming intersection, Sam could see a hitchhiker, standing at the side of the road. A weathered, brown shape among the dust and haze, with two bags lying behind his feet. But he was smiling, holding a cardboard sign that read, *Help me, I'm British.*

SIGN

34

'Thanks for that, love. Much appreciated.' The hitchhiker swung his legs into the car and pulled the door shut. With his bags in the boot, he snapped on his seatbelt and sat stiffly in the back behind Dettie, clutching his knees.

When Dettie looked down at the dried mud crusted on his shoes, it was as though there was something sour in her mouth. 'Our little Samaritan is the one to thank,' she said, gesturing back at Katie with her thumb. 'She would've sulked the rest of the trip if we'd left you out there.'

'In that case, thank *you* very much, young miss,' the hitchhiker said, nodding to Katie.

He *was* English, and when he spoke his voice sounded like he was about to break into a laugh. Sam turned to sneak a better look. The hitchhiker had a thick brown beard and grey eyes. He was thin, and his shirt hung too large from his neck, exposing the length of his clavicle, ballooning where it tucked into his pants. He smelt like linen warmed by the sun, and when he ruffled his hair flecks of pollen and dust came drifting out. When the hitchhiker noticed Sam peering at him, he smiled.

'Morning,' he said, raising his eyebrows. Sam waved back.

Dettie put the car in gear, pulled out from the side of the road and hopped back up onto the highway. Everyone jerked in their seats, and as she sped off, the motor howled, the shuddering inside it increasing. 'So where are you trying to get to?' she asked.

The hitchhiker folded up his cardboard sign and stuffed it behind his legs. 'Not any place in particular,' he said. 'Just travelling.'

Nobody said anything, so he cleared his throat. 'Spent some time up on your Gold Coast there,' he said. 'Bit of Sydney. Tried Adelaide out for a while. Thought I might head out west. A friend of mine said I should check out Monkey Mia. Have you been at all?'

'And that's what you do, is it?' Dettie snorted a laugh. *Travel around?*'

The hitchhiker scratched inside his beard. 'For now,' he said, shrugging, the gesture almost entirely muffled by the saggy mass of his clothes. 'Just doing the rounds.'

'And that pays well, does it?'

When he'd unwound a kink in his seatbelt, he looked around and smiled. 'And where are you lovely people off to?'

'We're going to Perth,' Katie said.

The hitchhiker whistled.

'Three days it's took so far,' Katie said, 'but we're going fast and not stopping. We sleep in the car even. And we bought new clothes when we needed them. Also, one time there was this boy who broke a tooth—'

'So have you got a name then?' Dettie's voice rose, drowning her out.

The hitchhiker was nodding at Katie, but he looked up. 'Oh, yes. Sorry, love,' he said. 'It's Jon.'

Dettie adjusted herself in her seat. 'Sorry, it's *Mr . . .*?'

'No, don't bother with the niceties, love. Jon's fine.'

She inhaled, loudly, through her nose. 'Well. Mr Jon,' she said, 'that's Katie in the back with you, and this here is Sam. He doesn't talk.'

Sam was expecting him to ask why, or to look shocked, but Jon only nodded. 'Had a good dose of sun there, me mate.'

For the first time that morning the sunburn on Sam's face throbbed again, and he dipped his head.

Jon began folding back his shirtsleeve. 'I grew up in Manchester,' he said. 'We see the sun there about twice a year if we're lucky. So you can imagine when I got out here, I was lily white. And the first day—the *first day*—I got off the plane, I got burnt worse than I ever have in my life. Just walking the streets. Giant blisters all over me.'

Dettie kept breathing loudly through her nose.

'A few days later, though, when the glow went down,' Jon held up his forearm, 'this was what was under it.' His skin was as brown as Sam's grandfather's had been after working all those years on the farm. 'You watch, me mate, in a couple of days you'll have a better tan than any of us.'

Sam felt his sunburn throb again, but this time it didn't hurt. He almost liked the tight feeling on his skin.

The car drifted towards the side of the road and kicked gravel up under the floor. Dettie stopped peering in the mirror, frowned, and jerked the steering wheel so that the tyres remounted the asphalt.

Jon was tapping on his knees, whistling. He fiddled with the ashtray near the doorhandle, and turned to look at Katie. 'So how about you, sweetheart?' he said. 'I bet you got all the boys running after you.'

Katie scrunched up her nose. 'Eww! No!' she groaned, but she was blushing.

'She most certainly does not!' Dettie snapped. 'And I'll thank you to keep a civil tongue in your head.'

'Sorry, love,' he said, puffing out his cheeks. 'Didn't mean nothing by it.'

When he noticed Sam looking at him, he rolled his eyes. Sam spun back around, covering a smile with his hands. Beside him, Dettie was glaring at the road, her expression narrowed and tight.

Jon grasped his shirt and lifted it up and down to fan his chest. He glanced around at all the windows, wound shut, and leant forward. 'Just realised I didn't catch *your* name, love,' he said, over the hiss of the vents.

Sam noticed his aunt's eye flicker, but she didn't respond.

A moment passed until Katie sat up again, bouncing in her seat. 'That's Aunt Dettie,' she said.

'*Dettie*, eh?' Jon leant forward against Sam's seat back and rested his chin on his arm. He whistled. 'Can't say I've heard that before. Is it short for anything?'

The plastic of the steering wheel squeaked under Dettie's grip.

Katie hummed, 'Um . . . nope. Just Dettie. Aunty Dettie.'

'It's Bernadette,' Dettie exhaled, shaking her head.

Jon tilted his ear towards her. 'What's that, love?'

'Bernadette. My name.'

'Oh.' Jon grinned at her, exposing a mouthful of cluttered teeth. 'Like the saint.'

sign

Dettie glared at him, eyes narrowed, but when he kept grinning back, her face softened. As she turned back to the road a faint look of surprise tickled her lips. They drove on, her shoulders relaxing more with every passing kilometre.

35

Ice cream ran between Sam's fingers and down his wrist. He licked the back of his thumb clean and watched the closest seagull squawking angrily, ruffling its feathers as it charged another bird. Katie's paddle-pop was sliding off its stick and she had to duck to scoop it into her mouth. Her chin was wet with chocolate ice cream and her shirt was stained. Almost breathless, she was slurping up as much as she could before it all melted.

Travelling through Port Augusta, having crossed one dried-up lake that had cracked into large mud plates, Dettie had decided to stop at the next shoreline. After crossing a narrow bridge, they'd pulled over near a small dock where people were using a concrete ramp to load their boats into the water, and where a pink Mr Whippy van had parked. Dettie had let Jon buy them all ice creams, and was nibbling her own lime-flavoured icy pole, holding it at a distance, one hand poised to catch the runoff. The car was parked behind them, near a pair of bins, and they were standing beside a long wooden jetty that reached out into the rippling water.

sign

For the first time in days Sam felt a crisp breeze creeping beneath his singlet and up his back. His teeth were numb as he bit into the last of the paddle pop, letting it melt away in his mouth. Jon had finished his in four lazy bites and was chewing on the stick. No one had spoken since they'd parked. Katie's attention had been on her ice cream; Dettie, who clutched her handbag tightly to her side whenever Jon was close by, had tested each of the car's wheels with her foot; and Jon strolled with his arms stretched out, tilting his head back in the sunlight to let the wind whip through his clothes, pinning them to his body.

In the sky two birds caught an updraft and were lifted higher, their wings trembling. Two long brown bridges, one newer than the other, both uplifted on crisscrossing pylons, snaked off into the distance, uniting both sides of the town. People as small as ants were fishing from the smaller of the pair, riding bikes and walking its length with dogs. Several white sailboats bobbed on the surface of the water.

'Is everyone done?' Dettie asked, winding the wrapper around her stick.

'Just a second, love.' Jon yawned. 'You might want to take a bit of a breather while you can. Look around. It's a hell of a view.'

Dettie cleared her throat, jerking her head towards Katie and Sam.

'What's that, love?'

'The *language*.' Dettie raised her eyebrows.

'Right.' Jon nodded. 'Sorry, love. *Heck* of a view, kids.'

'Just say "nice view".'

'Right.'

Dettie had stayed back from the water's edge, trying not to look out over the expanse. She hadn't even crossed the boundary of the dirt car park. They had been driving together for a few hours now, and gradually she and Jon had stopped talking so cautiously to one another. She'd even stopped flinching when he called her *love*.

The seagulls had given up on Sam and were crowding around Katie, cawing and twitching their open beaks.

Jon tugged a map from his back pocket and sat down, spreading it out over a patch of grass. Sam knelt beside him as he was pinning it down with his shoe and a couple of pieces of bark, and watched him hunt out a strip of road that followed the coastline. Sam leant over to read the name of the closest town.

'Wondering where we are, me mate?' Jon shielded his eyes. The sun had just swung out from behind a cloud.

Sam nodded.

'Well,' Jon bit his bottom lip as he turned the map towards Sam, 'it looks like we're smack in the middle of Port Augusta here.' He jabbed at the name.

Jon's map was a little smaller than the one in the diner, and had been folded and refolded until it was breaking apart at the creases. In the area of ocean he had written comments and drawn arrows that led to the towns he must have visited. Under Melbourne it said *Twisted ankle off tram*, and pointing to a town called Millicent he had scrawled *One eyed Geezer—story about shark hunt*.

Jon began tracing his finger along a highway leading west. There was nothing written yet under the arch of the Great Australian Bight.

Sam tapped the paper, and then pointed at the road and his watch.

'How long to go?' Jon asked, and went back to measuring out the distance with his thumb. 'I should say a good couple of days.'

Sam tugged at the grass, nodding.

Beside the car, seagulls had started pecking around the bins, snapping at one another. Sam watched them leaping into the air and gliding in small circles, but he became slowly distracted by his view of the car. Something about it didn't look right, he realised. It seemed to be exactly the same, the same make and colour, and there were no new scratches or dents—but something had changed, he could tell. Nothing seemed to be missing. The aerial was still there, and the mirrors, but he felt as though he should have been noticing something; he just wasn't sure what it was.

'So, do you know any sign language, me mate?' Jon said.

Sam blinked. He let the grass blades in his fingers tumble back to the ground. He remembered Tracey clasping his hands. The pamphlet she'd given him on sign language, with its cartoon people, stiff and grey and dead-eyed. He shook his head and stared again at the map.

'Never mind,' Jon said. 'A brother of an ex-girlfriend of mine— way back in the day—he was deaf. We all grew up together talking to him in sign. I know you're not deaf, but I was thinking I might get a chance to dust off some of that. See what I remember. It'd be nice.' He took a deep breath, held it, then let it out. 'Although, that's British sign,' he said. 'I don't know if it's different here.'

Jon kept staring up at the clouds drifting above them. He sniffed and scratched his nose. Slowly, his eyes eased down until they focused on the stick still clenched between his teeth. 'You want to see a dumb trick?' he asked, and grinned. 'Here, give us your garbage.'

Nodding, Sam wiped the spit off his paddle-pop stick and held it out.

'Oh, and I'll need . . . Could you ask Katie for hers? And see if your aunt has still got one too? Could you do that?' Jon wiped off his own stick and pinched the two together at a right angle.

Dettie and Katie followed Sam back over. Dettie had insisted on rinsing hers off and was wiping it dry with her blouse.

Taking the four sticks, Jon wound them into one another, their edges touching, the two inside sticks crossed. He had to strain to lock them in place, but when the four of them were knotted together they held, making the small frame of a boomerang. He lifted it up, hanging it on his finger.

Katie laughed and Sam raised his thumbs.

When Jon laid it down on the map, the tips of the boomerang stretched from the road they were on off into the midst of the Nullarbor.

36

The noise in the engine had gotten louder. It pattered, shrill and rhythmic, beneath the hood, and Sam wondered if something metal—perhaps something important—had broken loose and was thrashing around. It grew faster at higher speeds, and now that they were on a straighter patch of road, the sound was becoming impossible to ignore.

Dettie had snapped the radio back on to drown it out, and skipping quickly over any news reports or talkback programs, she settled the dial on a station that boasted it played only 'oldies'. At first syrupy love songs engulfed the car, overwrought duets that swelled with violins, and Sam could hear Dettie humming along under her breath. But when the lyrics to 'Yellow Submarine' began, Jon's eyes lit up, and he stretched forward, tapping the side of Dettie's seat.

'Oh, louder, love,' he said. 'Louder. Please.'

Surprised, Dettie chuckled a little, turning the music up, and by the time the sound of the waves had begun, Jon was singing loudly, swinging his fist through the air as though leading a sea shanty. His excitement was infectious as he leant over to sing close to everyone's ears, and soon Dettie was warbling along too. By the second chorus, even Katie had started, bopping her head and murmuring the tune when she didn't know the words.

Sam, of course, could not sing. And as he sat and listened, realising that for once he hadn't even bothered to try, an odd emptiness flooded through him. Suddenly, the crowd noise and the brass band behind the melody seemed creepy, almost ghostly, as he stared out at the empty roadside. He could feel the music wash over him, rhythmic and clanging, smothering: Katie's flinty tones; the deep voice, rumbling and low, that Jon was putting on to make them laugh; and Dettie's old-lady opera voice, trembling every time she held a note. There was a peculiar otherworldliness to the sound of it all. He couldn't add anything to the cacophony, but felt it stirring the atmosphere of the car, quivering on his skin. It was as though he were a drum, his sunburnt flesh pulled tight and the submarine noises, the distant clanks and groans of the ship, amplified by the hollow in his chest.

In the front seat Katie was rocking in place and smiling, and as Sam watched his sister and Dettie laughing together, he remembered—from what felt like months ago now—their strange dance in the kitchen when they prepared the apple pie for their mother's dinner party. He could still picture the way they had swept through each other's arms, powdered with flour and swapping spoons. For a moment they seemed to be back there again too, giggling at each other, sliding in and out of harmony.

The song faded away, to be replaced by a crooning boy group, and as Dettie lowered the volume, despite Katie's protests, she muttered something about smut. Slumping back in her seat, her arms crossed, Katie's smile drained away. But her body wasn't twisted as far away from her aunt as it had been before. In the sudden quiet, beneath the persistent hum of the air vents, the motor's clatter persisted.

'You know—if you want, love,' Jon inched forward again, gesturing through the windshield, 'I can take a look at that noise for you.'

'It's fine,' Dettie said. 'It's nothing for you to concern yourself with.'

He raised his hands. 'Righto. But my old man was a mechanic,' he said. 'Doesn't make *me* one, of course, but I helped out with plenty of repairs in his shop growing up. If you were interested.'

Dettie was silent, shaking her head, but as the sound droned on, Sam could see she was thinking it over.

37

The car looked like it was yawning. Sam felt as familiar now with its boxy, angular face as he was with his own, and as it cooled off in the shade of the petrol station, its doors open and its bonnet propped up, to Sam it too seemed to be exhausted, yawning. The station had a garage for repairs, and Jon had somehow talked the heavy-set mechanic into lending him some tools. So while Dettie and Katie emptied out the rubbish from the back seat and refilled their water bottles, Sam watched Jon circle the engine and poke around inside. He had already checked the oil and the tyre pressure, and now he was calling Sam over to show him the inner workings of the machine.

'What do you reckon, me mate?' he was saying. 'Think the fan is loose?'

Sam shrugged. He was still standing back from the car, stretching up on his toes. Jon gestured for him to come closer and look.

'Yeah. Not the exhaust,' he said. 'That would be up the back, wouldn't it?'

Sam shrugged again, but this time he felt surer of himself. He nodded.

There was more plastic and rubber hosing inside than he had expected, a brightly coloured battery bigger than a lunchbox, and what appeared to be a fat plastic water bottle. He was surprised at how quickly Jon's hands had turned black. The engine didn't look all that dirty, and he hadn't really seemed to have touched anything yet.

'What about the belt, eh? The fan belt? You think that might give us a rattle?'

Sam nodded, liking how even in the dry air the car's heat still radiated up under his face.

Jon leant in, taking what looked like a thin black strap between his fingers. 'Does that look loose to you?' He wiggled it.

Sam had no idea, but he nodded.

'I think you're right, me mate. We might need to give that a tighten.' Jon rose again, using his beard to scratch an itch on his arm. 'Could you grab us a screwdriver and a wrench?'

Sam hurried over to the toolbox and hunted through it. There were two kinds of screwdriver, a flat top and a cross, so he took one of each. The wrench was more of a problem. He didn't know exactly what a wrench was, whether it was like a set of pliers, or one of the long-handled tools hanging from the lid, shaped like little metal bones.

'Yep, that's the one,' he heard Jon saying, and realised he was holding an adjustable version of one of the bones in his hand. As he passed it over, Jon took the flat screwdriver and left the other for Sam to twirl about.

The station mechanic wandered out from the garage to see how things were going, and to check whether they were misusing his tools. He lifted his cap, rubbing the sweat from his forehead, and as he turned to head back inside he spat into the grass, nodding to his dog, a mangy brown animal that was skulking along the edges of the shadows. Across the yard, past the petrol pumps, Dettie and Katie had left the toilets and walked into the store, flicking their hands dry. A truck sped by on the road, sweeping a cloud of dust behind it, and for the first time since he'd sprinted across a soccer field, long before his operation, Sam enjoyed the prickly combination of dirt and sweat on his skin.

Jon was explaining to him all about the fan belt's nut and the washers. He showed him what a pulley was, and told him about the sheaves. He even let him press on the belt to see if he thought it was tight enough, and Sam agreed, without having anything to judge it against. Sam forgot everything Jon told him straight away, much of it while he was still talking, but he liked being there, listening, able to agree and interact. And even though he suspected that Jon had known what the problem was all along, he liked feeling that he was somehow part of finding the solution.

When the strap was tense enough, Jon wandered back to the toolbox and laid the things inside, wiping his hands on a rag. 'What do you think?' he said. 'Should we start her up? See if that's fixed it?'

Sam nodded, stepping back from the car.

'Wait a minute—where are you heading off to?' Jon gestured towards the driver's seat. 'I need a driver,' he said. 'I've got to stay out here and listen. Who else is going to switch her on?'

Sam shook his head, but Jon was already nudging him over to the door.

'It's simple,' Jon was saying. 'Look. The park brake is on. It's not in gear. You just sit in the front there, and when I say go, you turn that on.' He pointed at Dettie's key chain, dangling in the ignition.

Sam was panting through his vent, his eyes darting around, afraid his aunt would be watching. He couldn't see her through the glare on the store window, and as Jon helped him into the front seat, he ducked his head out of view. He reached for the seatbelt.

'Don't worry about that, me mate. Just flick her on. We'll have us a listen.'

Sam felt dwarfed by the seat. It was set back further than the passenger seat, and if he laid his back flat against it, he could barely reach the steering wheel. It was strange to look over at the passenger's seat, where he had been sitting most often lately, and see it empty. The doorhandle his knee was usually pressed against was so far away. When he looked in the side-view mirrors all he could see was the sky. Slowly, he stretched forward and took hold of the keys. Through the windscreen, Jon was giving him the thumbs up.

Holding his breath, he turned the ignition.

As the car sputtered the tiny St Christopher statue on the dashboard shook. The paddle-pop stick boomerang they had hung from the rear-vision mirror trembled and swayed. The engine coughed and died.

'That's okay. That's all right, me mate,' Jon was saying. 'You're half there. Almost. Next time just turn it all the way.'

Sam looked over at the store, but Dettie hadn't emerged. The large mechanic was still in his shed, and even his dog, where it was sniffing around a stack of wooden crates, barely lifted its head. No one was watching. No one cared. Sam lifted his arm again and took hold of the key.

This time, the car growled to life, and he was aware, more than ever before, of the tremor that ran through his seat when the motor began. Every part of the car was in motion, though it remained in place. The radio aerial quivered slightly, Dettie's cigarette packet shuddered from the dashboard and onto the floor, and he could even feel the keys still swinging between his fingers.

'You did it. Good work!' Jon was calling. He leant in towards the bonnet, his eyes shut. 'And listen to that,' he said. 'No sound. I think we got it.'

Sam laid his hands on the steering wheel. He could feel it pulse beneath his palms as the engine went on rumbling. It felt great. For the first time in as long as he could remember, he felt normal. When Jon spoke to Sam he didn't seem to be secretly pitying him. He didn't stare at his neck or ask stupid questions. He didn't treat him like he was made of glass. Sam was actually happy for a moment, and as the car fidgeted around him, it seemed happy too. Finally, Jon unhooked the bonnet, and eased it back down.

'Right,' he said. 'We better go wash up, eh? Before your aunty sees what a mess we've made of ourselves.' He waggled his blackened fingers in the air, and Sam smiled.

'You just switch that off, and we'll head over.'

Sam turned the key the other way and the motor stopped, sputtering faintly before falling silent. And as he stepped out of the car he felt another rush of power pulling the keys from the ignition.

'What's going on out here?' Dettie was wandering back with an armful of snacks, muesli bars, dried banana chips and drinks, her handbag still clenched tight beneath her elbow. 'Could you see anything wrong?'

'Just a fan belt, darlin'. Nothing too serious.'

She harrumphed. 'Well, don't fiddle with it, then.'

Katie was behind her, chewing on a musk stick, and as she saw the dog over by the shed, now lolling on its side and rubbing leaves into its matted coat, she slapped her knees, calling it to her. The dog perked up at the sound immediately, and ran over, leaping and circling her, its tail thrashing happily, licking her fingers.

'It's already taken care of, love,' Jon was saying. 'Quick tighten. That's all.'

'I hope so,' she said. 'I don't want to get halfway down the road and have the thing blow up around us.'

Jon chuckled, waving as he backed away towards the toilets. 'Also, love, your numberplate was a little loose on the front there. I screwed that back on too.'

Dettie stiffened. 'Good. Fine,' she said, tossing the food on the back seat.

Sam turned and followed Jon's scuffed footprints across the oil and dirt, but when he heard Dettie shouting, he stopped short.

'Katie! That dog is disgusting! Get away from it!'

He looked back to see his aunt kicking out at the animal and Katie yelling in protest. Dettie's foot missed, but the dog fled, barking, to cower behind a tree.

Suddenly, the mechanic stormed out of his garage, scowling at them all. Spotting the dog, he whistled. 'Come on!' he called. 'Come on! Get away!'

It scampered over, whipping through the garage door, its head lowered, its tail between its legs. The mechanic stooped to gather up his toolbox. He spat again, glaring at Dettie, and then disappeared back inside too.

Katie was pouting as she watched the dog slink away. And while her aunt lectured her about diseases and rabies, she rolled her eyes and pulled out her handkerchief to wipe her hands.

'Oh, don't use that, girl. It's filthy.' Dettie reached towards her.

'It's Mummy's.' Katie clutched it tighter.

'Yes. Well. Look at it. It's filthy. Look how much you've wiped your nose on it.'

'I don't wipe my nose on it.'

'Oh, really? That's not what I've seen. Now come on, why don't you give it to me? I can clean it up for you.' Dettie pulled something from her handbag. 'And in the meantime you can use these nice new ones I bought.' She held the package, a small cube of colourful fabrics wrapped in cellophane, out in front of her. 'Look at that one, it's got rabbits on it.'

The wrapper crackled a little beneath her thumb.

Jon had already disappeared into the toilets, but Sam lingered, watching the moment play out: Katie, winding their mother's handkerchief between her fingers; Dettie smiling, wiggling the fresh packet between them.

Slowly, Katie pushed the handkerchief up her sleeve. 'No.'

Dettie sighed. 'It needs a wash, darling. Just let me rinse it off.'

Katie shook her head.

Dettie chewed the inside of her cheek. 'You'll wash it?'

'I'll wash it.'

Dettie slipped the packet back into her purse. 'All right. If you're going to do it, come on, let's find a tap.'

sign

Katie was hesitant, but she followed their aunt over to a tap in the shade behind the garage. The tap spat, shuddering, and as Sam watched, together his sister and aunt ran the cloth under the hiss of water and wrung it out. Dettie directed Katie on what to do, pointing, but never reaching over to snatch the cloth away. And though he couldn't hear what they were saying, as Dettie turned off the tap, Sam saw Katie smile.

38

The motor continued its healthy purr for a couple of hours, delighting Sam with every untroubled acceleration and gear shift. In the front seats, Katie and Dettie were chatting happily for once. Katie was imagining what kind of dog she would like her parents to buy when they got to Perth—small and fat with big floppy ears. In the back, Sam and Jon played Rock, Paper, Scissors, with Jon calling a silly commentary on every throw, pretending it was all a dynamic clash of sporting titans.

They were well along the Eyre Highway, a long grey strip of road that appeared to float across the browned landscape before them, dissolving into a warbled haze up ahead. Only tufts of small green bushes and spindly sun-worn trees broke the endless breadth of flat earth and sprawling blue sky, and every kilometre or so a ghostly dirt track would lead off the highway into nothingness.

When the battle was over—scissors vanquishing paper in a controversial counting delay that, it was said, would go down in history—Jon playfully toasted his defeat with a sip of water. As he replaced the water bottle by his feet he resurfaced with the scrunched copy of Sam's *Tales of Fear*.

'Hello,' he said.

Sam watched him flick through its pages, through the sprays of blood and stilted dialogue.

Jon laughed. 'Look at this mess,' he said, turning the issue to show Tim's face being peeled away. 'Brilliant.'

He skimmed through a few more scenes, far more amused than repulsed. 'You like the scary ones?'

Sam shrugged.

'I like the pirate ones, me,' Jon said. 'Have you read any pirate ones? Or Batman. Do you like Batman?'

Sam jerked, grinning wildly, pointing at himself.

'Yeah? Batman? Bat car? Bat plane? Robin? Good stuff. Great stuff.'

Sam didn't like Robin so much, but he loved every bit of the rest. And he had a desperate urge to tell Jon why. Why Batman was the best.

Because he didn't have superpowers. Because he wasn't the strongest, or the fastest, or the best. Because he was *smart*. And he worked hard. Superman got all his powers from the sun. Spider-Man was bitten by a spider. But Batman had to train. He had to learn. That was what made him the best.

Jon was talking about the old sixties *Batman* show that Sam had only seen a couple of times in reruns. He kept describing how funny it all was, but Sam wasn't listening.

He looked down at his hands.

Batman had to *learn* to be the best. He lost something and worked hard to make it mean something.

Sam thought of Tracey again, and the therapy sessions he had refused to attend. His excitement dissolved. He felt a twinge of shame.

Batman would never have given up.

39

A little further up the road they stopped so Jon could buy them a proper lunch. He wanted to get fast food, but there was nothing around. Dettie insisted on another roadside café so that the children wouldn't be eating too much rubbish. Katie whined, but eventually they pulled up in a small town called Wudinna, in a place so close to the road that it trembled when trucks went past. The diner was small but almost empty, and the man who took their orders also cooked their food and cleared the tables. While they ate, he waited in the kitchen, hunched over his television set. Halfway through the meal a fire truck roared past the window and their cutlery rattled.

'He's in a bit of a hurry,' Jon said, adjusting the serviette in his collar.

'Fires up ahead,' Dettie said. 'Bad, apparently.'

'Mm.' Jon was chewing. 'Weather wouldn't help.'

'Yes. Well, they could definitely do with some rain.'

'And some cold,' Katie said. She looked proudly around the table and then shoved a forkful of carrot in her mouth.

Jon waved his knife, smiling. 'Yep. Cold would be nice.'

Dettie shook her head. 'What on earth does it matter if it gets cold?'

Looking up at her, Katie blinked a few times and swallowed. 'Because when it's cold,' she said, 'the fires go out.'

'Oh, how ridiculous,' Dettie sighed, carving into her slice of corned beef. 'Temperature doesn't have anything to do with fires.'

'Yes, it does. When it's cold—'

'You mean when it's *raining*.'

'No.'

Sam had lost his appetite. He pushed aside his half-finished meat pie and sat his chin on the edge of the table.

'That's why there aren't as many fires in winter,' Katie was saying, shepherding peas to the side of her plate. 'Because this guy at school—'

Sam could feel a vibration beneath his head, up through his jaw.

'Goodness me, girl, you have no idea what you're talking about.'

Dettie slipped a chunk of meat, glistening like mother-of-pearl, into her mouth. Sam laid his head down flat. The table's surface felt cool against his cheek.

'I do so. A guy at school—'

Around him, his aunt and sister kept squabbling, but Sam tried to block them out, listening instead to the sound of clinking forks and clattering porcelain beneath them—the rhythm they were making without realising. It was a dull, distant beat, but it filled his ear, magnified by the wood. And behind the clatter he heard a thrum, like the table itself was humming.

'Katie,' Dettie was sighing, 'it's just ridiculous to be arguing like this all the time.'

Feeling the table move under him, Sam eased his eyes open and saw Jon laying his head down too. 'Little quieter down here, is it?' he whispered.

Sam smiled and nodded.

'Yep. I think you've got the right idea, me mate. Keep quiet. Keep to yourself. Let everyone else wear themselves out.'

Sam closed his eyes again and they both stayed that way a moment, each with their ears pressed to the table, hearing the same clunks and hums through the heavy wood.

40

Back at the car, while everyone waited beside their locked doors for Dettie to tuck her handbag away into the boot, Katie snuck around behind her aunt and fished out a plastic bag.

'Do you know how to eat a mango?' she said, skipping back over to Jon and offering it up to him.

He had been drumming his thumbs on the roof, staring at a small aircraft buzzing overhead, and for a moment he looked puzzled, a smile tickling his lips as he watched whatever it was that she was unwrapping. His face lit up and he chuckled. 'You know what?' he said. 'I actually can.'

He explained about his time in a place called Noosa, just after he first arrived in Australia, where a group of fruit pickers had shown him the proper way to cut up a mango. There was a trick. It was lateral thinking, he said. He lifted the fruit from the bag, looking it over. It was the one Dettie had been trying to peel, before she gave up. The skin was more withered than it had been the day before, indented with small abrasions. There was a long mark down its side where

Dettie had traced her fingernail. A thin brown discolouration like a scar.

Katie had snatched some plastic knives and forks from the takeaway counter, and offered those up too. Jon slipped a knife free, tipped the fruit onto its side, and cut lengthwise along the line that Dettie had left, carving off a third of its mass, straight through. The flesh inside was bright orange, and still looked quite firm. He placed the section skin down on the bonnet of the car, its wet surface shimmering slightly in the sun, and sliced off a similar piece on the other side. He now had two portions, like two halves of a boiled egg, and a strange disk shape, surrounded by a thin strip of skin, that must contain the seed.

Having slammed the boot shut, Dettie wandered over, jangling her keys and tutting to herself. 'For goodness sake,' she said. 'We don't have time for this now.'

'Take but a second, love.' Jon held the third piece in his mouth, between his teeth, while he took up both convex portions and scored a crisscross pattern into their flesh.

'What are you—?' Katie was up on her tiptoes.

'Here we go, darlin',' he said, and suddenly pushed his fingers up from underneath, turning the mango inside out. Its innards unfurled in two bright, crosshatched fans. 'Right,' he said. He set them down on the bonnet of the car, two glistening orange turtle shells of cubed fruit, perfectly sectioned and offering themselves up as though spread on tiny serving plates.

Katie sighed with delight. Even Dettie looked impressed. Her arms were still crossed, but she nodded. Everyone crowded closer, and they stood together for a time, leaning against the vehicle, picking off squares of mango and letting them dissolve, wet and syrupy on their tongues. Jon ate the middle slice. He worked the knife around its edge, removing the peel in a long strip, and chewed it down to the seed. The breeze blew hot and dry, and a scent of petrol gave the sweetness a slight tang.

As they lingered, chewing silently, enjoying the flavour, Sam suddenly had the urge to laugh. It didn't make sense. He had no real idea of where he was; he wasn't sure how long it would be until they got where they were going. He was tired, and still blistered. He couldn't even laugh if he'd wanted to. And yet somehow, all of that just made the whole situation funnier. At that exact moment, as a fat chunk of mango sat in his mouth, as the four of them, still full from lunch, ate fruit off the bonnet of a car, he was beaming. A big, dopey, wet grin.

Jon smiled down at him. He sucked his thumb and index finger clean and then pointed back at his own chin. He kept doing it. Over and over. One hand holding the remains of his mango, the other tapping twice on his chin. Sam thought he was telling him there was food on his own mouth that needed wiping off, but that wasn't it. Jon seemed to be asking him something. Or testing something.

Two taps on his chin, his eyebrows raised. Nodding.

'Tasty,' he said, finally. 'This means *tasty*. Sign language.'

Sam's body tried to laugh, but couldn't, so he went on smiling instead. It *was* tasty, he thought, and swallowed, the flavour of sunshine tracing its way down his throat.

41

'Close. That's good, lad, but just . . .' Jon showed him again. He lifted his hands and gave his palm more of a smack. Two quick, firm slaps with three fingers. 'With more of a whack,' he said. 'Like you *mean* it.'

Sam looked down at the limp tangle of his own hands, one curl of digits collapsed inside the other.

Over in a small patch of grass beyond the toilet block Katie and Dettie were picking yellow daisies. The tension of the argument at lunch had finally faded, and now, after another couple of hours of driving and an early dinner of hamburgers, the two of them had been to the toilet and decided to take a walk while they waited for Sam and Jon to finish up. It felt to Sam like they'd been eating all day, but while he was stuffed full, Jon still seemed ravenous, hunting for every last hot chip in the corners of the paper wrapping.

Sam watched as Dettie and Katie searched among the bushes. Amid the haze of hot air, the colours of the scene seemed to bleed over one another like a comic-book page, vibrant but blurred and pulpy. Several long, sweltering hours had passed. He barely remembered the glimpse of the ocean they had caught outside Ceduna, and now, apart from the occasional sprout of small flowers, the land was tawny and orange. It was like the surface of an alien planet. Up in the food van, the cook was whistling along to the radio, the tiny fan above his grill just pushing steam into the back of his neck.

'Give it another go,' Jon said.

Sam opened his hands again, holding them up as if he were waiting to applaud. They still felt rubbery and weak. Still soft. Still timid. He inhaled.

With his left hand lying open he hooked his right pinkie over his left:

S.

With his index finger he pointed . . .

Jon smiled, reminding him with his eyes.

Sam pointed at his thumb:

A.

And with the final move, he slapped three fingers down on his palm:

M.

S. A. M.

'Good *work*, lad,' Jon said. 'Perfect. There you are. *Sam.* That's the way.'

Pinkie fingers, thumb, palm. His name. His own name. Not hissing across his tongue, not scribbled out on a page, but acted out. It felt almost like a code. Or the special signals he'd seen in baseball movies—the guy catching the ball sending little clues to the one about to throw. Except that this didn't feel pretend. Jon nodded along. He made it real.

sign

Sam put his finger like *this*, and Jon knew what it meant.

He'd *said* something.

Not *said* exactly. Not spoken. But—

Well, maybe it was. Maybe he *had* spoken. It was a word. It was letters. It was *him*. Not in his mouth, or his throat. Not even in his chest, or through some puffy whisper. In his fingers. His skin. Through the jolt in his arms. He'd pressed it into the air.

Pinkies, thumb, palm.

Sam.

'That's it,' Jon said, leaning down to take another bite of his hamburger. With his mouth full, he tried to lick a dribble of beetroot juice as it ran down his wrist.

Sam thought of Tracey again. Her shaping his limp hands into position. Back then it had all seemed so overwhelming. Like an impossible set of strict rules. Morse code or flag signals. In her cluttered house, surrounded by ghastly electronic voiceboxes and her peculiar burp-speaking, sign language had seemed alien and baffling. The hopelessness of learning it all had smothered him. Literally choked him up. Left him gasping and terrified. But here, with the sweet vinegar tang of tomato sauce still on his tongue, watching Jon's gnarled knuckles, the stubble on his face, his fingers stained vibrant purple, it seemed less detached and abstract. Jon would grimace or grin along with the gesture. His whole body seemed to weave and duck into whatever he was expressing. It looked natural. Not a substitute for words, but an extension of them.

Sam practised some of the other terms Jon had showed him again, trying to move more forcefully.

Good?

A fist with his thumb up; one pump forward. That meant *good*. It didn't feel so silly anymore.

Good. Good Sam.

From his perch on the picnic tabletop, Jon stomped his heels on the slats of its seat, trying to swallow faster, nodding. 'Smashing,' he said, mouth full, still chewing.

Sam clapped, twice, his right palm on top of his left.

Happy.

'Good stuff. *Happy*. Well done.'

Sam held his arms up, trying to remember—then tightened his right hand into a spear, running his index finger down his chin.

Sad.

'You got it, lad. *Sad*. Perfect.' Jon made the *good* signal, rocking in place, swallowing. 'Well done. You got that sorted right quick.'

A palette of sauces was swirled in his burger wrapper. He crushed the remains into a ball and set it aside. 'What else, what else, what else?' he said, rubbing his wrists down his thighs, clucking his tongue. 'Oh! Of course—'

He held his right hand up. Palm facing his neck. Fingers touching his chin. Then he lifted it and moved it down in a short, graceful arc.

'This is *thank you*,' he said.

He made the gesture again. Fingertips on chin, lifting them away. Slower this time.

'As in, *thank you* for this trip, lad. To you, your aunty, your sister. Thanks a lot.'

Sam smiled, and tried it too.

Thanks.

'That's the one.'

198

Thanks. You. Good.

Jon nodded. 'My absolute pleasure, lad,' he said, and smiled again, fishing the last two chips out of their paper and tidying the rest of the rubbish into a pile. 'Now, is there anything else you can think of I can try to remember?'

Sam looked over at his sister and aunt. They appeared to be squabbling again. Katie had found a tennis ball that she wanted to take with her; Dettie was wresting it out of her hand.

'You don't know where it's been,' she said.

'*You* don't know where it's been!'

'I know it's been sitting on the side of the road. Sitting next to a public toilet. So no, you are not bringing this thing with us in the car.' Holding it aloft with the tips of her fingers, Dettie hurled it off further into the scrub.

For a moment, it seemed like old times—the two of them bickering over how long Katie was allowed to stay up and watch television, or how big a slice of cake she could have before dinner. It had a familiar rhythm to it. But then Sam thought of the last few days. He remembered Dettie disappearing on them. The shadow outside the window. The scraping on the metal. He remembered the phone call to his father at the railway station. That confusion on the other end of the line. Dettie's face, flushed and furious. He remembered her pacing the highway in the moonlight, prattling to herself and hissing, shrouded in smoke. He remembered standing over the dead kangaroo, its flesh stripped, its teeth exposed. The heat and the maggots and the buzz in his head. What word did he want to know how to sign? He reached for the crossword puzzle book Dettie had left behind. He unfastened the pen, found a new, unblemished page, and printed six letters along its edge:

Scared.

Jon took a last swig of his soft drink and leant forward to read. Squinting at first, a look of surprise flickered across his face. He glanced at Sam, curious. He opened his mouth to ask something, but Dettie and Katie were wandering back to the table, already recovered from their spat. Dozens of small flowers were gathered in the front of Katie's shirt, and Dettie cleared a space for her on the table, helping her empty them all out onto the wood. Sam turned away, dissolving the word beneath a cloud of scribble.

'So what are you two up to, then?' Dettie asked. 'Secrets?'

Jon wafted the air. 'Just having a chat.'

'*Chat?*'

'Learning a few words—aren't we?'

Dettie's smirk froze. She eyed them both carefully as she directed Katie up onto the seat. 'Words?' she said.

'Yes. Sign language. I used to use it a bit,' Jon said. 'Back in the day. Thought I might try and dig some up out of the old vault.' He pointed to his forehead. 'See what my mate Sam here can use.'

Dettie blinked, her eyes rolling ever so slightly. 'Oh. Well, he won't want to do that,' she said. 'We tried once. It didn't work out.' Her lips pressed tight.

Sam stared at the remains of his burger, tipped over on its paper. The lettuce wilting into the cheese. A fly crawling across a pale sliver of tomato.

'He's taking it up marvellously.' Jon's hand clapped over Sam's shoulder. 'Quite the prodigy he is.' He gave Sam another pat and then swung himself off the tabletop onto the ground. 'Mind you, it's the sign language we use in England,' he said. He began crushing all the rubbish into a single bag and winding it closed. 'It's probably a bit different here. But it's something to be getting on with. Bit of fun, anyway.'

Dettie hummed. Katie was paying no attention. She was threading daisies, one through the other, into a chain, methodically splitting each stalk with her fingernail and sliding the next one through. She shielded the pile of waiting flowers as Jon came by to tidy up.

'Like what?' Dettie said.

With the table cleared, Jon wandered over to the nearest bin to toss their mess away. 'What's that, love?' he said.

'What are you teaching him *exactly*? What words?' Dettie picked at the strap of her handbag. 'Why?'

'Just whatever I can remember,' he said. '*Hello. Boy. Girl. Mum. Dad. Happy*. Nothing too strenuous. I've forgotten most of it.'

'*Dad?*' she said, tilting forward. 'Show me *daddy*. Sam, do you know that one yet?'

Sam shook his head almost imperceptibly.

On the walk back over Jon hiked up his pants and wiped his palms on his hips. 'Sure,' he said. 'Okay. I think—' He raised his hands, wiggling his fingers. 'Okay. Yeah.'

With his index and middle fingers of both hands pointed, Jon crossed one over the other, right knuckles lying on top of the left. He tapped twice. He waited. Sam, still sitting in place, copied the move.

Pointed fingers. Right crossed over left. Two taps.
Dad.

'Well, that's lovely!' Dettie laid her hand on the back of Sam's neck. He tried not to flinch, but it was tender. It tickled. She was too close. 'Katie, look at what your brother has done.'

Katie shrugged, still focused on her strand of flowers.

'That's just wonderful,' Dettie was going on. 'Oh, your father is going to be so excited to see that. He really will. Good work, Sammy.' She opened her handbag and scooped out her keys. 'You'll have to show me more in the car.'

'So. We're off?' Jon rocked on his feet.

'If everyone has had enough to eat. If we're all ready.'

'Couldn't eat another bite,' he said. 'Beetroot and pineapple on a hamburger? I don't know if you Australians are mad—or geniuses.'

'Yes. Well.'

'Let me just run to the lavatory,' Jon said.

'Hurry up. This was longer than I thought we'd be stopping.'

'Will do. Sorry. Sorry, love.' He started off towards the toilet, then stopped, turning in place and catching Sam's eye. With his right hand held closed he traced a circle, clockwise, on his chest. 'That one means *sorry*,' he said, and did the gesture again.

Sam nodded, tracing the same circle on his own chest in reply.

Sorry.

'That's it,' Jon said, and gave him the thumbs up. He turned again and jogged away, disappearing into the darkness of the corrugated toilet block. Dettie watched him leave before directing her attention back to Sam. She stood beside him, the leather of her handbag squeaking beneath her fingers, her smile lingering too long. Taut and strained.

42

In the dream a pair of galahs were following a twisting fence across the ocean. They hopped from one foot to the other along the barbed wire, and every time they tried to fly they fell fluttering and exhausted into the water. There was another bird too, a brighter one, like a rainbow parrot with sprays of coloured feathers, but as Sam woke the images started to fade and he couldn't remember what the other bird was doing.

He and Katie were in the back of the car resting while Jon and Dettie sat in the front seats talking. Outside the sunset was coming on and the edges of the clouds were seared orange. Jon had his legs crossed, clutching his shin with one foot up on his knee. Sam liked the look of his shoe. Its faded blue canvas was stripped white at the heel and it had different coloured laces tied together with a double knot. The sole was worn through to a thin honeycomb pattern in the rubber and Sam wondered how far Jon had walked in them before they'd picked him up.

'It's getting a touch stuffy.' Jon was lifting his beard so that the vent could hiss on his neck. 'Would you mind if I cracked open a window, love?'

Dettie winced, and slowly nodded.

'Just a fraction,' he said. 'Promise. I feel like I'm basting here.'

She clicked the fan to full power and turned both the vents above the radio towards him. 'I'd rather not if we can help it,' she said. 'There's all manner of bugs and fumes.'

He chuckled. 'Bugs and fumes? You are a mad old bird, aren't you?' His foot wiggled as he grinned at her.

Sam was surprised that Dettie didn't scold him or pull over the car. Instead she smiled tightly and shook her head.

'So what's got the lot of you headed out to the Nullarbor exactly?' he asked. 'If not for the air? I got the sense you're meeting up with family?'

Dettie straightened the paddle-pop stick boomerang still hanging from the rear-vision mirror. 'We're going home.' She sat up in her seat. 'The children are my brother's and it's time he was with them again.'

Jon nodded. He watched the way she fiddled with her wedding ring. 'So where's *your* old man in all this?' he asked. 'Waiting up ahead? Or watching over the home fires?'

Dettie stiffened. 'He's dead.'

'Oh God, I'm sorry, love.' Jon dropped his leg and sat up. 'Recent, was it?'

'A few years ago.' She sniffed.

They were silent. Jon mopped his forehead with his shirtsleeve. The car rocked as they descended a hill. Sam's eyelids were easing shut.

'He liked to travel,' Dettie said, raising her chin. 'Ted, that is. My husband.' She splayed her fingers to glance at her ring. 'We used to go on trips. Up to the Blue Mountains. Tasmania. Once to Tahiti. He was very high up in business. Had meetings all over Sydney. All hours of the day.'

'That's great,' Jon said. 'Good for you. Good stuff. Getting out. Seeing the world. So, what did he do?'

But Dettie was busy tapping the steering wheel. 'He used to wear all these ties to work.' She laughed. 'So many ties. All different kinds. I remember whenever we had an argument I'd just buy him a new tie. "You need these," I'd say. "You certainly lose enough of them all over the place." And he'd just shake his head and laugh. "You know me," he'd say.'

Half smiling, Jon fanned himself with his map.

'Then one afternoon,' Dettie said, 'he was in the middle of a very important business meeting—Ted was very important in the company, very respected—and when he leant against a window, the glass popped out. Twenty-three storeys he fell. Onto the footpath. And died.'

Jon coughed. He sat upright, staring at her with his mouth open, murmuring an apology. He obviously had no idea what to say. Sam didn't know either. He had never heard Dettie talk about the day Uncle Ted died. It was one of those things no one ever discussed. He knew something had happened around the time he started primary school, but it must have all been very sudden. He couldn't even remember a funeral.

'That's terrible, love,' Jon said, rubbing the hair on his top lip. He shrugged. He shook his head. 'Life, eh?'

Dettie's hand snaked into her handbag, scratched around and came out with the photograph of Ted. 'You have seventeen good years,' she said, 'and then—gone.'

Sam couldn't see the photograph from where he was sitting, but he knew which one it was: Uncle Ted in his brown suit, his sleeves pulled up too short, drinking a can of beer at a family barbeque. He was bald, but his hair was combed over on top, and in the photo the wind was lifting it slightly at the edge, like the lid peeling from a tub of yoghurt.

'He looks like a friendly sort.' Jon passed it back.

Dettie held the photo out a moment, glancing down at Ted's lopsided smile. He was facing away slightly, distracted by something beyond the camera. Her fingernail picked at the sticky tape that held its edges together, then she stuffed it back in the bottom of her bag. 'So what about you?' she asked.

Jon held up his left hand. 'There used to be a ring on here,' he said, 'but you'll notice there's not anymore.'

Dettie stared back at him. 'Is she dead?'

'God, no,' he said. 'No, she's in Liverpool.' He made a clicking sound in his mouth. 'Some people might argue that's much the same thing, though.'

She didn't laugh. 'And you took your ring off?'

Jon crossed his legs again. 'No point in keeping it, love,' he said. 'There was no more marriage, sad to say. That's partly why I came over here.'

'You left? You ran off on her?' Dettie was glaring.

'No. Untrue, love. No, I had the opposite problem. My lady didn't want me.' Jon was talking slower, picking at the hole in his jeans. 'Second year of marriage,' he said. 'Thought we were happy. Heading for kids and all. But the missus—apparently *wasn't* so happy.' He cleared his throat. His tongue ran across his lips. He swallowed. 'She did some things that weren't nice. I got upset. She told me to leave. And I left. All very civil. Very grown-up.'

sign

Dettie's face softened to a frown. 'She was cruel?'

Sam could only see the back of Jon's head. He had turned away from Dettie, towards his window. The side of his beard was twitching like he was moving his jaw, but he didn't speak.

Against his shoulder, Sam could feel Katie stirring. She was breathing in shallow gasps, her eyelids starting to flutter. He moved gradually, trying to nudge her off his arm. With Dettie and Jon concentrating on the road, he pushed slowly, quietly, easing her away. She slid softly against the opposite door, her head rolling on her neck, but as her cheek touched the doorframe, she kicked. Her foot clipped Dettie's seat and she shook awake.

Jon looked back at them and Sam squeezed his eyes shut. He heard Katie beside him, stretching, smacking her lips; then she settled in her seat and was quiet again. After a moment, Sam pretended to be slowly waking up, easing his eyes open, but Jon had already turned back to watching the road.

There was a soft thump on the windscreen. Sam could see a streak of grey where something small had struck. It was a moth. There were hundreds of them, a cloud rippling across the sky. Spots lit yellow by the headlights, whirling away into the trees. Another struck the glass in a dull pop, only a puff of smeared dust remaining.

'It's getting late,' Dettie said. 'If you wanted to head on with us tomorrow, we're probably going to just pull up along the road somewhere to sleep.'

Jon was flicking through Dettie's collection of cassettes.

'Or we could drop you off at a hotel along the way.'

'No, it's all good for me, love,' he said. 'If you don't mind the company.'

Dettie shrugged and scanned the rear-vision mirror. The sun had sunk below the horizon. The sky around it was a wash of orange dissolving into blue ink. Sam thought about his uncle Ted as he closed his eyes, the occasional thump of a moth hurling itself against the window punctuating the quiet.

43

Tomato soup. Lapping at his thumbs. Steam drifting towards his nose. The can lay in the garbage under the sink. Was the microwave door still open? He stepped slowly across the carpet, heel to toe. Katie was sulking in her room. Dettie was staying over. She was over a lot since his father left. She and his mother were on the veranda. They had hospital papers. It was a week until he had to go to hospital. He could hear them whispering.

'He's going through something terrible, Dettie,' his mother said. 'Maybe he needs you to talk to him.'

There was something about the papers. His mother was waving them. But the soup was almost spilling. It had dribbled around the handle of the spoon where it met the bowl.

'I wouldn't even know how to talk to him.' Dettie's voice was tight. She sniffed.

Sam's mother took a deep breath. She was leaning against the back of her chair. 'You're acting like he's dead or something,' she said.

Sam wasn't watching where his feet went. Katie had left out her shoes.

'He may as well be dead,' Dettie hissed.

The concrete bit into his knees, his hands were scalded. His mother jumped in surprise. She called his name and knelt by his shoulder.

But there was something before that—back when he was inching towards the glass doors. As the curtains quivered in the breeze. They'd been whispering. Arguing about something. He'd heard them. He'd forgotten.

It was hard to remember. They were talking so softly. And the bowl was so hot on his fingertips.

'He says he's worried,' he heard his mother murmuring. 'About you. About how you're dealing with things.'

His vision was filled with the ripples on the soup, but he could make out their voices.

'He shouldn't be asking.' Dettie was sniffing. But it might have been sobs.

Sam felt carpet between his toes. The fish tank bubbled by the window. He was almost at the door.

'He thinks he's made a horrible mistake.' His mother exhaled. 'I think he wants to try and make it up to you.'

'Not a mistake, Joanne,' Dettie spat. 'A choice. He made a choice. *His* decision. And after all this time? No.'

Then they were quiet. Sam was confused. He inched closer, balancing the bowl. If he looked up he could see their silhouettes. It reminded him of the conversation Dettie and his mother had had after his father left—except this time it was Dettie who seemed upset, with his mother consoling her. A bubble winked on the surface of the soup.

sign

'He's been going through something terrible, Dettie,' his mother had said. 'Maybe he needs you to talk to him.'

Dettie's wedding ring clacked on the handrail. 'I wouldn't even know how to talk to him.'

The hospital papers in his mother's hand. His papers. There was something written on them. It was written small. Written sideways. But as he got closer he could make it out. He tilted his head. It was his mother's handwriting. Two words. But they didn't make sense.

But by then he was stumbling. He felt the concrete.

When his mother knelt down he could see the papers lying on the ground in front of him. Scribbled in pen beside the doctor's contact numbers, on the pages she always left by the phone, his mother had scribbled and underlined two words:

Ted called.

44

Sam rolled over and was awake. It was night. The car was chilled and someone had laid a blanket back over his and Katie's legs. The front seats were empty. He sat up and spun around to peer outside. As he did, Katie moaned and yanked a handful of blanket over herself. Sam could feel moonlight on his face, its gleam tracing the outline of the window beneath his chin as he peered through the cold glass into the gloom.

There was a mumbling. A hacking cough. Someone spat into the dirt. Sam turned, slowly, and saw movement. Now there were two shadows. A metre or so from the back of the car. Two figures. One of them grunted, its hunched, gnarled shape elongating as it raised its head, stretching as if to howl at the sky. But smoke drifted from its mouth instead, and Sam could make out the spongy thatch of a beard elongating its chin. The second figure was squat and seemed to be pacing. It was Dettie and Jon, both with cigarettes, both talking. The trees behind them were twisted and still, their branches lit white. Sam allowed himself to breathe.

As he settled himself back under the blanket he recalled the uneasy feeling that had followed him out of his dream. There had been writing. Words, on some kind of paper. Or a sign maybe? Something he'd read? And something about his hands. A sensation of heat. His fingers. He looked down at them in his lap, grey in the gloom. As he turned them over, his watch face glinted.

His scratched watch.

Ted. Uncle Ted.

Ted called.

He was alive?

Dettie had always talked about Ted as though he had died. But as Sam thought about it, it occurred to him that there never had been a funeral. There was no grave to visit.

Ted had called Dettie. Even after he was supposed to be dead. Because he wasn't. He'd left. He'd left her.

Like Sam's father had left his mother.

Another cough—it was Dettie—filtered through the window. Sam crouched out of sight and crawled sideways over the handbrake to the front seat. Dettie's handbag was tucked beside the pedals. Keeping low, he unfastened the clasp and slipped his fingers into the bag. Smoke lifted in thin clouds outside, and Katie lay sleeping, her skin tinted blue, cold like marble. Sam felt something jab his palm. He pulled a screwdriver out of the bag and laid it aside. Reaching in again, taking out her purse, he found Uncle Ted's picture beneath a thin fold of cash and eased it free. Creases shone across it in the moonlight. The sticky tape at its edges rustled under his fingertips. He held the photograph closer to his nose and stretched his eyes wide, trying to focus. Ted was smiling, the hand holding his beer almost pointing at

213

the camera. His cheeks were plump, and though it was too dark to make them out, Sam remembered the blotches of red that would always stand out on his face. He could still recall the heavy way his uncle would breathe, sucking in dramatically whenever he was about to speak. The way he talked loudly, and had a barking laugh. How he used to tell jokes at the dinner table that made Dettie slap his arm and say, 'Oh, for goodness' sake, Ted.' The way that made him laugh even louder, until she placed her knife and fork together on the plate, excused herself, and left the table in a huff, Ted calling out to her that it was all just a *bit of fun*.

Dettie wasn't next to Ted in the photo, but when Sam lifted it closer to the window for more light, he thought he could see the shoulder of one of her cardigans in the background, an arm carrying a salad bowl. Sam turned the picture over and saw Dettie's handwriting in the corner. The words *Ted—45th Birthday* and the year had been scribbled over in red pen, and he noticed that one of the creases down the picture was actually a neat rip through its centre that Dettie had taped back together.

The car shook as Jon's silhouette leant against the door. Sam stuffed the photo back into the purse, shoved it and the screwdriver in Dettie's handbag, and clambered over to his seat to slip back under the blanket. He lay in place, eyes open and staring up at the unlit ceiling light. The murmur of conversation went on outside, a noise like a persistent guttural groan.

As though outside of himself, Sam realised that the very same sound, garbled and otherworldly, would have filled him with dread only one night ago, would have evoked images of rotten corpses and ravenous blood-drenched maws. He wondered if it was having Jon nearby—another set of eyes to keep watch, someone to help remind him it was just his imagination gone wild. Whatever it was, the thought of zombies seemed further away than it had for days, even as the car creaked and rocked beneath him.

Somehow the photograph of Ted tucked in Dettie's purse—suspended in time, still smiling, and alive out there somewhere—was far more disturbing. He just couldn't explain why.

45

A sliver of pale sky slit the horizon. The road they were on was bare, off the main highway. In the distance a bird squalled like a dying cat. Sam's neck was stiff, and he felt the bones clicking inside it as he stretched. In the front of the car, Jon was asleep, rolled on his side, snoring into his armpit. But the driver's seat—Dettie's seat—was empty.

Beside him, faced in his direction, Sam could see Katie's eyes open wide, white and glistening, staring past him at nothing. He took hold of the material of her shirt and pulled on it, but she stayed stiff and didn't blink. Eventually, she shook her head. He yanked again, but she lifted a finger to her lips and pointed through the window on his side. Turning, Sam listened too, until above the chittering insects and the warble of birds, he could hear a strained voice hissing insistently behind them.

'This is not the worst of it,' it said. 'There's more. More time. Just tired. Get through it. Halfway already. Still moving. On the way. Just never. On the way. Don't stop. Never. Keep watch.' Dettie's voice shuddered in a quick rhythm, the stream of words only broken when she gasped for breath. 'Should call again. Given him a chance. He'll know. He knows.' She sounded hoarse, as if she'd been muttering to herself for hours. 'Let him know. Worried sick. We're coming. Still coming. Joanne will have called by now. They'll talk. He'll have talked. Made it. They'll make it. All there. Still there.'

Sam stole a look at her through the back window. Strands of hair were pulled loose from her usually tight bun. She was sucking at a cigarette, hugging herself, bobbing while she walked. They were parked in a rest stop about the length of a soccer field from a cliff face, and Dettie was staring out at the hazy ocean.

Katie's bottom lip shivered. 'What's wrong with her?' she whispered.

Feeling a stinging heat rising behind his cheeks, Sam shook his head. He shrugged.

Dettie's shoes were grinding a tight circle in the grey stones beneath her. It was like watching an animal pace the edges of its cage. She was glaring, but her attention kept jerking from the trees to the road, to her hands. Smoke lapped at her face and she blinked heavily through it. Another mournful birdcall whipped the air and Dettie tilted upwards, listening, until suddenly she flashed a look through the car window at Sam.

He ducked, and Katie stiffened beside him, her clenched teeth showing between her lips. They could hear footsteps crackling towards them, and Dettie's voice dipped to an indistinct mumble. Sam realised that both he and Katie had their hands clasped tight on their doorhandles.

A shadow passed Katie's head and they jumped as Dettie leant in through the driver's side window.

'Good to see you're both up already. Bright and early.' She tried to keep her voice low, but it came out as a gravelled hiss. Her clothes stank of nicotine.

'How are you kids? You tired? Hungry? Do you want something to nibble on? I've got some Life Savers somewhere.' She opened the door and knelt halfway inside. The suspension squealed. 'Or there could be some biscuits. No, we finished those, didn't we? Good. Not filling. I had two. Jon had a chocolate one. And those horrid birds took the last couple, didn't they? Sixteen biscuits like that—gone.' She snapped her fingers.

In the car's cabin-light, blotchy shadows hung beneath her eyes. As she smiled, Sam could see a fleck of tobacco stuck between her front teeth. 'Here we go,' she said, holding out a scrunched tube of mints, torn open, on her palm. The wrapper and the foil clung to her skin.

Katie was sniffling, and Sam shook his head, kicking the back of Jon's seat until he began to stir.

Dettie picked the hair off one mint and pushed it between her lips, almost burning herself with the cigarette still in her fingers. She flicked her hand, loosening a spray of orange embers that tumbled over the upholstery.

'Oh, for pity's sake,' she spat, dusting more ash into the headrest.

Calmly stretching his arms, Jon sat up. As he did he made a noise in his throat like creaking wood. 'You right, love?' he asked, ruffling his beard.

Dettie coughed, surprised, and put a hand to her cheek. 'Oh, I'm fine,' she choked. 'Just a little—just tired. Couldn't drop off last night. Headaches.' She took two sharp breaths. 'But a drop of coffee and I'll be right. Right as rain.'

'Good to hear,' Jon said. He rolled over to look at Katie and Sam. 'And how about you lot? How'd you sleep?'

Neither moved. Sam kept glancing at Dettie, watching her teeter as she bent closer to them.

'I'm scared,' Katie finally whispered.

Jon tutted. 'You got scared?'

She tugged at her seatbelt. 'No—'

'We were just sorting out breakfast, weren't we?' Dettie said, popping open her purse to thumb through her cash. 'Trying to pick something to eat. Now Sammy, you'll want bacon and eggs, I know. And Katie, I bet you'd love an omelette and some orange juice.' Her voice was melodic.

Katie mouthed something.

'I think I remember a sign. Yes. I saw a sign that said there's a service station. Fifteen minutes or so up the road.' Dettie pointed with her dead cigarette.

'I want cereal,' Katie's voice creaked.

'Somewhere near that horse farm we went past, I think,' Dettie was rearranging the weight of the handbag on her knees. 'Great big sign it was.'

'What's that, my sweet?' Jon nodded towards Katie.

'Hmm?' Dettie spun towards him, her lips pursed. 'That huge *sign* we passed,' she sighed. 'Not far back. We're talking about eating something.'

Jon smiled, blinking at her, and gestured to Katie. 'Sorry, love,' he said. 'I meant our littlest lady.'

Katie lifted herself up on her arms. 'I don't want an omelette,' she said, her voice more forceful. More natural. 'Or orange juice. I want cereal.'

'*Cereal?*' Dettie scoffed. 'You don't have to eat cereal. We're on a big trip. Special. It's a treat. I'm treating you.'

Katie shook her head. 'Muesli.'

Dettie sighed. 'Well, they probably won't *have* muesli,' she said. 'Truck drivers don't eat it much.'

Scowling, Katie slumped, her head sinking into her shoulders.

'Goodness, girl, I don't know why you have to make things so difficult.'

'You know,' Jon cleared his throat softly, 'I think I've seen cereal for sale at those places. Little boxes.'

Dettie snapped her purse closed and waved it, her nails digging into the leather. 'Oh, fine. That's *fine* then. Whatever you all want. You decide. Just be sure to let me know. I am only the driver, after all.' She turned and settled herself behind the wheel.

Jon hummed, glancing briefly at the children. 'I can drive for an hour or two, love,' he said. 'If you want to rest a spell.'

'No, no, I'll do it,' she sang, almost laughing. 'I'll drive. *I'll* buy the food. I'll plan the trip.' She shoved the purse down into her handbag. 'And I'll be the wicked old witch while I'm at it too, shall I?'

She shot a glare back at Sam and Katie through the rear-vision mirror. Her expression was all the more frightening for its bloodshot eyes and the shadows that still hung on her skin.

As the car started, its headlights snapped across a fence just ahead of them. Dettie reversed and Sam saw a sheep's skull caught in a twist of barbed wire. Behind them the sky was seething red.

46

Katie ate two single-serve packets of honey-toasted muesli, and slurped every spoonful of milk, savouring either the sound, or the flavour, or the way it made Dettie fidget impatiently.

'Come on, come on, girl,' she said, pinching the bridge of her nose. 'We don't have all day.' She'd taken an aspirin, but it didn't seem to be working. She rubbed her eyes and drew circles on her forehead with her fingertips, humming a kind of tuneless music to herself.

Everyone else was done and their plates had already been cleared, so when Katie finally finished, they paid the bill and got up to go to the toilet. By the time Sam returned, Jon was already out in the car park, circling the car, examining it. Katie was with him, having not waited for their aunt, and was waving her arms dramatically as she spoke, bouncing, and holding up her handkerchief in the breeze to dry.

Sam watched her as he crossed the restaurant, through the jangle of the cash register and the burble of the television on the countertop, trying to work out what it was she might be saying.

He could still remember his mother giving that handkerchief to his sister while he was in hospital, the way she had closed Katie's fingers over it as she told her to keep it safe. About how it would hold her tears, and she'd be happy again when it dried. But as he thought back he found he was having trouble recalling the exact sound of her voice. Just as the tone of his own speech had gradually faded from his memory, it seemed his mother's was slipping too.

The thought made Sam's stomach lurch. He closed his eyes, concentrating, trying to hold on to the last of it, to summon it back to his ears. Suddenly it was important—desperately important—that he succeed. The thought of losing it was terrifying.

Then there it was. He could hear her clearly. So clearly she must have been standing in the room. Just behind him.

'. . . my children home,' she said. Her exact voice. Warm and flinty, and sounding oddly choked, but definitely her.

He turned, checking the restaurant tables. Two truck drivers and a man in overalls, a young couple, half-asleep, and the television, facing away from him, chattering on with some kind of news report. She wasn't there. But he could have sworn—

Dettie, who was waiting by the door, gripped his shoulder, hard, and heaved him out into the street. He tried to resist, pointing back inside, but she was striding towards the car, hissing. 'Come on. Get in. Everyone. Go. *Hurry.*'

'What's wrong, love?' John said, jumping down from the railing he'd been perched upon.

'Nothing. We just—we don't have all day. Now get in.'

She unlocked the doors, quickly, and ushered them all inside, desperately scanning the restaurant window behind her.

sign

And as the car wheezed to life Sam thought back to the moment she had grabbed him. About the spiteful, angry look she had been shooting at the television set.

47

The morning sunlight lay heavy on the backs of their necks. Patches of vegetation were giving way to long stretches of umber earth, punctuated by tufts of thorny brush and a sky so wide and blue it stung the eyes. Dettie was driving faster, more aggressively, overtaking other motorists and gunning the accelerator, but the pulse and sway of the car, sweeping across lanes, grumbling back into place, was oddly soothing. Jon and Katie were soon asleep again in the back seat, each slumped over, mouths agape. Sam watched the few trees that still peppered the horizon slash by. Many were tall, ashen tangles of branches, all erupting at once from ground level, as though their trunks had been sucked down into a dried-over riverbed, choked and seized in place.

The radio was on but turned low. Dettie kept one ear tilted to listen. When the news reports came on she would raise the volume slightly, her fingers clenching the dial from the moment the intro played until the sign-off trumpeted its way back to the music playlist.

sign

At first Sam had been thinking about how clearly he had heard his mother's voice—how peculiar it had been, as though she had crawled momentarily out of his mind, spoken, and then disappeared. It reminded him of the zombie comic. How the woman had heard the zombie's shadowy howls across the distant hills, echoing, but clear. He was tired of reading the comic, though, and his eyes were heavy in the warmth, so he just lay back in his seat, occasionally practising his name back to himself—pinkies, thumb, palm: *Sam.* Otherwise he just let the noise of the news drift over him, his gaze tracing across the same details of the car's cabin he'd been staring at for days.

The radio's hushed patter carried on, Dettie's face clenching into a panicked scowl whenever the news anchor spoke. A government official was reminding everyone of the strength and severity of the fire front. It was not to be underestimated at any cost, he was saying. There were still fire-fighting volunteers travelling in from other states, but more were needed.

Sam knew every millimetre of the car's cabin by now. The tear in the dashboard, its split plastic exposing an eruption of yellow foam. The floor mat beneath his feet, still marked with a lick of dried mud. The five-cent coin jiggling in the ashtray.

A farmer who had lost his property was being interviewed, his voice catching as he spoke. 'So fast,' he sobbed. 'No time to get the cattle out.'

The steering wheel was worn down in the grooves where Dettie had rubbed her thumbs over the years. A starfish crack at the edge of the window was lit gold by the sun.

A family had been reported missing—Dettie's hand shook on the dial, the volume dipping—after their holiday house was consumed at a caravan park. She let the sound rise again.

A single slat on the passenger side air vent was broken, slanted against the force of the fan gushing against it. The paddle-pop boomerang was marked with the indents of teeth.

Once the weather report was over—a total fire ban was in place, record temperatures expected—the music returned and Dettie lowered the volume, releasing the stereo knob and straightening herself to glare at the road ahead.

Sam felt the same itchy upholstery against his elbows as he lifted the hem of his T-shirt and directed the breeze onto his belly. He could barely remember a time when his body wasn't resonating with the ride, the car vibrating its persistent, deadening thrum beneath and through him.

Up ahead on the road, yet another mound of roadkill was emerging from the haze. It was a large kangaroo, torn open at the stomach. Two crows were perched on its flank, feasting. As the car sped by he saw one digging its beak into the wound like a knife. For the first time Sam didn't feel a lurch of revulsion at the sight. In fact, when he thought about it, it didn't seem that horrible anymore. With the stories of fires raging out there somewhere— people missing, animals being burnt alive, the numb fear in people's voices as they spoke into the reporter's microphone—the remains of some creature on the road wasn't so scary by comparison. It seemed natural, actually. The kangaroo was already long dead. The birds and ants and bugs needed to feed.

For all of her eccentricities, Dettie was right about one thing: they were out in the wild now. And there were worse things to worry about than a chunk of dead meat. Beside him, she shook her head ever so slightly to herself. A tiny involuntary twitch, persisting as she dug her thumbs into the grooves they had already worn into the steering wheel. She spurred the engine on.

48

'So what brought *you* out here?' Dettie was peering at Jon from the corner of her eyes, stirring her tea with its bag.

Sam was surprised they had even stopped. Katie had to plead for an hour to get something to drink, and even then Dettie only agreed to buy something from a service station if they waited to drink it at a rest stop further along the road. They were running late, she said, and had to make up time; but as Sam had held her styrofoam cup on his knee, watching it lap at the plastic lid and waiting to find somewhere to pull over, he wondered why it made any difference where they stopped—at the service station, or out on the highway?

'What brought me out here?' Jon looked up from untying his laces.

'Australia,' Dettie said. 'Why travel all the way from England to Australia?' She wasn't glaring exactly, but there was a stern look to her expression that made it seem like Jon was being interrogated. And while everyone else sat at the rest-stop picnic table, she hovered, shifting weight from foot to foot, watching every car that grumbled by. 'Why not Paris? Ireland?' She took a small sip and held the cup firmly between both hands.

Jon slipped off his shoe. He hummed. 'I guess the usual answer is probably the surf, isn't it?' he said. 'That or the beer. That's what the tourists say back home. Soak up the sun. Drink the beer. See the sports. Except, of course, I don't surf, or watch cricket. Your sun has already turned me to leather. And forgive me for saying, but I don't know what people are talking about with the beer. Your lager tastes like water.'

Jon had bought a lemon squash, along with Katie and Sam, and would periodically turn to swig the warm, fizzless drink. He lifted his foot, laying it on his opposite knee and dusting off the sole. Sam could see a hole worn into the edge of his sock, stretching the length of his big toe.

'Of course, it is lovely here. That's for certain,' he said. 'In England right now it's winter. Cold. Grey. Who wouldn't prefer a bit of light? But to be honest, growing up in the UK, it's—' He seemed to be about to say something, but exhaled instead. 'Well, I wanted to get away. Something different. But familiar, you know? Something not so—so rigid.'

Dettie's eyes narrowed. 'Rigid?' she repeated.

Katie had swiped five biscuits from the packet lying open on the picnic table, and was stacking them up on top of one another. She would take a bite from one and then move it to the bottom of the pile as she chewed, playing her own strange little tower game as she listened.

'See, you lot don't really have a class system here, do you?' Jon said. 'Do you know much about all that?'

Dettie tilted her head. It seemed she didn't really know, but wasn't going to admit as much.

sign

'In England everybody's obsessed with class,' he said. 'What class are you in? Upper class? Working class? They obsess about it. This old social pecking order—real ancient stuff—stretching back to the days of the landed gentry and working serfs. It's the kind of toffee-nosed, blue-blood, self-righteous system you would have thought they'd thrown out with powdered wigs. But no. There are people who are obsessed with it. They make sure it gets baked into everything. The schools you go to. The jobs you get. The clubs you get allowed in. Who you date. Where you live.' He grunted. 'Meanwhile, we have the bottle to call the French snobs.'

He fished inside his shoe, fingers scraping at something on the sole. 'It's exhausting,' he said. 'It wears you down. Makes you fed up. Makes you old before your time.'

A small stone tumbled down into the dirt. 'This cloud hanging over you every moment of every day,' he said. 'Knowing that no matter what—what you do, where you go, how much you make—you're going nowhere because some inbred wankers—'

Dettie snorted, coughing tea from her lungs.

'Sorry,' he said, quickly. 'Sorry, love. *Sorry*. Sorry, kids. I mean, wowsers. *Wowsers*.'

She caught her breath, theatrically flicking drops of tea from her fingers as she shook her head. Katie was sitting up, smiling widely, trying to remember what Jon had said that got such a reaction.

'It just gets frustrating when you see it everywhere,' he went on. 'Something that meaningless. Something so utterly arbitrary. All because a bunch of—' he shot Dettie an apologetic look, '*wowsers* don't want us poor trash getting a seat at their restaurant. Breathing all their rarefied air.'

He took another mouthful of lemon squash and swished it around his teeth. 'It's just nice to be over here for a little while,' he said. 'To be out from under all that for a spell.'

Dettie's lips were curled, but she offered him a quick nod.

Katie went back to absently scratching two biscuits together, making a small pile of crumbs on the table. 'So if you don't have any money,' she said, 'you have to stay having no money?'

'Sort of, sweetie. A little bit.' Jon slipped his shoe back on and began retying his laces. 'Only, it's not really money, so much. It's the way people treat you. You can get rich—people do. Actors, writers, sportspeople. But if you were born working class—even if you were born middle—anyone who thinks they're an upper-class person will look down on you as worthless. Unworthy. You're born in your box, you'll stay in your box.'

'That sounds horrible,' Katie said.

'We're England, sweetie. I suspect we invented horrible.'

Dettie sighed, rolling her eyes. 'Well, yes, I'm sure there are some who abuse their place,' she said. 'But it's hardly all bad. There is refinement, isn't there? Breeding and civility. And there's something to be said for aristocracy. For having people to look up to.'

Jon slumped back against the table. Over on the highway a couple of cars fizzed by. He gave a grim smile and shrugged.

Katie stared over at Dettie like she had just spoken a foreign language. 'What?' she said.

'Kings and queens, dear. A whole history—a living history—reaching back to the very birth of the country itself.' Dettie was peering off into the distance, out at the baked brown undulations of the horizon. 'It's all very romantic.'

Jon stood up, rolling his shoulders. 'But it's all just an idea, love,' he said. He stretched his back and started pacing, very slowly, in place. 'Some mad nonsense someone dreamt up back in the Dark Ages. Royal bloodlines. Heraldry. Family crests. All just excuses for one group of posh tossbags to push everyone else around. To say *get off my land, don't touch my stuff.*'

Sam had gotten used to watching Jon's hands when he talked, and even though he wasn't signing anything, his gestures showed he was getting agitated. They sliced at the air. His fingers were stiff. Even his elbows seemed locked tight.

'And they learn it so young,' he was saying. 'I was a white-van man for a while. My dad, he was a white-van man, after he finished up at the mechanics. Do a bit of handiwork. Fix your car. Make you a shelf. Build you a rabbit hutch. That sort of thing. If you could see the way these toffs look through you. Even their little prep-school kids. Like you're not even there. It turns your blood cold.'

Dettie stared down into her cup. The tea had already cooled. She was actually nodding, but Sam noticed the deliberate, delicate way she was holding it by the rim, her pinkies very slightly raised.

'Still,' she said, 'I think there's something to be said for breeding.' The string of her tea bag hung matted in a stain of dried milk on the side of her cup. 'Wish we had a little more of it in this country. Civility.' That last word she seemed to want to hold on to as she spoke it, stretching it out. Sam thought of Roger. Dettie's insistence on those 'cultural differences' Roger and his mother had supposedly faced. How 'unfamiliar' he apparently was.

Jon sighed. 'Oh no. No, don't wish for civility, love. You don't know how good you've got it here. You lot are young. You're not

231

stiff and decayed like us.' He looked out at that same horizon Dettie was peering into and clearly saw something else. 'The way I figure it,' he said, 'two hundred years ago we packed up all the interesting people and sent them out here. And the best thing you lot did—the *best* thing—was toss all that lords and gentry nonsense in the bin.' He yanked the waist of his pants. 'Still got Her Majesty's head on your coins,' he said. 'Looking a might younger than in reality, I'll add—but otherwise you've gotten on with it.'

Dettie's face was drawn. She set aside her drink and dusted imaginary crumbs from her lap. She seemed to be auditioning to be one of those ladies Jon had just banished from history.

'Besides,' Jon said, turning and waving at the makeshift picnic strewn across the table, 'wouldn't you rather sit here with us? Enjoy this sunset? Eat a few Jammie Dodgers? Sip from a styrofoam cup? Rather than nibble half a cucumber sandwich with some sorry Jane Austen rejects? Living your whole life propped up on the reputation of dead people you never knew?'

She blinked, slowly, staring at the ground. 'If there's one thing the world could use more of,' she said, 'it's good manners.'

He smiled. 'Well, I can say *jolly good* and *pip pip* occasionally, if it'll make you feel better, love.' He caught her eye and held it, raising his eyebrows. 'M'lady?' he said, and faked a bow.

Dettie's expression softened and she smiled too.

'Cucumber sandwiches are gross,' Katie said.

'Exactly,' Jon said, and laughed.

And to Sam's surprise, Dettie and Katie laughed too.

49

Dettie had put Sam up front with her again, and was telling him about the trip she and Uncle Ted had taken across Western Australia for their honeymoon.

'And it was just like this,' she was saying. 'We'd drive and drive, and stop if we saw something. And at night we'd fall asleep in the first hotel that we came to. We didn't map it all out, you see. We just went. Like us now.' She lifted her fingers from the steering wheel, holding on underneath with her thumbs. The road raced towards her open palms. 'Like explorers,' she said. 'That's how Ted described us. He said your aunty was an explorer. He always said funny things like that.'

Sam wasn't paying attention, but he kept nodding. He was concentrating on the conversation Jon and Katie were having behind him. Jon was telling her all about England, about their money and their black taxicabs. About his two pet dogs—Yorkies—who had proper little stuck-up British barks, he said. About all the different kinds of slang they used at home.

'Bollocks,' he said. 'That's another one. See, if you know that someone's telling you fibs, and you want to let them know, you say, "That's *bollocks*," or "You're full of *bollocks*."'

Katie giggled. 'Bollocks,' she said, slowly, plopping out the word on her tongue.

'And if that person is really thick—you know, *stupid*—you can call them a berk.'

Dettie's head jerked. Her lips were pursed as she strained to listen. 'What on earth are you teaching her back there?' she called.

Jon looked up and grinned. 'Nothing, love. Nothing. Just telling her more about the mother country.'

Tugging some slack in her seatbelt, Katie sat forward. 'I know what bollocks are,' she said.

Dettie clicked her tongue. 'Well, I need to concentrate now,' she said. 'So if everyone back there could just settle down.'

Her eyes were bulging in their sockets, and when she blinked, her face tightened around them. Sam would catch her starting to yawn, but then cover it up by biting her lip.

For another hour they drove without talking, the trees and the bushes lining the roads getting drier and more withered the further they went. They were actually in Western Australia now, heading towards its capital city, as Dettie kept reminding them. It was hard to imagine what the definition of a city even was anymore. Each town they passed through seemed smaller than the last, hugging the road for a few hundred metres before dissolving away in the distance. Cars seemed to be kicking more dust into the air behind them, and for a while they followed a tourist bus that belched black fumes Sam could taste through the air vents. Above him, the paddle-pop stick boomerang shuddered almost imperceptibly, turning in slow circles. When he got especially bored, he scanned the dashboard, looking over the knobs and dials, settling finally on the radio. He sat forward and flicked it on, raising the volume.

'—fears that without further information forthcoming on the location of those who have disappeared—'

Dettie muffled a yell and slapped the radio quiet with her palm. 'We might leave that off for the rest of today, sweetie.' She chewed her lips. 'My headache and all.'

Sighing, Sam flopped back in his seat and watched the last ribbons of cloud dissolve beneath the sun. Out in a distant field, thin sheep meandered through the latticework of shade cast by a lone, half-dead tree. They passed another exit, leading off to a town called Madura, where several cars appeared to be pulled up together for a picnic. A sign telling them to *Slow Down* whipped by, followed by another, larger sandwich board that read: *Random Breath Testing Ahead*. Suddenly, Sam could feel the car slowing down. Dettie's breath was starting to quicken. When he looked over, he saw that she was shaking, slumping in her seat, staring at another large sign as it approached them along the road.

It read: *PREPARE TO STOP.*

A car soon overtook them, and when the truck behind began blaring its horn, weaving across the road, Jon leant over. 'Everything good up there, love?' he asked. 'People seem to think we're dawdling.'

Dettie was gaping at the road ahead. She murmured, 'There's just a—' Her eyes flashed along the edges of the road. She wasn't blinking. 'There's a stop. Up there. For drink driving. Breath tests.'

Jon ran his hand over his beard. He chuckled. 'What's the matter? You nip off to the bar when we weren't looking? Had a couple of pints?'

The car was moving so slow, veering across the gravel, that the truck sped around them too, beeping furiously. Their motor sputtered, and Dettie's head jerked as she scanned the highway ahead. Another truck thundered past and Sam could feel the wind of it shake the car.

Jon was still smiling, but his voice had a slight quiver. 'Love, I think we might want to go a touch faster now, eh?'

In the distance, Sam slowly made out the shape of a parked vehicle and two figures waving down traffic. Dettie saw them too and the car rattled off the bitumen and into the dirt.

Katie squealed. 'What's happening?'

'Nothing, honey,' Jon hushed. 'We're just—what, love?' He tapped Dettie on the shoulder. 'Engine trouble? Petrol?'

'Police,' Dettie whispered.

The hush and scrape of earth being kicked up by their wheels went on beneath them. Jon looked puzzled. He started to laugh but the sound faded away.

'Mummy says to do what the policeman tells you.' Katie's voice was tight.

'Shut up,' Dettie snapped. 'I don't want to hear about your mother right now.'

'*Love,*' Jon said. 'She just—'

'Shh. Quiet.'

The remains of Jon's smile hung on a little awkwardly. He glanced from Sam, to Katie, to the flashing lights up ahead, and his eyes widened. When he realised Sam was peering back at him he forced an unconvincing smirk.

sign

The car skidded to a stop. A cloud of dust rose beside Sam's window and Dettie twisted around. She set the car in reverse and drove backward a hundred metres or so. An oncoming car swerved around them, honking. Katie screamed.

Jon was holding her hands. 'It's okay, love. It's all right.'

They reached a kink in the highway, out of sight, and Dettie skidded, wrestling the car into first gear, and U-turned swiftly onto the opposite lane. Panting, her eyes flashing to each mirror, she sped back the way they had come. The engine howled. The police faded from view. The paddle-pop stick boomerang swung awkwardly, slapping the glass.

50

'It was nothing,' Dettie chuckled. 'I was being silly, that's all.' She sipped from a bottle of water and wiped her forehead with her wrist. 'Now, don't you kids run off now!' she called.

Jon was standing in front of her, scratching his eyebrow with his thumb. 'You just seemed a tad jumpy, love.'

'Oh, goodness, no.' Dettie screwed the lid shut. 'My licence,' she said, and swallowed. 'I left it at home. My licence.' Her smile crept wider. 'A couple of *thousand* kilometres away.' She giggled, a sound Sam was sure he had never heard her make before. 'And I didn't particularly want to turn around and drive all the way back to get it.'

Jon was nodding, but he didn't say anything. His eyes flickered towards Katie and Sam, who were taking turns sipping from a plastic travel mug.

Dettie had driven east almost twenty minutes before finding a side route over some raw, unpaved roads that led around the police block. She'd spent the detour muttering to herself and telling Sam not to worry, while Jon distracted Katie with a whispered game of I Spy. Now they were stopped on a country lane that fed back onto the highway a few dozen kilometres along.

'I tell you, I'm a complete duffer sometimes.' Dettie tossed the bottle through the open door and tugged a cigarette from her handbag. She offered one to Jon, but he shook his head.

Katie, meanwhile, had turned her back on them and huddled closer to Sam, almost pushing him back against a wire fence, whispering, 'She's getting really strange.' Her eyes were wide and wet.

Sam nodded. He felt a drop of water roll down his neck.

'Have you seen how her head wobbles?' Katie said.

He looked over at Dettie, who was clutching her cigarette with both hands and leaning on the car. Jon was watching the way her foot kept scratching at the dirt, shuffling it into small mounds and then dusting it flat.

'I know you wouldn't have wanted to worry the kids,' he was saying, speaking slowly. 'But I think they might have been a little confused.'

'Oh, no.' Dettie picked at her tongue as if there was a hair stuck to it. 'No, they both know they can trust me.' She nodded.

Katie slurped from the cup and dried her lips with their mother's handkerchief. 'I heard Mummy talking on the telephone to Uncle Ben once.' She leant even closer to Sam's ear. 'She said Aunt Dettie needed to go see a doctor. About being sad. She said she probably should have kept going.'

For a moment Sam wondered if that was why Dettie had been so against him visiting Tracey at first. Did it remind her of some therapy she had needed once? But as he glanced up he realised that their aunt was staring straight at them both, her

239

cigarette smouldering in her hand. He felt his chest tighten, and his legs. His whole body clenched in place, electric. When she didn't look away he raised his arm, timidly, to wave. She didn't respond, though, and slowly he realised she wasn't staring at him, but rather was fixed upon Katie's hands and the small white embroidered handkerchief she was gently folding away.

51

Beneath Sam's seat, behind his legs, was the cardboard sign Jon had been carrying when they'd picked him up. It tickled the back of his knees, and as the car rumbled along the track, he lifted it up and set it on his lap. Everyone was quiet, and Dettie was watching Katie intently up front, repeatedly wafting her hands away from the radio dial. Jon was staring out the window at the trees and mounds of dirt flashing by, his thumbs buried in his beard, scratching his chin.

Sam turned the sign in his hands, reading it over. On one side was Jon's large, looping writing in thick black texta, *Help Me, I'm British*, but the other side was blank. Leaning back down to the pile of papers and wrappers on the floor, Sam found Dettie's crossword-puzzle book and slipped the pen free from its pages. He tested it on the corner of the cardboard, and then tapped Jon's leg to get his attention.

Will you come with us to Perth? he wrote, and held the words out.

Jon read the message and smiled, sadly. 'We'll see, me mate. We'll see.'

'What? What's that?' Dettie stretched back in her seat, cocking her ear towards them.

'Nothing, love,' Jon said, taking the sign and pen from Sam's hands.

For a moment they sat motionless as Dettie fretted with the rear-vision mirror. When the car had settled back into its familiar drone, Jon scribbled something on the sign himself. He tapped Sam's knee with his knuckle and held it out to read.

You asked before . . . This means SCARED.

Sam looked up and Jon was signing. Both hands were curled up like bear paws, fingers hooked like claws. He tapped them on his chest, twice, the right hand higher than his left. He tapped two times, silently, his eyebrows knotted together.

Sam mirrored the movement back at him, tapping twice. Then again. He felt the tiny flutter upon his chest like a heartbeat.

Jon nodded and turned back to the window. Folding the sign in half he tucked it away beneath the front seat.

52

After pulling into so many service stations Sam had developed a rhythm. As the motor coughed to silence he would tumble out to use the toilet, splash the stickiness from his face, and check his stoma in the mirror, trying to clean the uncomfortable redness that was steadily expanding around his vent. He would then head inside, out of the heat, to check the magazine stands for another issue of the zombie story. There would usually be a glass refrigerator stacked with colourful drinks to lean against for a moment and feel the chill through his shirt. There would always be some kind of fan or, if he was lucky, a rumbling air conditioner, churning the air. And there would be men's magazines, with waxy-looking women in bikinis and high heels draped over motorcycles that he would have to push aside to find the comic books.

This station was different, though. They had just pulled up in a place called Caiguna, at the only building visible in any direction: a structure standing alone beneath a span of blue sky that had steadily widened the further west they travelled, and that to Sam now seemed to envelope his entire vision. There had been no more police breath tests, and hardly any traffic at all. As they parked at the pumps, the building appeared lopsided, one corner of the corrugated roof sagging by the toilets. As Sam entered he could see that the walls had been built from thin wooden planks that had shrunk, letting the sunlight slip between them. The whole place, inside and out, was painted a bright yellow and looked as though it could crumble in a strong gust of wind. The only reading material for sale was a pile of old car magazines stacked near the door, and everything was covered in dust. The doorways were hung with plastic streamers, and when the shopkeeper emerged from a back room she was wearing a faded blue singlet and guzzling from a beer bottle.

Dettie was outside wiping the windscreen and Jon had opened the boot to pull a change of shirt from his bag. Nailed to the wall above Sam's head was a two-year-old calendar with curled corners. It looked brittle, flecked with the sunlight streaming through the walls, and in its photograph—a faded image of the ocean—a thin yacht was sailing out towards the horizon. He heard the shopkeeper behind him sorting her papers as she drank.

Dettie had started to fill the car with fuel, watching Katie and Jon make barnyard noises at one another. Katie was a pig, pushing up her nose and snorting, and as she ran past, Dettie watched her, pulling the petrol hose out of the car and holding it limp in her hand. Jon clucked like a chicken as he closed the boot, and Katie mimicked the noise, giggling as she ran. On her way past Dettie, Sam saw his aunt lift the nozzle and very quickly spray Katie across the back with petrol.

Katie stopped. For a moment she stood frozen, her mouth agape, eyes wide. She lifted her wet arms, tugging at her clothes. Then she screamed.

Jon, who was doing up his shirt buttons, looked over. Dettie dropped the hose, ran towards Katie, and grabbed her shoulders.

'What happened?' Jon's voice was almost a shout. 'Are you all right?'

Dettie was crouching beside Katie, trying to hush her.

The shopkeeper rounded the counter and stepped through the doorway, shielding her eyes. 'What?' she grunted.

Sam followed her out.

Looking up at them, Dettie rolled her eyes. 'Oh, the girl here was flapping about,' she said. 'She knocked me and got a splash of petrol.'

'Petrol?' Jon knelt. 'Where? On you? On your skin?'

Katie was howling, wriggling under the damp patch on her shirt. 'I didn't touch anything,' she whined.

'We just need to wash up.' Dettie had to wrestle a better grip to keep her niece close.

The smell had already hit Sam, and Katie was gagging, trying desperately to pull off her top.

The shopkeeper shrugged and waved them inside.

Dettie pushed Katie along, her fingers clamped tight on her shoulders. 'We'll try not to be too long, Sammy,' she said, rolling her eyes and tutting. And as they disappeared through the streamers at the back of the store he heard Katie's moans as Dettie chastised her for 'mucking around'.

From behind him, Sam heard a scrape as the petrol hose was lifted from the ground. Jon washed off the nozzle and finished filling the car. He looked at Sam and exhaled loudly. 'That aunt of yours, eh?'

Sam scuffed his feet, watching as the breeze raised wisps of dust from the ground. He wanted to talk to Jon about

245

Dettie. To tell him he was worried. To explain why he was so scared.

Jon screwed the petrol cap on and slid the nozzle back in its pump. He ran his nails through his beard and stretched. 'If all the excitement's died down, I might take a stroll,' he said, leaning into the car and pulling out a cigarette and a lighter. 'Will you be good here for a minute, matey?'

Shrugging, Sam stared at the car's bumper.

Jon wandered down the road to light up, but Sam stayed standing where he was, his eyes still unfocused on the car. He heard a muffled yell from inside the store, then quiet. The car sat in place, encrusted with dust, and a familiar sensation crept over him. There was something wrong with it. With the car. Something was different. Not with the colour or the shape. It was smaller than that. But it was wrong. His eyes flashed across the wheels and the lights and the wipers. Everything appeared fine. Then he settled on the numberplate.

It was wrong. The plate was wrong. They were supposed to have his uncle Ted's initials, but these letters were different. Unfamiliar. Even the numbers didn't seem right, though he couldn't remember what those should have been. He scanned the car again, checked both front and back. It was definitely Dettie's, but the plates weren't what they were supposed to be.

He thought about the lurching shadow of the zombie. How it had tugged at the car. At the bumper bar. The scraping sound of metal. He remembered how Dettie had been gone. How she'd disappeared. He remembered the screwdriver in her handbag. His temples throbbed. His mouth was dry. Dettie had changed the numberplates. For some reason she'd swapped them with some other car's plates. They were the same colour, the same

sign

state—but more scratched up and bent. Jon had even noticed that they were loose. He'd tightened them up before they'd fixed the fan belt. Sam's eyes were stinging but he didn't want to cry. He heard his vent whistle.

From somewhere inside the store there was a gush of water and more of Katie's shouts. Tentatively, he crept back through the doorway, inching closer to the back room to try to see what was going on. The shopkeeper stood behind the counter, clearing her throat. She was tidying up, gathering handfuls of paper, scrunching them together, and tossing them into the bin. Behind her, Sam could see a telephone hanging on the wall. He needed to call someone. He needed to get the shopkeeper to call someone. His mother. His father. Anyone. Someone needed to know how Dettie was behaving. The talking to herself. The sneaking around. The spraying Katie deliberately with the petrol hose. That she was back there now, clawing at her, washing away the proof and blaming Katie for playing up. He needed someone to know where they were—wherever Caiguna was. Jon was just a silhouette, too far away to help, and Dettie would be back any minute, so Sam stepped across the store and approached the counter.

The shopkeeper's skin was leathery. Sam could see old tattoos, wrinkled, on her arms. As he stood across from her she sorted a stack of receipts into a drawer under the register.

Sam tapped on the counter and waved.

The shopkeeper stopped, looking up at him. She offered a tight, quick smile, and then went back to her papers.

Sam knocked again.

The woman exhaled. 'Yes. Hello,' she said, keeping her eyes down. 'What do you want?'

He pointed at his throat, right at the strap around his stoma. He shook his head, and then gestured to the phone.

The shopkeeper glanced at his neck, her eyes widening in surprise, then blinked and sipped her beer. 'Your grandma will be out soon,' she said.

Mouthing the word, *No*, Sam mimed Katie being sprayed with petrol. He squeezed his finger like he was pulling a trigger and pointed it at his clothes.

The woman blinked. She tapped her foot, frowning. 'Yes, I saw,' she said, monotone. 'Very exciting.'

Sam knocked. He was bouncing on his toes. He pointed out at the car. *The numberplate*, he thought, hoping she'd understand. He tried to shape the words with his lips.

'Look, little fella, I don't have time to play games.' She rolled the bottom of her bottle around on the cash register.

Sam searched the counter for a pen. There was nothing. He mimed scribbling something in the air.

The woman pretended not to see and stared over his head. One more muffled shout echoed from behind the streamers. It was Katie.

Sam slouched, feeling the breath in his chest slip away. He mouthed, *I need to call my mother*, but the woman was intentionally not looking now. He signed, *Mother*—three fingers slapped twice on his other palm—then mimed the handset of a phone up to his ear.

Mother. Phone. Phone Mother.

The woman nodded and looked away.

'Hmm. Yep,' she said.

He banged his fist on the counter.

Help.

He made a thumbs-up sign and slammed it on his other palm, just like Jon had shown him.

Help. Help.

His left hand stung. His whole body was clenched, pricked with sweat.

'What? Do you want some chocolate? Here.' She pulled a Mars Bar down from a shelf on the wall and set it in front of him, pushing it closer. 'Now go away. I'm busy.'

He kicked the counter, ran around to the phone on the wall and lifted the receiver. He held it out to the shopkeeper.

'Hey! Stop messing around! That is not a toy, damn it!' she said, snatching it out of his hand and hanging up. As she shoved him back around the counter, she noticed something outside, and sighed. 'Go play with your dad out there.' She was waving towards the doorway, and as Sam turned, he saw Jon strolling back to the station, peering out at the horizon.

Sam felt himself smiling. Fine. He could explain to Jon. Get him to make the call. But just as he started to jog towards the entrance, the plastic streamers scattered and Katie returned, stomping her feet, with Dettie behind her, puffing and flicking her hands dry. Both of their faces were flushed.

'Well, that was an adventure.' Dettie scratched through her handbag. 'Sammy, I hope you didn't get into any mischief.'

The shopkeeper grunted and dropped the Mars Bar back into its box.

'How much do we owe?' Dettie asked, waving her purse.

Leaning in the doorway, Jon told her the final price and Dettie started counting out the cash. There wasn't enough. The stack of notes was depleted. She was seven dollars short. With her face suddenly tense, she fished out her chequebook.

Katie's clothes and hair were soaked, and she still smelt strongly of petrol. She was shivering, and when Sam touched her arm she choked and ran out to the car.

The shopkeeper punched the price into the register as Dettie wrote out the cheque. With it signed and dated, she slid her license from her purse and set it down on the countertop.

Jon stepped forward. 'Huh,' he said. 'There's your licence there.' He pinned it to the wood with his finger. 'Guess it wasn't lost after all.' His expression was blank.

Dettie paused, staring down at it. She opened her mouth and closed it again. She narrowed her eyes.

They watched each other a moment, neither one moving, until the register dinged. 'That'll do,' the shopkeeper said.

53

The blanket, their pillows and the first-aid kit had been thrown into the dirt beside the petrol pumps. Katie was clambering over their seats searching for something. Snivelling, and not bothering to wipe the tears from her eyes, she had tipped over the floor mats and emptied the glove box. The pages of her colouring books were torn and scattered across the upholstery.

'What in blazes are you doing?' Dettie shouted, wrenched her from the car.

Katie squirmed. 'I've got to find it!' she shrieked. Strands of wet hair clung to her cheeks.

'And you're just going to pull the car apart?'

'Wait. Wait, what's the matter?' Jon stepped between them, kneeling. 'What have you lost, sweetie?' He lifted Dettie's hand gently from Katie's neck.

'Her—her *han*—ky—' Katie could barely speak through her juddering breaths. 'Her hanky—it's gone.'

Dettie rolled her eyes and wandered away.

'Whose hanky, lovey?' Jon asked softly.

'Mummy's,' she choked. 'Mummy's hanky. She gave it to me.'

Dettie was gathering up their things from the ground and dusting them off. 'We don't have time for this silliness,' she said. 'We have to get going.'

Katie noticed the tiny smile curling at the edge of her aunt's lips and her expression hardened to a glare. 'Where's Mummy's hanky?' she hissed.

Dettie waited a moment, shaking out a blanket before turning. 'What?' she said. 'I don't know why you're asking me.' She folded the square into a tight bundle and placed it back in the car. 'I can't be taking care of all your things, girl. If you can't look after them—'

'Where is it?'

'All right now.' Jon's hands were raised, palms open, to both of them. 'We can't have lost it. It must be in the car somewhere.'

'Well, there's no time to be hunting for it now.' Dettie tossed a handful of colouring-book pages into the bin.

Katie's fists were shaking. 'You don't care! You're happy it's gone!'

The shopkeeper, Sam realised, had appeared in the station doorway to see what all the noise was about. She leant against the frame, one hand parting the streamers and shielding the sun from her eyes.

'We are driving across the Nullarbor desert, young lady.' Dettie pointed towards the horizon, her teeth clenched. 'It's long. It's unpleasant. It's going to be stressful for at least another entire day. We have got more important things to worry about than some silly bit of cloth.'

'We can have a look though, love,' Jon soothed. 'It'll just take a minute.' He lowered his voice. 'I'm sure it's about. Somewhere. And if it'll calm her down.'

sign

Dettie crossed her arms and squeezed her elbows. 'Fine! *Fine,*' she said. 'You want to waste your time, go ahead. But don't expect me to help.'

So as Dettie stood aside, strumming her fingers on her handbag and continually examining her watch, they searched the car. Sam checked beneath the front seats and through the paper bag they used for their garbage. Jon flapped out the other blanket, and Katie ran her hands along the creases of the seats. They hunted through the boot and Katie even ran back inside to the sink where Dettie had helped her clean up. Finally, slumped on the back seat, his legs dangling out of the door, Jon blew out a long breath.

'Nowhere,' he said and looked up at Dettie. She was still fixed in place, tapping the hard leather of her handbag. 'Unless,' he nodded at her, 'what if? Maybe it fell in your handbag, love.'

Dettie laughed. 'Oh, I don't think so.'

Raising himself from the car, Jon edged closer to her. 'Probably not, love, I'm sure,' he whispered. 'But to put her at ease.'

'No, no, no.' She clutched her strap to her chest. 'No. I'm not having *children*—and some *stranger we picked up on the side of the road!*—ferreting through my belongings.' She kicked backwards and started to pace. 'Anyway,' she said, 'I've looked. I looked before. It's not there.'

'You're sure?'

'I tell you, it's not there!'

'You took my shirt to wash.' Katie was pointing at her across the bonnet. 'You were holding it. With my hanky.'

'So now I *took* it!' Dettie voice was cracking. 'Stole it, did I?' She slipped the bag from her shoulder, stomped to the back of

253

the car, and tossed it into the boot. 'This is ridiculous. I am *fed up* with being blamed for everything on this trip.' She slammed the lid down. 'Now we are *getting* in this car, and we are *driving* to Perth, and I am *not* going to hear any more nonsense from anyone.'

She rounded the vehicle, dropped into the driver's seat and wrenched the door shut.

Katie stepped up to the passenger side window and sucked in a deep breath. 'You're *bollocks!*' she yelled, her eyes squeezed shut.

Dettie's grip fell from the steering wheel. She nodded slowly, and when her mouth closed, a sick smile crept over her face. She blinked, kept nodding, and turned to stare at Jon. 'Oh, I see,' she said.

'Come on.' Jon led Katie away from the window. 'Let's all calm down now, eh? I bet it'll turn up,' he said. 'Just when we're not looking for it. That's how it always goes.'

After watching the commotion in front of him for so long, Sam was suddenly surprised by the sight of a large red tractor that had turned off the road and into the station. There was an old man in overalls driving, bouncing in his seat, and as he pulled it to a stop beside the furthest pump, he waved. Jon noticed, and shot him a quick nod.

Dettie fussed with the mirrors and jangled her keys.

'It's a hot one out today.' The old man whistled as he climbed down from the tractor.

Jon agreed, and popped open the back door for Sam to get inside.

'In a hurry, I see,' the old man said as the dirt crackled under his boots. 'Fair enough. I don't want to keep you.' He smiled. 'Just wanted to warn: if you're heading anywhere west, be careful. Those fires are getting pretty bad out there. News reckon it's the worst in a generation.'

'Scary stuff,' Jon said, hoisting his boot up into the doorframe.

'Too right, mate. Already lost some fireys, they say.'

The car roared to life and Dettie revved the motor. Jon called out a thank you and slid in beside Sam on the back seat.

Dettie stretched over to open the front passenger door, but Katie ignored her and leapt into the back with Sam and Jon.

'What is this?' Dettie snapped. 'What? Am I diseased now?'

Jon sat forward. 'No, love. Sorry. I should have jumped up front.' He leant across Sam to open the door, but Katie grabbed his arm and hugged it tightly.

Dettie huffed. 'Oh, forget it.' She stomped on the accelerator. The car's wheels spat dust across the old man's legs as he scampered away, and they skidded out of the station, swerving onto the road, heading west.

54

The horizon only continued to flatten the further they travelled. The colours of sunset faded from a dense red cloud in front of them to a serene purple shadow, glistening with stars behind. Aside from the engine, the only sound was Katie, kicking the seat in front of her. They still hadn't found her mother's handkerchief, and she was lying half asleep on her side, quiet, her leg still giving the upholstery an occasional half-hearted thump. The road had been straight and long, and Sam would catch Dettie yawning every few minutes, letting the car roll off to one side of the lane before shaking her head and jerking the wheel back to the centre.

When the sun had sunk completely, the air cooled, and Dettie drove for a while with the air vents switched off. For a while the absence of their hissing seemed alien to Sam and he considered how strange it was to hear the crackling of their tyres over the bitumen.

Finally, they pulled into an old rest stop, little more than a beaten-up wooden table, a tap, two garbage bins and a pile of metal someone had discarded beneath a tree. There were no toilets, so Dettie left the car lights on while they used the bushes. This was where they would spend the night, she said.

An unfamiliar cold wind gnawed at their clothing, so Jon decided to build a fire in an old ten-gallon drum he found by the scrap heap. Dettie reminded him of the fire ban, but he promised to keep watch the whole time and not let things get out of hand. Nonetheless, Dettie made them fill up every water bottle they had at the tap and lined them up on top of the picnic table, just in case.

Jon found branches and wooden scraps lying around, and after snapping them in two with his boot and stacking them up, they soon had a small blaze to light their faces and warm their hands. Dettie tried to wrap a blanket over Katie and Sam's shoulders, but Katie threw it off. As the children sat on the edge of the concrete table, Dettie and Jon turned two bins over and used them as seats.

The fire crackled and popped. Something inside the drum settled, sending lit ash up through the smoke. Sam's toes were cold in his shoes, but his nose glowed and the smell of burning wood watered his eyes. Between the heat of the fire and the cool of the air, his neck, which had been getting increasingly irritated, was a peculiar wash of tenderness.

'Who wants to hear a story?' Jon inched closer to the fire.

Katie said that she did, and Sam nodded.

'All right then, what do you want to hear?'

His sister hummed thoughtfully to herself, but Sam waved his arms in the light, trying to remember the sign Jon had shown him. He held his fingers like bear claws and tapped them to his chest. Was that right?

Scary. Scary.

Jon nodded. 'Okay. Good. What kind of—' he signed back.

'What's *that?*' Dettie said, leaning forward. 'What are you doing? What are you talking about?'

'Nothing, love. It means *scary*. A scary story.'

'No.' Dettie shook her head.

'Yes!' Katie snapped. 'Scary. I want to hear scary.'

Jon waited, surveying their faces. When Dettie didn't object further, he took a breath. 'What kind of scary story?' he said.

Sam held his arms out in front of himself, rolling his eyes back. He tried to groan—couldn't—and stuck his tongue out instead.

'A sick story?' Jon said.

Sam shook his head. He pretended to bite.

Jon still couldn't get it, so he held out his hand. 'Here, my old mate. Scratch it out on this then.' He pointed at his palm.

Sam took Jon's palm, and by drawing each letter slowly inside it with his fingertip, he spelt out a word.

'Zombies.' Jon grinned.

Sam nodded.

'Of course. Zombies,' Jon said, scratching his eyebrow. 'Oh, I can tell you zombie stories.'

'No, you *can't*,' Dettie snapped. 'He doesn't need any more of that terrifying the life out of him right before bed.'

Jon smiled. 'It's just a story, love. Make-believe.'

'Does it have to scare them silly, then? I don't want them up all night, petrified.'

'I want to hear it!' Katie yelled.

Dettie leant back, crossing one leg over the other. 'Fine. Your decision,' she said. 'You all do whatever you want.' She lit a cigarette and sucked at it dramatically. 'Never mind me.'

sign

Jon waited, smiling. 'Come on, love. It's just for fun.'

She waved him away, so after a moment more, he nudged closer to the fire, his face lit gold by the flames, and with wide eyes, started to tell them the story.

It was a true story, he said, of a young couple he'd known in England. One night, they had driven out to a secluded lookout in the wilderness. On a date, he said. And while they were sitting, watching the stars, they heard a news report come on the radio. A deranged killer—a *zombie* by all accounts, he said—had been seen roaming the exact area where the couple had parked their car. The zombie, the report informed them, could be identified by its missing hand. It had been chopped off, Jon said, acting it out by pulling down his sleeve and leaving only a pinched stub. Instead, he said, there was just a long metal hook stuck in its place.

From out of his sleeve, two fingers appeared, curled together like a question mark.

'Oh, for goodness sake,' Dettie muttered.

'So when the couple heard the news, the girl got scared. She told her boyfriend she wanted to go home. Pleaded with him. But the boyfriend didn't want to. It was a nice night, he said. There was no such thing as zombies, he said. Eventually, they had a big argument. They yelled at one another. She demanded that he take her home. And the boyfriend was so mad that when he started the car he sped off. Fast-like.' Jon slapped his hands together. 'He tore off down the road, and drove all the way home like that.

'And all the way home, both heard a clinking sound. Coming from the car. A *ting, ting, ting* noise. On the outside of the door.

'When they pulled into her driveway,' he said, 'when her boyfriend walked around to open the girlfriend's door . . .'

Jon paused.

'He found—'

He stretched towards them.

'Hanging from the girlfriend's doorhandle—' Jon raised his arm, his fingers still curled, 'was a bloodstained . . metal . . . hook.'

Katie gasped, holding on to her ankles. Sam was smiling.

'The zombie had been just about to open their car door before they drove off, you see.'

It was a silly story, but Jon told it so well that for a moment the old thrill of the undead surged through Sam's belly again.

'Is that true?' Katie was rocking herself against Sam's side. 'That's not true!'

'Of course it's not true,' Dettie snorted. 'It's ridiculous.'

'Oh, no. It's true.' Jon's eyes widened in the flickering light. 'They still have the hook. Hanging over their fireplace. They showed it to me.'

Katie squealed into her hands.

'*Congratulations.* Now they'll never get to sleep.' Dettie flicked the ash from her cigarette.

'Another one,' Katie giggled. 'Tell us another one.'

'Okay, darling,' he said. 'You pick this time. What's the story going to be about?'

'Um . . .' She twisted a finger through her hair. 'I don't know.'

'How about a lost kitten that finds its way home?' Dettie offered.

'Come on, love,' he said. 'Let her choose.'

'We haven't got forever, and she obviously can't think of anything.'

'A crazy old lady,' Katie said hurriedly. She kept her eyes directed at the tips of her shoes.

sign

Dettie was staring over the flames at her. She closed her mouth. Her chin jutted out slightly. She flicked her cigarette again and fussed with the neck of her blouse.

'Crazy ladies?' Jon snapped a stick and fed it into the fire. 'Crazy ladies . . . Not sure if I know any stories about—oh, wait,' he said, dusting off his hands. 'I do have one. But it's a bit gross.'

He looked over at Dettie for approval, but she had turned away to look at the stars, still fiddling absently with her collar. He began.

There was once this young woman, he said. He'd read about it in the newspaper. Famous story from a few years ago, he said. She had a spoilt little poodle that needed lots of attention. It was fed treats all the time. It had expensive haircuts and toys. So whenever the woman had to go out anywhere, she would leave someone to watch it. Like a babysitter. But for a dog.

'Anyway, one night,' Jon said, 'she was going out to a dinner party, but her regular dog-sitter was busy. So she asked the old lady next door if she could do it for her. Just for the night. But what the young lass didn't know was that the old woman needed pills. Medicine, to stop her being crazy. And in all the excitement that day, she'd forgotten to take them.'

Dettie's lips were pursed tightly. She wasn't facing them, but she was listening. She sat still. Exhaling into the dark. Unaware that the cigarette seized in her fingers had turned to a column of ash.

'After a couple of hours of watching the dog, the old lady was feeling strange,' Jon said. 'But she was so happy—so grateful— to be out of the house, that she wanted to do something nice for the young woman when she got home. *I'll make a roast chicken*, she thought, and got out all the pans and spices she needed, and set the oven. And so, she prepared the meal and popped it in the oven.'

Jon's voice got slow again, stretching the moment out. 'Eventually,' he said, 'when the young woman got home that night, she could smell something burning. As she walked into the house she found the old woman in the kitchen. She was sitting at the table, covering her face. Crying.

'Slowly,' Jon said, 'the young woman opened the door of the stove—' He mimed the action for them, leaning in, peering into the campfire. 'And then she saw what the crazy old woman had done.' He recoiled in horror. 'She had plucked, and stuffed, and roasted, the woman's pet poodle.'

'*Good heavens!*' Dettie snapped, leaping up. 'That is the most hideous thing I have ever heard in my life!' She was clutching her arms, shaking.

'Eww!' Katie had her knees hugged to her chest.

It *was* gross, but Sam was smiling.

Jon hid a huge grin behind his wrist.

'No more stories!' Dettie spat. '*No more!* That is it!' She flicked her dead cigarette into the dirt.

'What did it look like?' Katie whispered.

'You are *not* answering that!' Dettie pointed at Jon. She dusted off the back of her legs. 'Disgusting, terrible story,' she murmured. 'That poor woman.'

'Tell another one!' Katie pleaded.

Dettie spluttered and shook her head. 'Absolutely not,' she said. 'That was ghastly.'

'Maybe your aunt's right, darling.' Jon winked.

Whining, Katie rolled back against Sam's arm, clomping her heels. 'Never get to have fun.'

sign

'I think somebody's getting grouchy,' Dettie sang, and began rolling up their blanket over her arm. 'I think it must be time for bed.'

Sam's legs were sore from sitting on the table, but he didn't want to leave the warmth of the fire. He liked watching the different colours of the coal, whiter the deeper they were, throbbing in the heat. Dettie had to prod the children back to the car to settle them down, and she sat with them until Katie could barely keep her eyes open and Sam pretended to be asleep. When she finally left, pushing the door closed softly behind her, he heard Jon call out, 'See you in the morning, kids!' and then Dettie hushing him quiet.

55

'They're just stories, love,' Jon was saying.

Sam had inched the rear window down to listen, but their voices were muffled and he had to strain to make out the words. The sound of the fire was soothing as it popped and crackled and, even in the chill, Sam had to sit up to stop his eyes from sliding shut. Dettie was perched on the picnic table beside Jon, gazing into the flames.

'What kind of person would find that amusing?' she said, shaking her head. 'Who would even want to *think* such things?'

He chuckled and picked at the hole in his jeans. 'It's not real, love,' he said. 'That's the point. They're fantasy. Zombies and crazy old women. Ghosts and murder. There's no harm in them. Just scary yarns to tell at night. To give you a thrill. To make life a bit more exciting.'

'To warp your mind.' She shuddered.

Jon stoked the fire with a sizzling branch. 'Well, they're not everyone's cup of tea,' he said, watching the leaves ignite. His face yellowed and, as he let go, the branch curled into the metal drum.

sign

They sat quietly for a few minutes, and Sam watched the smoke fleeing the illumination of the fire. Occasionally, Dettie would jerk around, wide-eyed, to check the surrounding bushes; whenever she did, Jon would steal quick glances at her, dipping his head. He drew a deep, long breath and blew it out.

'It's a pity we can't find that handkerchief,' he said.

Dettie stiffened. She bent to lift a long stick from the ground. 'Well, if the girl hadn't been running riot the whole trip . . .' She stiffened, her neck straight, her chin dipped.

He sat motionless. 'Yes, it's definitely strange,' he said, slowly. 'Just losing it like that. After treasuring it for so long.'

Dettie pushed one end of the stick she was holding into the dirt. It was a broken tree limb, and it reminded Sam of a baseball bat as she rolled it in her hands. 'Children are reckless,' she said. 'No sense of what's important.'

Jon didn't say anything for a moment. He just watched her from the corner of his eyes. When he did speak it was too soft for Sam to make out anything except the word *kids*.

'Me?' Dettie's voice squeaked. 'No. No, Ted and I never did. No time for them really. What with us always on the move. Travelling. And Ted's work. And my—'

She broke off. She went back to grinding her stick into the earth. She hummed. 'And then the way Ted's death came up on us.' She was smiling, but the flickering across her face darkened her eyes. 'Quite a surprise.'

Sam tried to read the expression in her voice. She was saying it again—that Ted was dead. He couldn't tell if she believed it, or it was just something she'd gotten used to saying. He wondered, briefly, if the difference mattered.

On the back seat, Katie was rustling under one of Jon's flannel shirts.

'But it was no big issue in the end. It just meant I was always there to help out Joanne—Donald and Joanne—with the kids,' Dettie said. 'Babysit for them. Drop the kids at school. Pick them up. Do some dinners and housework. Even helping Joanne through that sorry business with Sammy's voice.' She looked over at the car and Sam had to duck. 'She and Donald were going through a rough patch at the time. As you would, of course. All that stress and worry. And afterwards. With work. But I was there. To help. Helping. As best I could, anyway.' She let out a long, slow breath. 'It almost feels like they're mine,' she said. 'Sometimes.'

She withdrew a crumpled packet of cigarettes from her sleeve and offered it to Jon. They each lit one and she crushed the empty packet and threw it in the fire. They both sat smoking silently, and as he waited, Sam felt himself start to drift off to sleep. A warm quiet slipped over his mind and he had to keep shaking himself awake.

Jon was turning the cigarette in his fingers, watching it smoulder. He seemed to be thinking something over, nodding to himself. Finally, he cleared his throat.

'Here, love—I want to ask,' he began, slowly.

Dettie straightened herself to face him.

He took a long drag of smoke and let it drift casually from his mouth. 'The little ones. Their mother—Joanne?' He picked at the hole in his pants. 'So she—? She does know they're going to Perth?' His head was shaking very slightly. His eyes remained locked on the fire. 'She knows where they are, doesn't she?'

Dettie choked, clutching her neck, and coughed. She tried to swallow down her hacking. When she'd finished her face was drawn. 'Why—what makes you say that?' she wheezed.

Jon eased forward with his elbows on his knees. He didn't look at her as he inhaled. 'The children's clothes,' he said, and gestured to the car. 'They haven't got much else to put on. Just a couple of shirts and things. Not even pyjamas. No luggage.'

'Well, we were—it was a great shock. A hurry,' she stammered. 'Their father. *Donald.* Their father's very sick.' She coughed again. 'In Perth. My brother. Which we're—is why we're going—and—' She was lifting the stick and tapping it on the ground. She took a breath. 'I'm sorry,' she said, 'are you accusing me of something?'

'No. No. Course not. Just—just curious,' Jon said. 'Just curious.' He ran a hand through his beard. 'One of those funny little oddities, you know? Gets you thinking.' He gave a quick smile that slid from his face as though it were melting. 'Besides, I mean, it's none of my business, right?'

'Exactly,' Dettie snapped, brushing the ash from her lap. 'I mean, not that there's anything—' Now she wasn't blinking. 'I mean, it's fine,' she said. 'The children. Their mother. Everything's *fine.*'

'Oh, I know.' Jon still hadn't turned to face her. 'Of course it is. Silly of me, really.'

She was nodding, more to herself than to him. 'Everybody's fine.'

There was a moment of silence.

'Except their father,' Jon said. And when Dettie didn't respond, he added: 'Because he's sick.'

'Oh, yes. Yes,' she said. 'Except for him.'

Gradually, Jon looked towards the car, and after a moment, Sam realised that Jon was nodding straight at him, through the window, a vacant expression on his face. Holding his stare, Jon drew a small, clockwise circle on his chest.

Sorry.

The window fogged beneath Sam's chin where his stoma was breathing on the glass. His fingers remained hooked over the edge of the door, fingernails picking at the rubber seal. He wasn't sure what to sign back. He wasn't even sure how to. He returned the nod, feeling a strange mix of fear and reassurance. Jon knew. He was worried about Dettie too. Worried for them. But just as he was wondering why Jon would need to apologise, he saw Dettie.

She had turned in place, watching Jon's face, trying to read his expression. Had she seen? Had she seen him signing? She straightened, following his line of sight, peering over at the car. Squinting through the smoke. Sam ducked out of sight. The ghostly puff of condensation on the window above him shone white against the black sky.

After a minute he inched his way back up. Dettie and Jon were still beside one another. Still silent. Neither looking at the other. Each taking slow drags from their cigarettes. Finally, Jon stretched out his arms and crushed the last of his butt on the edge of the table.

'Well, Dettie,' he said, standing up, 'I'm knackered. Fancy I might run off to the little boy's room, then turn in for the night.' He pointed into the bushes.

Dettie stared at him, her jaw hanging slack. A flicker from the campfire suddenly gnarled her face. From the angle of the light it almost looked like a sneer.

'You—you called me Dettie,' she said. Her voice was colder than it had been. Not angry, but somehow disappointed. 'Isn't that funny?' But it didn't sound like she found it funny at all. She sighed a laugh. 'You don't usually call me Dettie,' she said. 'Usually you call me—' She hiccoughed, and a vague, gaunt expression hung on her face.

Jon didn't appear to be listening, and nodded, shooting her a half-hearted smile. Excusing himself, he pushed through the branches and out of sight. Sam watched the leaves rustle back into place behind him. When the orange throb of the fire glistened over them, the bushes seemed to ripple.

Dettie stood, momentarily unsteady on her feet. She lifted the stick and began lurching towards the car. Sam huddled down even further, slipping the blanket over his arms, shutting his eyes, and trying to will the muscles in his shoulders to go slack. He didn't dare even sneak open one eyelid, but he could hear her—the scrape of her feet, the drag of the stick, the snuffling and huffs of her heavy breathing. A current ran through his body. He could feel every fibre of the blanket against his neck, could smell the faint vinegar tang of potato chips from an empty packet on the floor. His own heartbeat thundered behind his ears.

Swaying slightly, Dettie began muttering hoarsely to herself, but even this close, straining to listen, Sam couldn't discern what she was saying. It seemed to be a long, unbroken stream of words. Eventually she shuffled away, still murmuring, back over to the table. She stood awhile, her eyebrows twitching, her lips moving rhythmically. Staring into the glow. Unblinking. There were tiny holes in the metal drum, and Sam could see the red coals burning within, could imagine them surging white.

His head felt heavy, so he laid it back on the seat, peering through the window with one eye open.

Sam lay for a moment, feeling his eyelids dipping shut. He could hear Katie's breath, and as it mingled with the light-headedness of sleep, he recalled again the girl behind the curtain. It was almost her raspy breath that he was hearing again—the way it had started to fade that last night she was in hospital. Before she had disappeared, been moved to wherever she went. He could almost see her glazed expression as her chest rose and fell. So gently. So heavily. Nearly still. Her eyelids half open. Dry and rubbery. Her thin hand limp as the doctor placed it back on the mattress. She'd gotten better, they'd told him. And as he gave in to the sensation of sleep he accepted, in a detached way, finally and completely, what he already knew.

They had lied.

She was dead.

An unsettling calm washed over him.

Dettie dropped her cigarette butt and rolled the heavy stick around in her hands. She squeezed it tightly and let it go, shaking her head from time to time as though a shudder ran through her whole body. Eventually she moved off again, taking the stick with her, and followed Jon into the shadows. The fire snapped and hissed, and just before he surrendered, he thought he heard a sheep bleating wearily from a nearby field.

56

The engine growled to life. Sam was aware, suddenly, of Dettie's gasping, and the scent of ash on her clothes. A door slammed, then they were moving. He sat up. It was still before sunrise, and as the headlights swept across the picnic area he saw a wisp of smoke curling from the now-darkened metal drum. Katie was murmuring something, but the car jerked, and Sam had to grab for his seatbelt. They lurched to the left, the tyres crackling, and as they sped off he thought he glimpsed two lumps of luggage tipped over on the road.

Katie started shouting. She was telling them that Jon wasn't in the car—calling out so loud that her voice cracked. When Sam turned, he saw that the front passenger seat was empty. There was no sight of Jon anywhere—even out on the road— and one of his shirts was still wound up into a ball on Katie's lap.

The car hit a deep pothole and the children were thrown about in their seats. Katie squealed.

'Where's Jon?' she said, twisting in her seat.

Dettie hissed through clenched teeth. She was frowning.

Her head lolled as though she was struggling to hold it up, but her fingers were tight on the wheel.

'Where's Jon?' Katie screamed, drumming her fist against the door. 'Where is he?' She kicked as hard as she could at the front seats. '*Where?*' Her thumping went on, hard enough that Sam could feel it ripple throughout the entire car.

'He's gone,' Dettie said, quietly.

'Where?' Katie kept kicking. 'Where *is* he?'

'Gone.'

'*Where?*'

'He's *gone*, Katie. He left!'

'No, he didn't—'

'Yes, he did!'

'No!'

Dettie twisted around, her eyes swollen as she snatched Katie's ankle and pinned it down. 'He left us!' she said. 'He did. He left. That's what people—' Her breath caught like a hiccough. 'That's what he did.'

Katie kicked free. 'No, he *didn't*. Where is he?'

'He's *gone*,' Dettie barked.

The car lurched right, and Katie yelped. Sam grabbed for the ceiling and Katie at once, his stomach turning. The tyres drifted across the dividing line of the highway, the cabin wobbling. In the distance, up ahead, an oncoming Land Rover flashed its lights. Dettie's breath shuddered. She cleared her throat. Blinking. Licking her lips. She gripped the wheel again, steering the car back onto their side of the road.

'People leave, girl,' she said. 'That's what they do.'

Katie was crying—tears running down her face freely. Her expression was blank. Her face slack.

sign

'I don't know why you have to keep fighting me all the time.'
Dettie was sitting forward, taking short, sharp breaths. '*I'm* not
the one who left,' she said, blinking hard, her head shaking in
a tiny, rhythmic quaver. 'That was *him*. I'm the one who stayed.
The one keeping us together. Keeping this family together.'

The Land Rover shot by, still flashing its lights, the driver
frantically waving. Sam was still holding on to Katie, but it felt
like she had wilted. Her arm, prickled with sweat, hung limp.
He squeezed her hand, but she didn't respond.

'That's why family is so important,' Dettie was saying. 'Family
doesn't leave. Family *stays*. That's why we're going to Perth. Why
your father is there. Why your mother is meeting us. Where
she's waiting for us.'

Sam squeezed again, but Katie didn't move. She was
shivering, staring through the back of the seat in front of her.
As if through the upholstery and the padding. Through the
dashboard. Through the engine block and the duco shell.
Down, out and beyond the car. Down to the black, cool asphalt
whipping by beneath them.

PERTH

57

For almost two hours they drove without talking. Katie had pressed her face in the seat, sobbing, and Sam was turned towards the window, tears blurring his eyes, watching the sun slowly lift into the sky. Jon was gone. And just as Sam's house had appeared larger and more alien the day his father had left, so too did the car. The night before it had seemed so crowded and lively; now it was cavernous. Emptier. Looser. Since they'd hit the pothole, the rattling sound had returned to the engine. It was soft, almost unnoticeable, but Sam could tell it was building, and as they continued on with the ventilation fans turned down and the radio off, it was the only sound they could hear beside his sister's strangled gasps.

As the shadows shrank towards the horizon, Sam could see in their place expanses of scorched fences and blackened trees. They were driving towards an area already charred by bushfire and he could still smell the melted tar beneath their wheels. He had no idea where they were. A half-destroyed sign said something about Dundas Nature Reserve, but he had no way to tell if they were in it, or near it, or had already passed through. The landscape all around reminded him of a documentary he'd seen once about an erupted volcano that had swept a village away, leaving nothing but charcoal and dust. Smoke was darkening the air above them, and all around, spotting the fields, he could see lumps that were probably once animals, smouldering, the same colour as the ground.

He remembered the first afternoon of the trip, and Dettie dragging them out onto the road to stare down at the dead kangaroo. He remembered what she'd said about it. That it had given up. Given in. Surrendered to death. But as he looked out at these animals, their smouldering husks, torched into the dirt, Sam knew they couldn't have fought to stay alive—even if they'd wanted to. They didn't slink off to death. It came for them. He could only imagine what it must have been like. Trapped behind their wire fences. Pacing the locked gates desperately. The flames chewing up the ground. Gushing over them. The bleating and shrieking as they cowered, engulfed by the blaze.

The seatbelt fixed him in place, constricting his chest. The heat muddled his head. He felt the quilt—the quilt Dettie had made for him months ago—tucked tightly around his legs. It strained across his knees, stretching out the stitching on its dozens of embroidered squares.

In one square, a tiny knotted figure that Dettie had intended to represent him was flying, its arms spread wide among the birds. Sam stared down at it: a silhouette in the sky. Just like all the other cheery, impossible scenes she had painstakingly crafted. That she had tried desperately to will into being. But he was a sheep. Sweating into his wool as the grass blades ignited under his feet. The birds were overhead as they scattered, soaring to freedom.

For a moment he wasn't sure if he was awake or still dreaming.

58

A smaller fire had swept around the next store they visited, and the owner was still outside with a hose, spraying down the walls. There was a stench of charcoal and smoke in the air.

'Not heading west, are you?' the man said. 'It's getting ferocious out there. Almost took this whole lot.' And as he directed his hose back onto the roof, his teeth showed, speckled with ash and grit.

Out of habit, Sam found himself standing in front of a comic-book stand, his eyes scanning the covers. To his surprise, he finally found, tucked at the back, with its pages crumpled and bent in half, an earlier edition of *Tales of Fear* than the one he already owned.

Dettie hovered behind him, and when she saw what he was flicking through, snatched it from his hand. As she held it up to look at the drawing of a car on the cover, her face softened. She crossed to the counter to pay for the comic, and bought a packet of Chico Babies for Katie.

When they were back on the road his sister, who had not

said a word for three hours, rolled down her window and hurled the Chicos as hard as she could from the car. Sam was surprised that Dettie didn't comment—about the window, or the lollies, or the quiet. She just rubbed her eyes and twitched, and kept on driving.

59

Reading the second comic was nothing at all like the first. Now there was no thrill. Nor any fear. No swirl of nausea at the thought of the blood. The pictures of the corpses were all scratchy, and the colours were too bright. The woman with the torn shirt looked ridiculous, pressing the back of her hand to her forehead and screaming. It was an expression that was supposed to represent terror, but looked more like she was singing. That, Sam thought, was not what terror felt like.

Even the zombie's eyes, which he had perceived at different times as bloodthirsty or sorrowful, just looked surprised now. They were empty, and they gawped at the world, perplexed. The slobber running down its jaws was almost funny. The zombie no longer reminded him of himself. His operation. His lack of voice. Tracey. But it made him think of something—he just wasn't entirely sure what.

From the bowels of hell I spurn thee, Sam read, and gave up. He flashed through one final time to see if any of the zombies had metal hooks for hands, and when they didn't, tossed the comic to the floor.

It landed on a piece of bent cardboard sticking halfway out from beneath his seat. Even before he had bent down to pull it up, Sam knew what it was. Jon's sign. *Help me, I'm British*. Sam's own small scribble on the back.

Dettie watched Sam unfold it, and adjusted herself in her seat. She cleared her throat. 'You know,' she called, 'I wasn't sure if I should tell you two this. But last night, Jon decided to catch a bus back to Sydney. That's why he had to go so suddenly.'

She tapped her thumbs on the steering wheel. 'Yes,' she said. 'He decided all at once. He was so excited. Told me he was going to fly back to England. To be with his wife again.' She stretched up in her seat, trying to see Katie in the mirror. 'Did you know he had a wife?'

The rattle in the engine was rising again as Dettie's foot pressed harder on the pedal.

'He asked me to say goodbye to you both, though,' she said, nodding. 'He did. He was going to do it last night, but you were asleep and he didn't want to wake you.' She hummed, her eyes back on the road. 'He said, tell your two special ones thank you. And have a fun rest of the trip.' She was nodding away. 'So you see—there's no reason to be upset like this. That's not what he would've—'

She stopped and pursed her lips.

'Why don't we—when we get to Perth—why don't we see if we can write him a letter? What do you think?'

Katie was stretched out on the back seat, clutching Jon's shirt to her chest. 'You're a liar,' she whispered, exhausted. 'I hate you.'

Sam spun around to look at her, but Katie was perfectly still. Her eyes were puffy from crying and she kept them closed.

283

Dettie's shoulders fell, but she didn't say anything. She slumped back down into her driving. Sam could see her lips trembling. Her nails dug into the plastic as she tightened them on the wheel. She sniffed.

Watching her, part of him wished that he could hate her too. Even just a little bit. So many times in the past—and particularly the last few days—he had wanted to scream at her, to rage or run, to tell her to stop and listen. But as he watched her now—her body bent, her thin, dishevelled hair being battered around by the air vents, the bandaid twisted and blackened on her finger—she looked feeble. Tattered and withered and sad. He couldn't stop thinking of the yellowing photo of Ted in the bottom of her handbag. The sticky tape that ran behind his face. The story she told about the way he died. He remembered all the times she had told him about her heart operation and the scar that stretched down her chest. The wedding ring she would never take off that had tarnished on her hand.

His whole life she'd been so large. Old-fashioned. Stuck in her ways. Afraid of fuss. Fierce. But he had to admit that she was warm and welcoming too. Familiar. Secure. When they got home from school she would be there. When he heard his mother crying at night it was Dettie who would make tea and sit with her. Talk her through it. Even after his operation, having Dettie tell the awful story about her heart attack over and over again did, somehow, make the whole experience less frightening. She'd been through something even scarier and survived, after all. She hadn't given up.

But as he looked at her now, she looked impossibly fragile. Her fingers were stained yellow with cigarettes and speckled brown with instant coffee. Her dress was smudged with charcoal. She

284

was a bundle of frayed hems, bandaids and laddered pantyhose, worn down by this endless, exhausting trip.

She'd told them they were going to see their father. That their father wanted them. That their mother was waiting for them there too. Now Jon was supposedly on his way to Sydney.

But she was a liar. She'd lied the whole time. From the first morning, lying on the phone, all the way through. She seemed to be held together by hundreds of lies. Lies she'd wrapped around herself to make sense of the world. Comfortable and numbing lies. Their father hadn't abandoned them. Her husband was dead. Jon was fine. Her lies were all she had left.

Perhaps that was why she favoured Sam so much now. His silence. She could lie to him all she wanted and he couldn't talk back. Katie, on the other hand, was all questions, clarifications, pushback. It grated on her. Made her wallow in the fraud. Stopped her forward momentum.

And Perth, Sam realised, was simply the biggest lie of all. A hope she had committed them to, that she could no longer abandon. It was just a dream. An idea. A word on a road sign— no closer or further away than it had ever been. But for Dettie it had become the confirmation of something bigger than any of them in that car could ever understand. It spurred her on, but Sam realised that if they ever actually did get there, something inside her might irreparably break.

He heard Dettie's breath shudder, and saw a tear welling beneath her eye. He felt a falling sensation chilling his stomach. It wasn't repulsion exactly—more the shock of realisation. The disappointment of an inevitability. Like the day after his operation, when, bandaged and groggy, he had tried to speak for the first time and nothing happened. Dettie was trapped. She'd set herself on a course that had no ending, and from which there was no turning back.

As he stared at her, watching her fidget, blinking sweat and tears from her eyes, he realised that it wasn't just her. It was words. All words. *You'll be good as new.* People were only attracted to what was familiar. The girl behind the curtain was just getting her own room. Words were just lies inherited. The product of desperate people pressing their desires onto the world. Remaking it how they longed for it to be. And Sam was tired of lies. Comforting words. Empty sounds with no more substance than breath.

His gaze dropped and he saw his mother's blue-embroidered handkerchief, the one Katie thought she had lost, tucked in Dettie's lap. It was between her knees partially covered by her skirt. And somehow that attempt to hide it seemed so pathetic that Sam felt a fresh rush of pity for her. Her expression was empty. She was gawping at the world. Perplexed. He lifted his hand slowly and petted her elbow. It was a moment before she felt his touch, and when she did, she smiled and wiped the moisture from her cheek.

Their mother had no idea where they were.

They had to get away.

60

The red glow in the distance grew into smoke and forest fire. They could smell the fumes of it through their vents and the only traffic on the road was driving the opposite way. Other cars, loaded with luggage and pieces of furniture, beeped at them as they roared by, but Dettie kept heading forward, towards the blaze.

The weight of the sun made Sam's eyelids heavy, and when he tried to remind himself of being at home, he found he couldn't remember the sensation of anything in particular. The smell of their kitchen, the feel of his mattress, his mother's voice; all he knew now was the numbness of his car seat, vibrating, rocking him ever so slightly, and the heat. There had always been this heat. Always the dust. And always the three of them.

For a moment he wondered if Jon had just been a dream from which he'd woken. Another lie. The memory of his accent seemed so strange, like some tropical birdcall. But he could feel the cardboard of Jon's sign between his fingers. He could see the tiny boomerang swinging from the rear-vision mirror. And behind him, he knew Katie was still clinging to one of Jon's weathered flannel shirts.

The grinding in the engine went on, even louder than before, and when Sam placed his hand on the dashboard he could feel the vibration of the fan belt. He could picture the way it was thrashing about beneath the bonnet.

A handwritten sign whipped past, warning that the road ahead was closed, but Dettie didn't flinch or even slow down.

'Oh, my head,' she groaned, digging deeply into her temple, her papery skin stretched. 'My head.' Her teeth were clenched. 'That blasted noise.'

Another sign—this one singed at the edges—shot by.

'Jon could have fixed it,' Katie said. She spoke quietly, her lip trembling, but she was staring at her aunt's eyes in the rear-vision mirror.

Dettie looked dazed. Her hair was matted into knots and her skin was pasty. When she spoke she seemed to be returning from somewhere far away, retracing every sentence in her mind. 'Pardon?' she said.

'Jon could have fixed the noise. He did before.'

Dettie scoffed. A laugh that turned into a cough. 'Well, if he did, he didn't do a very good job.'

'Yes, he did!'

Dettie sighed heavily. It took a moment for her eyelids to lift again. 'I honestly don't know why you keep getting so worked up,' she said. 'He went his way. We went ours.'

Katie sat forward, stretching her seatbelt. 'What did you do to him?'

'I mean, it's not as if he's your father—'

'What did you say to make him go away?'

sign

'Please. Stop this, girl. Stop it.' Dettie's voice trembled.

'What did you say?'

'We've made it this far now. Just—*please*. You'll be back with Ted soon enough.'

Katie's face fell. Her fists, balled white, released. 'Who's Ted?' she said, her eyes wide, welling with tears.

'What?' Dettie rubbed the bridge of her nose.

'You said *Ted*. Who's Ted?'

'Roger, I said.' She thumped the wheel with her palm. 'I mean, *Donald*. Back with Donald. Your father.'

'Why did you say Ted?'

'Katie! That's enough!'

When Dettie yelled the car shook, lurching across the road and into the path of an oncoming ute. The driver beeped furiously, flashing his lights, and the caravan attached behind lurched heavily. Dettie yelped, wrestling the car back in place, and Katie screamed, clinging to her seatbelt. The ute roared past, still honking.

'You *see?* You see, girl? Do you want us to get killed? I am too busy to be playing these games all the time!'

Trembling, Katie sat back in her seat, silent, and began stuffing blankets and clothing around her self. Sam's heart was racing, and the rattle in the engine suddenly seemed more ominous, as though the car were about to shake apart at any moment, scattering itself across the gravel.

They drove on that way for another few minutes, the air becoming ferociously hot. Ahead of them, parked halfway into the dry scrub, a small fire truck stood at the base of a large plume of white smoke. It looked abandoned, but its hoses were still fixed to its taps, throbbing like fat yellow snakes, stretched across the steaming road and into the bushes. Sam couldn't see the fire-fighters through the haze, but as Dettie slowed to pass the truck, he could hear shouts through the crackle of flame. Amid the shifting blurs of orange and grey he thought he could see silhouettes.

Once they had rounded the blockage, Sam caught a glimpse of more blackened animals fallen in the dirt. This time it was birds, their bodies charred, what was left of their feathers splayed and smouldering. The sight of so many at once made him want to vomit. He had to choke down the sensation, his head heavy. It was just like the first time he'd seen the dead kangaroo, but this time his vision didn't fade. He could see it all clearly, without wanting to turn away. Somehow he wanted to remember it.

And as he stared at their shrivelled, steaming forms, illuminated by shafts of sunlight that cut through the smoke, Dettie kicked at the accelerator and the car sped on.

61

They were pulled over on a blackened stretch of road so that they could pee. Dettie had become so impatient, so jittery, that she now left the car running. It shuddered in place with the handbrake on as she stalked off to squat behind a cluster of scorched bushes.

To Sam it felt like the end of the world. Like a page from one of his comics brought to life. Another small fire front had just swept through the area. The air remained heavy with smoke, and a crisp heat radiated up from the ground. There were no animals in sight. No sound of birds. Even the flies that usually pestered his face were gone. No traffic came from either direction, and the last building Sam could recall had been a farmhouse a few minutes back, as yet untouched by the fire, where a farmer was hosing down his buildings.

Sam stood waiting for Dettie, basting in sweat, staring in through the front door of the car as it yawned before him. For one wild moment he thought about jumping in and driving off. He felt every muscle in his body tighten. He could do it. With

Dettie staggering around in the bushes, metres away, he and Katie could leap inside, snap down all the locks, and tear off, abandoning her behind them in a cloud of dust. As he stared in at the dashboard display, he tried, frantically, to think of which lever to pull, what pedal to press, to make the car go. He remembered sitting in the driver's seat when Jon was fixing the engine, and turning over the ignition. He remembered barely being able to see over the wheel; feeling his legs waggle, toes centimetres from the pedals.

But he had to do something. It had gone on long enough. The whole trip. All of it.

It had to end.

The keys dangled in the ignition. Poised. Waiting.

He looked at Katie. She was scratching the toe of her shoe into dirt beside the highway, exposing the red earth beneath its charcoal crust. Further back, a few dozen metres down the road behind her, he could see the burnt-out husk of a vehicle, partially nosed into the scrub. Like everything else around them, it too had been overwhelmed by flames. Lopsided, with no tyres, its glass shattered, the roof partially collapsed in on itself.

It wouldn't work. He'd fail to get the car in gear. He wouldn't be able to steer. And then they'd still be stuck with Dettie. Watching her get even angrier. Seeing her lose even more control.

Maybe if they could run, he thought. If they could make it past the wreckage of the car, out of her line of sight. From there, they'd be able to scramble into the skeletal remains of the foliage, could make their way from cover to cover, to try to get back to that farmhouse. Maybe even wave someone else down on the way. Whatever. Anything. They just had to do it. To go. Now.

sign

Before he lost his nerve, Sam took a breath, grabbed for Katie's hand, and sprinted. She gasped, but didn't shout. He couldn't see her face behind him, but she gripped his fingers tightly in return and pumped her legs to keep pace. The atmosphere was dense and sweltering. He could feel the soot spattering his skin, coating him. His lungs ached, his head throbbed. Tiny fireflies danced across his vision—or maybe they were brushfires, still smouldering somewhere nearby. He couldn't tell. The ground crackled under their feet like it might shatter at any moment, giving way beneath them. But finally they were away.

They made it to the other side of the burnt-out wreckage and Sam ducked, dragging Katie down with him. Her cheeks flushed, her eyes wide and already bloodshot. Her breath was short and panicked.

'What?' she said. 'What's happening?'

He put a finger to his lips, hushing her, his chest blazing as he tried to stifle a cough. He pointed, back towards Dettie and their car, and shook his head. He mouthed, *Liar.*

Liar. Not safe.

'What? Lost?'

No. He waved his hands. He curled them up like bear claws, just as Jon had showed him, and thumped them on his chest. Two short, hard taps:

Scared. Scary.

He spun a finger around his ear. *Crazy. Scary.* He gestured to her, and back at himself, then mimed running with his fingers.

'I don't . . . Sam?'

He looked around for a stick that hadn't been incinerated so that he could try to write in the dirt, but there was nothing

293

nearby. Suddenly, behind them, he heard Dettie shout their names. Her voice cracked.

He grabbed Katie's wrist and scrambled off into the bushes.

Everything was black. Grey. Twisted charcoal branches clawed at his skin, snatched at his hair. No animal sounds, no sky above. Just grey and smoke and ash. Heat still radiating up from the ground. The crush of their footfalls. The skittering snaps of twigs reclosing behind them.

He felt a snag on his neck, but kept on. His ankle rolled on uneven ground, but he kept going. His legs were whipped and scratched, but he kept kicking his way through. His hands were covered in dust and smears of black soot. His throat was parched and tight. His eyes stung with ash. Both arms, he realised, were lit red with scrapes and cuts. His flesh seeped. Grazed pools of sweat, pink with blood, seethed like daubs of alcohol. But they were free. They were out.

Katie was becoming a weight, lagging behind, not lifting her feet as she ran. He pulled at her hand, desperate. She was crying. He broke through another cluster of dead brush into a small clearing. There was still no sight of the farmhouse anywhere in the distance. How far had they driven past it? How long would it take to get there?

He stopped, checking that the road was still visible on his right side, letting them both catch their breath.

'We have to go back,' Katie was moaning. 'We've got to go back.'

He turned and looked in her eyes. He looked deep in her eyes. He shook his head.

No. Scary.

Katie crumbled. She twisted in his grasp, letting out a long, howling whine, collapsing to her knees.

He pointed again, off into the distance, to the farmhouse he hoped was closer than it seemed. They were free—

'We can't,' she sobbed. 'No . . .'

He could see the fear in her face. That long empty expanse before them. The danger. They were in the middle of nowhere. Under the sun. The temperature surrounding them, pressing in like a fever. No food or water. Alone. He wasn't even sure where he was dragging her. He couldn't even *tell* her why. He snatched a stick from a nearby branch and began writing in the dirt, but Katie wasn't even looking.

In the distance, further away now, Dettie was still shouting, her voice clipped and hysterical. She was weeping as she spun in place. Calling out. Desperate.

Katie was sobbing into her wrist, her whole body jolting with each breath, hair matted against her wet face. She was saying something, the words so strangled at first they were inaudible.

'We can't leave,' she said.

Sam stopped. Stopped tugging at her arms. Stopped trying to lift her up. Stopped pointing. He turned towards her. The thunder in his head went pounding on. Her face was streaked with black tears. She shook her head. 'We can't.'

'We're family.' Her voice bit the words with tremors. She was shaking. 'Family doesn't leave,' she said.

The sun burned on overhead. The landscape around them, blistered and warped and corroded, stretched on in every direction. That farmhouse, even if it was still there, suddenly seemed as much of a dream as Perth. Sam was nodding. He didn't realise at first, but he was.

His neck was red and inflamed. The vent was soaked with sweat and ash. His skin stung ferociously, slick, as though he were bleeding. His chest jerked. Sucking at the air. His lungs were on fire. He couldn't breathe.

Couldn't catch his breath.

He heaved. Shallow. Jagged. Useless intakes. Hot and harsh.

It was like Tracey's house again. But much worse. His vision clouded. Fireflies buzzed in his eyes. His body went numb.

They were trapped.

No hope. No escape.

He was weeping. Silent. Choking. He was ashamed of himself. Furious. He was an idiot. He had tried to save Katie too late. He'd only realised what Dettie had done when there was nowhere for them to go. His throat wheezed. Louder. Shrill. It was all he could hear.

They were going to die.

He punched the ground. His whole fist cracked through the black crust, scorching his knuckles. He kicked it. He hissed. Folding over onto his knees, he ground his teeth until it felt like they would snap. His world shrank in on itself until he was just a raw, furious nerve, doubled over and silently screaming. It was a moment before he could even feel Katie's arms around him, hugging his back.

At first he felt dead inside. Defeated. Another shambling zombie. But eventually, he noticed something else: his heart was beating on behind his ears. He could feel it shuddering, hot and insistent, in his throat. He couldn't shout. He couldn't talk. He couldn't even moan. But he could feel that pulse. Beneath and behind everything else. That urge to survive. He felt it burning. Hot and restless and alive.

Gradually his breathing settled. The hiccoughing subsided.

sign

The fog started to clear. The world around him resolved into view. And with Katie still clutching him, he looked up.

Above him the air was still pale with smoke, but beyond that was the sky. A bright, saturating blue. All the more dazzling for the tears in his eyes.

Suddenly the enormity of it bewildered him.

He had seen world globes. He sat beside one at school. He had traced his finger along the shape of Australia. He knew that the world was not flat. But here, looking up at the sky—blue everywhere; the essence of blue—the ground beneath him sloping away in every direction, he felt the nature of the earth as never before. Spherical and drifting through space. It was a peculiar sensation—his entire world expanded and shrank simultaneously. He seemed to be looking down upon a miniscule image of himself, looking up. He knew himself, all at once, to be no more than a speck on a ball, spinning in place, impossibly clinging to its surface. Always about to be flung off, out into that incomprehensible vista of blue.

He felt light. Oddly light and wide. As though he could stretch his fingers out and take hold of each side of the horizon, could cling on tight to the world itself if he wanted to.

But he didn't.

He kept looking up and the earth spun on beneath his feet. He knew that beyond that blue sky was a void of stars and cold, indifferent black. And he didn't care. Suddenly he just wanted to let go. To spin off into nothing and see where he landed. The car, the drive, Perth, all dissolved. He was still aware of them, but somehow they weren't so oppressive as they had been. Everything that had weighed upon him, that made him feel trapped, was now just floating along with him in the same void; little more than thoughts passing by, that he could leave unexamined. The constraints seemed to have slipped. The seatbelts and stoma guards and Dettie's grasping hands were far from him, and he had the sky to himself—the sky that was everywhere and his alone.

Once his breathing had calmed down, Sam helped Katie up again and they made their way out to the road, following it back the way they had come. By the time they reached the car, which stood still, grumbling in place, they found Dettie sitting in the dirt, clutching her chest. At first she was so lost in her own thoughts that she didn't hear them coming, but sat staring ahead at the road's tar, shivering. Alone.

As they drew near, Katie ran ahead and rushed to hug her. Dettie, looking up, broke down and smothered her with kisses.

Sam, walked slower, staggering, one foot dragging after the other. The breath through his neck was a fluttery whistle. Every part of his body was sore, speckled with grime and blood. Dettie gathered him into a hug, crying and whispering, 'Thank you.'

He was numb.

He had delivered his sister back to Dettie. Back to the car. Back to this insane trip. Back to the lie of Perth. And yet, in a puzzling way, he felt freed of something. Dettie was wiping her eyes on her wrists, Katie was begging her not to be angry anymore, and the car waited, still idling, for whatever would happen next.

62

The heat eased off slightly, but the sky had darkened. Sam couldn't remember the last time he had seen anything but smoke above the horizon, and as they pushed on, more of the landscape became stripped and charred around them. Whole paddocks were decimated, fences sunken and collapsed, livestock burnt. Road signs were folded over, melted in the heat, and Sam saw a whole house that had been reduced to a smouldering frame, its corrugated roof tumbled in upon itself.

A little further on a barricade had been set up to block traffic, propping up a large yellow sign that read *Road Closed*. Even the sandbags that held it in place had been scorched. As the car pushed around it, Katie started to speak, but Dettie shushed her quiet.

Sam's rage had faded, but he was not yet sure what had replaced it. In the midst of his new, peculiar calm he was realising that his anger had been with him a lot longer than just the past day. Long before they'd abandoned Jon. Even back before the entire journey began. The cold sensation twisting in his belly had been there since at least his operation. Perhaps even before. Since he and Katie had sat on his bed, reading his father's letter aloud. He wondered if that was why he had believed Dettie.

Her story was preposterous. Their parents had gotten back together with one phone call, after years of shouting arguments and conversations seething with unspoken accusation. The memory of his father sleeping on the couch for months. Roger, and his father's job, and the months that had gone by without even a word from him. Sam had wanted so badly to undo it all that he never stopped to properly think it through. He'd embraced the lie. Like everyone else. He'd let it calm the rage that so often pinned him in place, left him breathless and terrified.

And it had.

For a few days, even with his skin pulled tight and peeling, he'd no longer felt so much like a shell of himself, lost and echoing with empty fury. The thought of his father's return seemed to have filled in that hollow for a time. But in truth, beneath it all, the ache had remained, gnawing at his gut, tethering him to the past like the blankets tangled at his feet. Like the belt that pinned him to his seat.

Looking down at his greyed knees, at the black soot up his arms, he realised: he was just like the burnt-down house that had slipped by on the road. Eaten away. Exposed. Everything stripped from him. Everyone gone. His voice. His home. His father. His mother. Jon. All gone. Gone wherever Dettie's husband was. Wherever the girl behind the curtain had been led. Perhaps dead, perhaps missing, but lost either way. He couldn't run to them, or rely on them. He couldn't will them back into being, no matter how much he thrashed and sulked.

sign

He was burnt down, his emptiness exposed. But as he sat, swept along by the shudder of the car beneath him, it no longer hung upon him like a weight—the pain of what was lost fixing him in place, breathless. Instead he felt unburdened. It was the curious sensation of freedom that had made him woozy as he peered up at the blue sky.

Sam had spent the past several months grieving for what had been taken from him. But this trip, this journey into Dettie's fixation on the past, her deluded longing to bring it back into being, had liberated him. He could no more change what had happened up to this point than he could open up his mouth and sing. All he could control was what was to come. Because Katie needed him. He was still afraid. For her. For himself. But it no longer paralysed him. He would be ready.

He groped around on the floor and gathered up Jon's hitchhiking sign and a stray dark green colouring pencil.

Keeping the cardboard tilted away from Katie, so as not to frighten her, he changed *Help Me, I'm British* to *Help Us! Kidnapped!*

'What you doing there, Sammy?' Dettie said, angling to see in the rear-vision mirror. 'You doing some drawing?'

He glanced up at her. He nodded.

'Good. That's good. That's something nice and quiet to do. Good boy.'

He finished up the thick lettering and tucked the sign back behind his legs.

Ahead of them, the road disappeared into a wall of smoke. The cloud lay across the ground, motionless in the breeze, and within it Sam could see specks of flame lapping at the outlines of trees. The air was suddenly like a furnace. He felt it scalding his face. And he knew immediately that behind that curtain of smoke was the fire front. He stiffened, felt the heat in his lungs, and then they were inside it, swallowed by the white.

When the landscape disappeared, all at once, Katie shouted.

'Katie, I said be quiet.'

'No! Don't!'

'We'll be through in a minute.'

Sam couldn't make out anything, just grey smoke winding through white, flickers of orange, and the occasional flash of blistered roadside poles.

Embers swam in the air, peppering the windshield. Dettie snapped on the wipers, but it only smeared the soot around. The car swerved and pitched on the road, and Sam wasn't sure how his aunt even knew where she was going. Their tyres sounded wet through the tar, and something crackled against his door.

Katie was screaming, hysterical.

'Shut up, girl! Be quiet!'

Smoke blasted through the vents. Sam was holding his breath. He reached for Katie, holding her hand while bracing himself against the door.

'For goodness sake! Enough!' Dettie was reaching back, slapping her hand on the back seat. 'Shut up, damn it!' Her palm thumped on flesh. 'Listen to your brother!'

Sam was clutching the doorhandle. He could feel the tension in his chest, the urge to cough. He would have been screaming too if he could. His eyes were screaming. He couldn't afford to dissolve into a hacking fit. He squeezed Katie's hand and refused to let go.

sign

The clouds parted momentarily to show a lacework of fire eating the scrub. Katie thrashed and shrieked, and it was gone again.

Dettie shuddered behind the wheel, squinting. Her lips were pressed tight, coughing into her neck. Her whole body leant with each turn, the car lurching. Katie's tears tracked black lines through the ash on her face.

Everything was gone. The road. The sky. Everything beyond the window was white, and eerily bright. Almost luminescent. Sam was wheezing. His stoma felt raw and torn. His eyes stung. For a moment it was like being back there. Like waking after his operation. The white. The sweat. The pain. No shadows. Fluorescent bulbs. Just whiteness and blur. He blinked his eyes into focus. Squeezed Katie's hand until she turned and looked in his face.

He nodded.

The clouds swelled, and Dettie swerved to miss a charcoaled branch on the road. She yelped, and Katie shrieked. As Sam was thrown against the door the wind was knocked from his chest.

63

They came through it, bursting out of the cloud all at once, just as they had gone in. The sky was still blotted from sight, and in the distance the glow of flame was so intense it was like watching the sun itself tip over and collapse among the bush. There was a strange calm all around them. A quiet had settled all along the empty road. Everything they could see of the landscape was black. Tree branches stripped bare. The ground dusted with ash. It was as if the world had just stopped somewhere behind them and this was all that remained. And yet it was strangely beautiful. With a soft haze lingering in the air, the sky was split with shafts of blue sunlight.

Dettie was laughing, wiping tears from her eyes. 'I told you,' she said. 'See? We're fine. We made it.'

The car sounded heavier, the engine straining a little more, the clatter of the fan belt grinding even louder, but they were still in one piece. The edges of the windows and all around the air vents were stained black.

Sam realised he'd been chewing on the inside of his lip

when he tasted the blood. The feeling stung his eyes, but he was enjoying, in an odd way, the rusty taste that soaked his mouth. He thought again about the dead kangaroo, its stiff limbs and the dried patches of fluid on its fur. The blood he could taste now was fresh. When he sucked at it, and swallowed, he felt new warm blood taking its place. And there was something vital in that, something making it taste almost sweet. His blood. His life. And he felt it pulsing on quietly while Dettie sat up front, chuckling to herself, her gaze sweeping the landscape, with no idea of the sensation in his throat.

Far ahead of them two square shadows emerged from the blur. Vaporous in waves of heat, they eventually resolved into red metal. A pair of fire trucks, parked sideways across the road, blocked any oncoming traffic. As the car drew closer Sam could see a group of firemen rolling up the hoses on the truck. It appeared that they had just contained a burn and were now stacking their helmets and packing away their gear. One of the men looked up from splashing the ash off his face, and when he noticed their car approaching, he leapt up and started to wave.

Dettie was slowing down, a weary groan easing from her chest, but as more of the firemen began turning and calling out, gesturing for her to stop, she started looking around frantically for a way to get by the trucks. The car swayed as she swerved back and forth across the asphalt, speeding and slowing in jerks. When one of the closest men—Sam could clearly see the moustache on his face—dropped his bag and stepped forward, holding up his hands, Dettie swept off the side of the road just in front of him, skidded over the loose dirt and tried to thread her way around the truck on the left. But as she mounted the dip the wheels kicked burnt sand into the air, the tyres slipped, and the wheel snapped out of her hands. Growling, the car spun and slid into a mass of twisted bushes. They jerked violently to a stop, and the boomerang tied to their mirror whipped against the window and shattered into sticks.

Winded, Sam felt the seatbelt against his chest and the vent almost wrenching from his neck. He looked up through the burnt twigs littering the windscreen. There were more flames peeling into the sky ahead of them and the wind pushed ripples of heat in their direction. He could hear the firemen's shouts and their boots approaching across the gravel. They'd stopped. The car had stopped, and gradually the rattle in the engine slowed and settled to silence. Dettie had dark tears streaming down her face, but she wouldn't wipe them away. Her foot was still pinned to the accelerator. Her hands stayed hooked on the steering wheel. It looked to Sam like she might never let go.

64

The fireman's voice was muffled through the window. 'Hey! Are you right? You okay?' The crackling of the leaves and branches sounded heavier as they slid down the glass, tiny embers tumbling in their wake.

The fireman's glove was resting on the windscreen as he kicked away the scraps and charred foliage from under the front wheel. 'I think you're all right!' he was shouting. 'It's not a blow-out.' His eyes narrowed. 'Can you hear me?'

Dettie was staring straight ahead at the palm of his hand on the window. The glove was filthy. Even on their streaked glass it left a print. She was panting, and there was a slight squeak in her throat like something was caught there.

'I said, can you hear me?' He leant down to look through the side window. He tried the doorhandle. It was still locked.

Katie was stirring, groggy, as though she'd forgotten for a moment how to talk. She was pointing up at his face. Sam scrambled for the sign at his feet. It had been knocked forward, under the front seat.

The fireman tapped on the window. Dettie was stiff, her chest heaving. Slowly, she nodded, and jangled the keys in the ignition between her fingers. There were more firemen milling around the car, looking it over. Even covered in soot and ash their orange uniforms seemed to shimmer in the light.

The man by the door tapped again. Harder. He gestured for her to roll down her window. 'Lady!' he said.

Dettie raised a hand and waved, still focused on the edge of the fire truck and the trees. Measuring the gap with her eyes.

There was a loud clanking. The fireman had knocked that time with an axe, and was still holding it against the glass. 'Lady. Roll down your damn window!' he said, his voice sounding distant.

Dettie turned to face Sam and Katie. 'Are you kids hot?' She was forcing a smile. 'I might just give us some air for a minute, okay? So you sit tight while I talk to the nice man.'

Turning back, Dettie opened her window a few centimetres. 'Oh. Hello,' she said.

'*Hello?*' The fireman looked mystified, glancing at one of his companions, shaking his head. 'Is there anyone hurt in there?' he said again, louder than he needed to.

'Oh, no, we're fine. Thank you for asking.' Dettie was trying to be cheerful, smiling, but her throat was raw. It made her voice sound thin and hoarse.

With the window down Sam could hear the distant roar of the bushfire. It grumbled, like a long, slow peel of thunder. He could taste the steam in the air and the smell of melted tar. He unclipped his belt to get more reach and scratched around beneath the front seat.

'Well, if no one needs any help, you should turn around and head south,' the fireman said. 'Drive back about thirty kilometres or so—'

'Yes, yes, we *would*,' Dettie hiccoughed, 'but we just have to get through.'

'You're not going through anywhere,' the man with the axe said. 'That's what I'm saying. No one's going that way. It's a nightmare up ahead.'

Dettie hummed and ran her fingernail along the steering wheel. 'Yes, well, we *have* to get through. So if you could just—'

'Jesus, lady.' The fireman bent down to get a better look in the car. 'It's *no access* through this road.' He was speaking slowly, one word at a time. 'You shouldn't be here. There were signs all over the place. Road blocks.' He thumped twice on the roof. 'You've gotta turn your car around, and go back. Now.'

Sam brushed aside stray lolly wrappers and dishevelled maps. He stretched his arm as deep under the front seat as he could. More of the firemen had started wandering back to the truck. One laughed while another was squeezing a hiss of water over his face from a water bottle. Sam felt cardboard on his fingertips.

As the man with the axe stepped away from the door he noticed Katie wrestling with her seatbelt in the back seat. The man seemed puzzled, and as he crouched to look in closer, Sam, who had just popped back up, met his gaze with wide, pleading eyes, waving his piece of cardboard and mouthing the same word over and over. Sam set the cardboard in his lap and made a thumbs-up sign, stamping it pointedly on his palm. Again and again. Deliberately. Mouthing the same word. The fireman looked him over. He saw Sam's lips shaping out the message.

Help.

The fireman read the cardboard sign, a fusion of black texta and green pencil:

Help Us! Kidnapped!

He glanced again at Katie, turned to get a better view of Dettie, and then darted his eyes back in at Sam. He wiped a smear of ash across his face. 'Oh, Jesus,' he said. 'You're—'

He leapt up and shouted to the other men. 'Tim! Wayne! Move your arses! Get over here!'

Dettie's elbows were shaking. The squeaking in her throat was rising to a loud, choking sob.

'We're fine,' she hiccoughed. 'You can see we're—we're fine.'

Katie had slumped against the door and was running her hand across the glass.

'Now, I'm not trying to alarm you,' the fireman was saying loudly, but gently, 'but I think there are some people looking for you.' His arms were spread wide, inching closer to Dettie. 'There's nothing to be worried about,' he said. 'Just some people want to talk, that's all.'

Dettie bowed her head. She exhaled.

Suddenly, the fireman leapt at the car, hooking his right arm through the top of her window. He was making a grab for the lock, and Dettie shrieked, slapping at his glove and winding the gap smaller, squeezing his shoulder. Then the car was surrounded—orange suits were knocking at the doors, blocking off the rear bumper. Dettie twisted away from his elbow and tried to fire the car's ignition, but it spat and died. A man with a beard was whispering to Katie by her door, trying to get her to undo her lock. There was another man beside Sam, clearing out the branches in his way.

sign

Finally, the doors were open and Dettie was wheezing, hugging the steering wheel to her chest. The horn blared. As they pulled Sam from the car, she reached back, snatching at his wrist, her nails digging into his skin. 'Sammy, no!' she shrieked. 'Don't you! Not you! Sammy, stay! We don't break! We're not broken!'

Katie was already in a fire-fighter's arms, squealing back at her aunt, telling her to stop. Calling her a liar. Dettie's face was damp and bright red, her jaw speckled with spit. Her hands shook. Her lips, thin and white, were seized in a sneer, yellow teeth exposed. She was incoherent. Wild. Thrashing about in the firemen's arms. Her grip twisted the last of Sam's sunburn into a scalding sting. As she turned, forcing a desperate smile, he had one last flash of a cartoon zombie, and someone tugged his arm free.

After they'd taken her keys and radioed the police, it took three firemen to lift her from the car. They had to pry her fingers loose as she kicked and scratched and bit. One of the men—the one with the moustache—led Sam and Katie to the back of a truck to get them some water. As they walked, he steered them by the shoulders, shielding them from their aunt's view with his body as she yelled instructions to them, telling them to stay strong—that they'd be with their father soon.

'Sam!' she called out. 'Sammy, you'll tell them the truth! You tell them where we're going!'

65

The police station was yellow. The desks and windowsills were a lime green, but the yellow seemed to bleed over them and everything else. On the table in front of him, Sam had a mug of hot Milo that the officers had made, and even the cup was soaked in yellow, showing up the cracks in the porcelain. Everything looked old: the large grey typewriters that filled the air with clacking, the withered papers on the noticeboards. Even the officer they were sitting with looked years older now than she had driving over with them in the squad car. Her badge said *Barnes*, but when she introduced herself to the children it turned out her name was Sam too.

Sam had refused to let Katie out of his sight from the moment they had been led from Dettie's car. He hugged her and shared his water with her while they waited for the police to arrive, shielding her from the sight of Dettie ranting and screaming over at the next fire engine. He'd held her hand throughout the entire ride with the police officers. Across several dozen more kilometres of blackened earth, past signs warning of

sign

extreme weather conditions and total fire bans, to a town called Merredin, where a small police station sat in the shadow of the boxy courthouse next door.

Officer Samantha had let Katie and Sam have showers in the locker rooms. When they were both washed up and the nurse they called had helped clean Sam's stoma with antiseptic and ointment, Samantha gave them each a change of clothes from the station storeroom. Katie's T-shirt, PCYC written in huge letters across the front, hung down past her knees. Sam's was an aqua colour and had a drawing of a constable on it. The cartoon cop had a huge grin and sunglasses, and he was pointing out from Sam's chest, saying, *Cops are cool*. It looked like the officer who was over at the front desk speaking on the telephone, the one whose Adam's apple kept bobbing above his collar.

On a table beneath the window, the clothes Sam had been wearing for the past few days were packaged into piles. He could see his *Australia* singlet folded up inside a plastic bag that said *Evidence*. In another bag beside it was his old shirt, the one he'd thrown up on—the one Dettie had been washing when she cut herself on the sink and bled. The pale brown stain left in its fabric was exposed, and glowed almost purple under the fluorescent lights. Katie's clothes were folded beneath the window too; even though they were sealed up with tape he could still smell the petrol.

Sam reached for his Milo and took a slow sip. His hands still trembled, and as he set the mug back down he could see long red marks on his arm from Dettie's fingernails. The hollow sensation was still in his belly, and the warmth of the Milo didn't reach it. It reminded him of the moment before a roller-coaster first tips downhill. He was burping like he needed to throw up and his skin was clammy. It felt strange to be in the one place for so long, not moving. It sent a relentless tingle through his muscles—as though after driving for so long he now had motion sickness from keeping still. He almost missed the rumble of the car beneath him. To be sitting in a crowded yellow office where nothing on the desks rattled, and no trees flashed by, seemed unnatural. He tightened his fingers on the two paddle-pop sticks he'd managed to grab from the car. The others were probably still scattered on the dashboard, but he could press the two of them together and recall the shape of the boomerang.

Officer Samantha opened a packet of biscuits and cleared a space on her desk for them. Katie grabbed two and dunked them in her drink.

'Do you guys know what's happening now?' Officer Samantha asked, leaning forward in her chair, her elbows on her knees.

Katie was tapping her heels together. 'I want to talk to Mummy,' she said with her mouth full.

'Of course, sweetie. We're doing that. We're trying to get her on the phone now. See that officer over there?' Samantha pointed at the man at the front desk, the one who looked like the picture on Sam's T-shirt. 'Soon as we get in touch with her, you'll be the first to hear about it. So don't you worry about that. But that's not what I mean. I'm talking about your Aunty Bernadette. Do you know what's happening to her?'

Katie shook her head. Sam shrugged. He had watched two officers lead Dettie into the second squad car back on the road. She was still shouting things at them that Sam couldn't hear, and they seemed to be listening to her and nodding their heads. One of them was even writing things down. But since they'd arrived at the station they had kept her in another room, somewhere out the back.

'All right, guys,' Samantha said, 'well, it's like this.' She dragged her chair closer and the wheels squeaked. 'Maybe you realised, or maybe you didn't, but your Aunty Bernadette isn't very well.' She tapped her fingertips on the table. 'Your mother explained all of this to the police in Sydney. She said that your aunty needs to take medicine because sometimes she gets very sad.'

Katie was nodding.

'Now, she's done that for a long time,' Samantha said. 'But your mother says—and we all think she's right—that it's likely your aunty hasn't been taking her medicine for a while. That maybe that's why she decided to take you guys on a trip without telling anyone. Even your mum.'

'I knew it,' Katie said. 'I knew she didn't tell Mummy.'

'That's right,' Samantha said, touching Katie lightly on the knee. Sam felt himself tense, but Katie was fine. 'Your mum came home and you guys weren't there,' Samantha said. 'There wasn't even a note or anything. So for a long time she didn't know what had happened. She was very worried. She contacted her local police. They let all of us other police officers know, and we've been looking for you ever since.'

Katie was breathing heavily. 'Does Mummy know now?'

'She will soon. If she doesn't already, I promise, she will very soon. So don't let that concern you. She knows you were with your aunty. She knows that you guys were heading this way.'

Officer Samantha told them about how Dettie had phoned their father; about how she had called to tell him she was bringing his children to live in Perth. Their father had told her

315

she was being silly, Samantha said, and once he'd hung up, he called their mother to let her know where they were. While Samantha spoke, Sam remembered Dettie's face as she hissed into the phone near the railway station, her shoulders knotted and her finger jabbing at the air. He'd been so scared then that she might look over and see him. She'd seemed large and forceful, ready to snatch their whole trip away in an instant; but looking back now it was all so feeble. A scared old woman pleading into the phone because she had nowhere else to go.

'Because of that call your mother knew that you guys weren't hurt. And I know she's going to be very, very happy to hear that you're safe with us now.' Samantha smiled. 'So we're going to make sure we take good care of you until she gets here, all right?'

Suddenly, Sam sat up and gestured for a pen. When she realised what he wanted, Samantha took a biro from her top drawer and gave him the back of an incident report. 'Is that good?' she asked.

He nodded. The pen was dry and he had to scratch it angrily on the corner of the page before the ink started again.

What happened to Jon? he wrote, the nib digging into the page.

Samantha looked confused.

'Jon?'

He travelled with us. Hitchhiker.

'Where's Jon?' Katie perked up. 'Is Jon here?'

It took a few minutes—Sam writing; Katie excitedly filling in the gaps—but eventually Samantha got the idea. They had picked up Jon along the way and he'd gone missing the previous night. Sam was unable to tell her exactly where they'd last seen him, but he knew it was after Caiguna, somewhere near the Dundas Nature Reserve. To Sam's surprise she didn't seem as concerned as he would have expected, but she promised to have the officers interviewing Dettie ask what had happened and let them know.

'Is Daddy coming home?' Katie asked.

Samantha puffed out her cheeks. 'Oh, that I don't know,' she said. 'I don't think that he's—' She leaned over the desk towards them. 'You know what? How about if I get someone to check that, okay?'

Katie's expression collapsed into a heavy frown.

Sam was clutching the pen so tightly his fingertips were white. Their father was a waste of time. He wanted to keep talking about Jon, but Katie's eyes were filled with tears. Samantha smiled tightly.

'But until we hear back from your mum, why don't we start to talk about what happened on your trip, hey? Can we do that?' She lifted out another pad of incident reports, and scratched around in her drawer until she located a short, chewed pencil. 'So what happened, guys? What happened with your aunty? From the beginning.'

The children sat picking at their clean police T-shirts. Katie put her hands around her Milo mug, but didn't pick it up. Sam wondered how to start, drawing a circle around Jon's name with his pen.

'She was angry,' Katie said.

Samantha nodded. 'Yes,' she said. 'Yes, she was. She is. But she's not angry with you, sweetie. At the moment she's just a very upset lady. Very confused. And we can try to help her by being very honest about everything that happened, okay?' She wrote the date and time up in a corner of the notepad. 'So your mummy went to work that morning, and then what?'

Slowly, Katie started to answer the questions Samantha was asking about the trip, and Sam, writing on his pages, would clarify details. About where they'd travelled, as best they could remember; how long Dettie would drive before stopping. Samantha asked whether Dettie had yelled a lot, and why Katie's clothes smelt like petrol. A couple of times she asked whether they had seen Dettie taking any pills, even if they were just vitamins, and whether she'd ever gotten lost or confused on the roads. Mostly Katie just answered yes or no, and Samantha would nod, scribbling down whole sentences on her pad while shielding the words with her hand. Sam's recollections were more specific, and he tried as best he could to offer the names of every town he could recall and roughly when they were there.

When she'd finished, Samantha stood up to go and type her notes. Sam grabbed her shirt as she moved to leave. He pointed at what he had written, slapping his pen on a single word, circled several times:

Jon?

66

For over three hours Sam and Katie waited at a conference table by the station's kitchen. They had sandwiches and orange juice and chocolate bars. A fan fixed to the wall in a corner hummed down at them, slowly shaking its head. Officer Samantha helped Katie plait her hair into a French braid—something Sam had never learnt to do properly—and found them a handful of pencils and a stack of printer paper with which to amuse themselves.

At first Sam spent his time writing down every detail he could about Jon. That he was from England; that he'd been to Noosa; that he was heading west. He described his canvas shoes and his scraggly beard. The colour of his dusty luggage. He wrote down words Jon had used like *hard graft* and *wowsers*. It began as a way of giving the officers something to search for, but it soon became a kind of sprawling portrait, a repository of everything he remembered about Jon from the past couple of days. That his father had worked as a mechanic. That he'd been married once, but his 'missus' had not been very nice. That his ex-girlfriend's brother knew sign language. Samantha said that what he had written would help, and even took a blurry photocopy of the first few pages, but by the time he was writing down Jon's technique for cutting mangos and the nervous way he chewed his thumbnail, she lost interest.

After a while, as he thought of anything else to add, Sam started doodling around the edges of the page. Bushes and trees. Birds. A car. And beside the car, because he could think of nothing else, a zombie. He used a green pencil for its skin, like they had in the comic book, and drew long, spiky nails and teeth. And it looked terrible. Not scary or threatening at all—even with a scribble of red gore on its lips it seemed more like an angry green man with silly hair. Even the hook he scribbled on the end of one wrist looked awkward.

On a counter beside the station's microwave was a small black-and-white television that Samantha had turned on so they could watch afternoon cartoons. During the ad breaks it kept showing news bulletins that updated the progress of the fires. Sam saw images of fire-fighters shouting out orders and firing hoses into the blazing scrub. He watched for their faces, wondering if he might recognise any of the men who'd stopped their car, but most were wearing masks or sitting in the shadows of their trucks, sucking oxygen from bottles. There was footage of a huge helicopter that inched across the sky, dumping water into the largest flames. Smaller planes were circling the smokier areas, opening their bellies to release water that turned to white foam the moment it touched air.

With the television's sound down low, and the noise of the office surrounding him, the footage of the fires seemed eerily calm, like a dream. Most peculiarly, during one newsbreak he actually saw himself and Katie. His and his sister's faces were up on the screen with the word *FOUND* written beneath them. The pictures were old school photos—the one of Sam was before his operation, with short hair and no stoma. Sam tapped Katie to get her attention, but by the time she turned to look a team of football players were practising on a field.

Sam went back to drawing. On a clean section of page he started drawing flames—red and orange flickers, like leaves. As he coloured over them with yellow, he thought about the campfire Jon had made for them at the rest stop the night they had left him behind. He tried to draw Jon into the image, in beside some bushes. He pencilled his flannel shirt and his ripped jeans, and carefully outlined his jaw with brown whiskers. He remembered the way Jon's eyes had shimmered in the light of the fire, like they were wet—but he didn't know how to draw that, so he left them plain. When he was done with the shape of Jon, he tried to sketch Dettie in beside him—her cardigan and her messed-up hair. But when it came to her face, he wasn't sure how to draw her features. He held the pencil above the oval shape of her head, imagining her smiling, imagining her snapping at them. At times she'd been ferocious, cornered and feral, like she was when the fire-fighters had dragged them free of the car; other times she had been sweet, cradling the red-haired boy who had fallen from the train, picking daisies with Katie. He could see her yellow smile and her narrowed eyes. He saw her singing along to the radio in her shaky opera voice, or smoothing aloe vera on his arms. There didn't seem to be a single Dettie to draw, so he left most of her blank.

When Officer Samantha noticed the first picture she was winding a rubber band onto the end of Katie's plait. 'Oh, that looks nice,' she said. 'Is that your car?'

Sam nodded.

'That looks good,' she said. 'Oh dear! That's a zombie, isn't it?'

Sam smiled politely, but he suddenly had the feeling she was patronising him somehow.

'He's very scary. What's he saying?' Samantha's voice was a little too soft. Too soothing. Aping surprise.

Sam shrugged. He wrote on the bottom of the page:

Nothing.

'That's right. I forgot,' Samantha said. 'Zombies can't—'

She stopped. She swallowed and leant over to point at the second picture, of Jon. 'And who's this coming out of the fire? Another zombie?'

Sam shook his head, but Samantha was busy straightening Katie's braid.

'He looks even scarier than the other one, I think,' she said, nodding. 'I bet you're going to be an artist when you grow up.'

It was the kind of compliment he would have once puffed up to receive, but now it rang hollow, an empty platitude to keep him sedate.

Sam wrote Jon's name in large letters and drew an arrow. Samantha, meanwhile, had turned towards the front desk where the officer was waving for her to come over to the phone. She squeezed Sam's shoulder and lifted Katie off her knee. As she rose, he slapped his hand upon the table, startling both her and his sister. He pointed again at the page.

She read the name. 'Oh. Okay,' she said.

He drew another large question mark.

'I know. I know. I promise, we'll ask.' Samantha nodded and crossed the station floor to take up the phone receiver.

Katie climbed back up onto a chair and helped herself to some pencils and paper. Far behind her, on the opposite wall,

sign

Sam saw an interview-room door opening and Dettie slowly emerge. She seemed shrunken. When two officers guided her to one of the desks on the furthest side of the room, she sat silently in a metal folding chair, stiff, with her eyes half closed. They'd taken her handbag, but she was still twisting Katie's handkerchief in her fingers, staring down at it. Sam had to lean around an office partition to see what was going on, and if he strained he could hear the droning voice of the police sergeant who was reading something to Dettie, pausing only occasionally to clear his throat.

Finally, the sergeant stopped, straightened the handful of yellow papers he had been thumbing through, and sat up in his chair. 'Ma'am,' he said, fitting a paperclip over them, 'is this statement—which I have just read back to you—correct, as to your recollection, in its entirety?'

Dettie gradually emerged from her daze. She nodded.

'Then can you please sign your name here at the bottom?' the officer asked, sliding the statement over to her and laying a pen on top.

Dettie eased forward in her chair and folded her arms tightly across her belly. Hunched, she leant across the corner of the desk and stared down at the papers, unblinking, for almost a minute, before lifting the pen.

'It's Bernadette,' she said to herself as she slowly completed her signature. 'Like the saint.'

The corner of the sergeant's mouth twitched and he took back the pen.

Sam couldn't hear all of what he said next, but he heard something about theft and child endangerment, and offering to speak to a lawyer.

Sam waited for Dettie to say something in reply, but she closed her eyes and nodded.

'Hey, kids!' Samantha was calling to them. 'Come on. Come over here, I've got a surprise for you.'

They both turned in their seats. Samantha was standing by the front desk waving them over. In her hand she was holding out the phone receiver.

Katie leapt out of her chair so fast she stumbled. Sam pushed back from the table, scattering his pencils. They scrambled over and pressed their ears together above the earpiece. Katie held her hands over her mouth as she trembled with excitement.

'My darlings? My babies?' Their mother's voice, thinned out through the speaker but warm and familiar, warbled on the other end of the line. She was laughing and weeping and breathing deeply.

Katie whined and collapsed against Sam's side.

'Sweetie, Katie, don't cry,' their mother was saying. 'It's all right. You're safe. And I'm on my way.' She sounded breathless.

Sam tugged the phone closer and tapped the mouthpiece. He made a popping sound with his lips.

'Sam? Honey, is that you? Sweetie. Oh. Thank God. Thank God. I should never—Sam, I'm sorry. I'm so sorry. For everything. Mummy's going to be there soon, okay? Mummy's going to be with you really, really soon. I love you. Make sure Katie—Katie? I love you both so much. I'm so sorry.'

She was talking almost too fast for Sam to make out, and Katie was howling beside him.

'You be strong,' their mother was saying. 'I couldn't be more proud of you. Of you both. I'm so sorry. I didn't know.'

sign

Clutching the phone in both hands, holding it up for Katie, Sam glanced up at Dettie. Through his blurred vision he could see his aunt still sitting at the sergeant's desk. She had turned to look at them both, holding a lit cigarette in her fingers. Her face was drawn and thin, and it too was wet with tears. As Sam wiped his eyes, she turned away.

Samantha left them to talk. When Katie had calmed down enough to speak she clutched the phone tightly to her head, telling their mother hurriedly about the trip. Sam tried to listen in, but Katie was so eager she eventually twisted the receiver from his hands. She mentioned the boy with the chipped tooth and Sam throwing up. The firemen, the handkerchief, how Dettie never let them wind the windows down.

'She was scary,' she said. 'She'd get all mad. All the time. We went to a petrol station at one place and she sprayed it on me. The petrol. All on me.'

Katie waited with her mouth open as her mother said something.

'Yeah,' she said. 'And I kept asking to call you, but she said you already left to go to Perth. That you went already. And I said, "No she didn't," but she yelled at me. She yelled all the time.'

Their mother was talking again.

'No, don't cry, Mummy,' Katie said. 'She was like that to everyone. She even made Jon leave.'

Their mother must have asked, because Katie explained all about Jon. All about his wife, and his stories, and the way he said *bollocks*. It made them laugh, and Sam could tell that somehow it was helping his mother to relax on the other end of the line.

Katie talked for almost an hour, and finally Samantha had to come back and take the phone from her hands. Their mother promised she would be there soon; she was flying, and they had to wait for her plane, but the three of them would travel home together.

Sam wondered what would happen to Dettie, but he was too tired to find a way to ask.

67

Later that evening the children lay on foldaway beds in the station interview room. Katie was asleep but Sam was lying still, staring at the ceiling, when he heard the door creak open. A tall silhouette peered through the frame. It was Samantha, asking in a whisper if he was still awake. He propped himself up on his elbows. Their father was on the phone.

Katie rolled over to face the wall when Sam tried to wake her. 'He doesn't care,' she said. 'He's not coming back.' She pushed the pillow to her ear.

Sam didn't want to leave her, but he was just going to the next room, and it was quiet and safe now. He rose from his cot and followed Samantha out into the office, shielding his eyes from the light.

The room was emptier than it had been during the day. The television was off, and when his eyes had adjusted it seemed like the yellow walls had darkened to a pale orange. The phone was off the hook on the front desk, and as they crossed the floor he remembered the old cassette tape he had found in the laundry cupboard. The one with him and his father singing 'Mary Had a Little Lamb'. On it, his father's voice had seemed flintier than he recalled, and it had been difficult to align it with the image he tried to keep of him, larger and more sonorous, in his mind. But now his father was close again. Just on the other end of the phone. Waiting.

Samantha wheeled over a chair for Sam to sit on, and then lifted the receiver to speak.

'Hello?' she said. 'Yes, sorry about that. I've got Sam here. I'll just put him on.'

She winked and passed Sam the phone. As he took it, he squeezed so hard the plastic squeaked.

'Hello? Hello, are you there?' It was his father's voice. But it sounded even thinner than it had on the tape. 'Is anyone there? Hello?'

Sam made popping sounds with his lips into the receiver. He felt the muscles in his throat tightening, trying to talk. He wished, once again, that he could whistle.

'Am I on hold—? I think they've put me on hold.' His father was talking to another voice in the background. A female voice.

Still popping, Sam tapped on the mouthpiece.

'What's that?' his father said. 'Hello? Is someone—Sam? Oh, it's you, buddy. Of course. No one was talking so I thought they'd—' He cleared his throat. 'Hey, how are you? Eh, buddy? I've been worried sick. They couldn't tell us anything. Are you all right? How's your sister? Is she there?'

Sam was nodding, shrugging, clicking his tongue; trying to make any noise. He had the phone pressed so hard to his ear that it hurt.

sign

'Sam, I said, are you all right?' His father's voice sounded distant through the crackle on the line. 'I'll tell you what,' he said. 'You knock once for yes, two for no. Are you good?'

Pausing a moment, Sam looked up at Samantha's face as she smiled back down. He thought of Dettie, being held somewhere else in the building, dishevelled and suddenly aged. He thought of Katie, quieter, more insular than she had ever been before. And Jon—who knew where?

'Are you good, buddy?'

His father clearly wanted the lie. But Sam was done with lies. He tapped the receiver with his knuckle, but before he could tap a second time, his father let out a lengthy sigh that filled up the line like static.

'Oh, that's fantastic, mate. That's just great. That's good to hear.'

Sam didn't bother correcting him. There was no point. He wasn't listening anyway. And there was nothing left to say.

68

It was six months before Sam and Katie saw their aunt again. There had been no need for long court proceedings or investigations. Dettie pleaded guilty and never changed her story. She had taken the children to be reunited with their father. She had done it without permission, and had misled Katie and Sam and their parents. But she was trying to save her family, she said, and she would never apologise for that. As part of her agreement she was placed in a hospital facility for rehabilitation.

Sam and Katie's mother made sure to explain to them exactly where Dettie was and all that was going on throughout the whole process. At Sam's insistence she didn't lie or dumb anything down. There had been enough lying, she agreed. Dettie was sick. She had been sick for a long time—since before Ted had left. She suffered from a form of mental illness that gave her mood swings, but she had never done anything like this before. It was called a 'manic episode', their mother said. Because she wasn't taking her medication properly, because she was agitated and stressed, she'd done a very stupid, very dangerous, very frightening thing. And she was going to stay in a safe place until she was back to her old self. If, Sam thought, she ever came back to herself.

'But the thing to also remember,' their mother said, 'is that your aunt Bernadette does love you.' She did not call her 'Dettie' anymore. 'What she did was inexcusable. Unforgivable. But in her own very, *very* misguided way, she did it because she loves you both very much.'

To Sam's surprise, it was only a few weeks before Katie softened towards their aunt again. Based on what their mother had described, Katie seemed to feel sorry for her, and was soon sending letters and photographs in care packages, wishing her well and keeping her informed about school or what was happening around the house. In return, Dettie would send letters that Katie would read aloud to Sam, after struggling with their mother to disentangle the uncharacteristically sloppy script.

Sam's feelings were more complicated. He was never sure which image of his aunt was going to surface from the complex tangle of memories in his mind. The stuffy, sombre oracle, warning him not to give in to death after his operation? The kindly guardian, plying them with lollies and ice cream, trying to keep their spirits up? The dishevelled, rambling creature clinging to a past already faded? Eventually he came to accept that she was all of them, and none, at once. This was just the way people were. Messier and more complicated and self-deluded than they themselves ever realised.

He'd thought much the same thing when they'd briefly met up with their father. It was for just an hour, immediately before flying back to Sydney. He'd met them for a short lunch at the airport cafe. Their parents were quiet and stiff with one another, and his father looked thinner than Sam expected. He had a moustache. He talked about how busy he was at work. He couldn't believe how much the two of them had grown. He was friendly and smiled and marvelled at how brave they had been. But at the same time Sam could feel his father staring at his throat, could sense the discomfort in his posture as he tried not to look like he was turning away from him. When they said goodbye, and he promised to all meet up again soon, Sam knew it was just another story, more comforting words that he was telling himself as much as them.

The same was true of the news media and everyone at school. The week after they returned home, a television reporter had interviewed Sam, Katie and their mother for the news. But when they saw the report broadcast, they had edited out all mention of Jon, kept showing footage of their mother crying, and claimed that Katie and Sam had been afraid the entire time, continually cutting to some weird black-and-white slow-motion footage of a car driving through the woods. Their classmates had found it all fascinating, and were soon happy to make up their own stories about Sam driving the car to safety himself, or Dettie getting into a shoot-out with the police.

As the weeks passed, Katie and Sam would occasionally speak to Dettie on the phone. The conversations were always short, and their mother would make sure to stand beside them, letting them lean against her for support if they needed to, listening in on a second handset, and reading aloud whatever Sam wrote down to say. Sometimes it would take Dettie a long time to respond. Katie would ask her something—what the weather was like where she was; what did she have for dinner—and it would take a moment for their aunt to take the sentence in, think it over, sometimes repeating a few words in a slow moan, and then reply. She'd occasionally even forget the question, or repeat something she'd already told them. Their mother explained it was because of all the medications she was taking. They helped her stay calm, she said, but they also made her tired. Made it hard for her to concentrate. Mostly Dettie just talked about the other patients, many of whom, she said, complained too much.

Sam's questions were almost always about Jon. What had happened to him. Where he had gone. But the few times Dettie seemed to hear what his mother was asking for him, her story remained the same. Exactly what she'd told the police officers, the doctors and the judge. Jon had decided to travel on his own. He'd taken his bags and hitchhiked the rest of the way alone. She would get confused and upset if they pressed her further.

For Sam, Dettie's voice now was somehow even more unsettling than all the murmuring and frantic twitching he had seen overtake her in the car. At least then she had focus. Even in the last, crazed moments when they ran off the road, her snarling and clawing at him, the desperate, terrified look in her eyes. Now it was hard to tell what she believed. What she knew, what she had told herself or couldn't recall. The truth had become even more slippery and unsalvageable.

He realised, finally, the true horror of the zombies that had lurked beneath the campy schlock in his comic book. Under the lumbering and the sharp teeth and the gore, what was so haunting wasn't the threat of death, but the unhealthy clinging to life. To what had passed. He'd been afraid that it somehow represented him. Silent. Angry. That he, like the zombies, had been changed into something unfamiliar, something strange. But it wasn't the changing that was so frightening—it was being unable to let go. He was now no longer clinging to some lost image of himself. Dettie, however, was lost. Wilfully detached from the truth. Hungry to be believed. Empty and thoughtlessly wheezing over the phone. She was still trapped, cold and haunted on the other end of the line.

Their mother was eventually able to contact Ted and fill him in on everything that had happened. He visited one afternoon for a cup of tea, to catch up and talk things through. Even he seemed surprised about what was happening to Dettie. Things were bad in the old days, he said, but she had never strayed so far from herself. He did laugh, however, when their mother said Dettie was telling people that he had fallen to his death from a skyscraper window.

'Wishful thinking,' he said.

69

No one else was ever able to explain what had happened to Jon. Nothing was ever found and no one seemed to have heard or seen anything the night Dettie left him behind. Sam had his mother call the police to check up every week. He wrote letters to different stations at every town along the roads they had driven on—even to places in and around Perth itself, but he received few replies. A bulletin had been circulated along with a sketch a police artist had made from Sam's description, but no one ever came forward and no new information appeared.

Jon had just vanished.

It was like that with tourists from overseas, one officer told him in a letter, two months after Sam had returned home. Often a traveller will just get on a plane and fly home without telling anyone, not thinking anyone will miss them. Most of the time there's no one to tell. The police kept assuring Sam that they would make some inquiries in London, but nothing seemed to come of it. He was just gone. Somewhere. And to Sam it seemed that nobody else was that concerned. Jon returning home—being fine—was all just another comfortable fiction everyone was constructing to avoid dealing with whatever was real. Strangely, even Katie started to believe that nothing was wrong. Sam wondered whether anyone would have believed Jon existed at all if they hadn't found his shirt and sign in the car.

Sam had kept the paddle-pop sticks from the boomerang Jon had given him. He made sure to remember the way they had slid together, fixed in place, bending into each other. And once he was home he had wound them together again himself and fixed them with glue. The boomerang hung from his ceiling now, and he would watch its shadow turn slowly above him each night as he lay in bed. He still remembered watching those sticks shudder above him as the car tore along those endless patchy asphalt roads, spinning in the sunlight. Sometimes he wondered if he would always feel that vibration running through his skin.

It was a surprise to Sam to consider that his mother had never known Jon. In a few days he had become such an indelible part of his life, and yet she'd never even seen his face. Perhaps never would. Ironically, after all of Dettie's panic about him, Roger and Sam's mother had drifted apart over the following months, and when Sam let his imagination loose he couldn't help but wonder what might have happened between Jon and his mother if they had met.

In many ways it was because of Jon that Sam asked to work with Tracey again. *Because Batman doesn't have superpowers*, he had wanted to tell Jon. *He has to work for it.*

Although he tried them both for a time, he discovered that he didn't like either oesophageal speech or the electrolarynx that Tracey lent him to try. Trying to swallow air made his stomach feel sick and sore, and the electrolarynx's unnerving sizzling sound still made him uncomfortable. But more than that, he felt like they were both just attempts to keep using old words—the same feeble words that the people around him kept using. Filled with soothing lies and misleading euphemisms.

Instead he wanted to learn sign language. To take on a new language, one that was fresh to him, while he got by, for the time being, with the old. His mother didn't quite understand, but she was completely supportive, and even learnt along with him as best she could. He worked with Tracey after school, and his mother bought him a few books for home.

Over many weeks, practising every day, he slowly became quite good. He even started signing in his dreams. It turned out that most of the signs Jon had shown him were at least a little bit different. In Australia they taught Auslan. Some of the signs were similar—*thank you* was much the same, as was *mother*, and *scared* was just one hand tapping the chest, not two—but even when they were different, Sam tried to remember what Jon had taught him as well, as best he could.

The more he practised, the more he liked the way it felt to sign. The rhythm of it running through his body. The muscles in his arms tightening or easing depending on how expressive he wanted to be. Sharing simple conversations with other members of Tracey's Auslan class. Recognising expressions. Pressing his meaning into the world with action.

Sam's mother announced that she was going to visit Dettie a week before she went. It was winter, half a year since their aunt had been hospitalised, and Katie had been asking, more and more frequently, to see her. There was no obligation for Sam to go, if he didn't want to. His mother said that she would absolutely understand.

Except Sam wanted to go. Because he still wanted to know. *Needed* to know. For himself. For her. So that it could end, whatever the answer.

He would ask her, this time in person. She had never told anyone else—but somehow Sam knew that she would tell him. He wasn't sure why, but he knew that if *he* asked her, if it was *him*, if he was right in front of her—not on the phone—she would say it. He would look her in the eyes, and she would look back. For once he wouldn't break her gaze, and he would ask her.

And he would see the truth in her face.

He practised his question for the entire week. As he showered and dressed and had breakfast, he practised it through. He wanted it to be automatic. Clear. Even if she didn't understand him at first. He wanted to sign it properly.

What happened to Jon?

He'd also written it down on a piece of paper, so that his mother could read it aloud for him too—but he was going to ask it. He would feel it through his chest and up the back of his neck. He would ask and she would tell him.

By the end of the day he would know.

When they arrived at the hospital, Dettie was sitting by a window, her shoulders slumped, the blanket over her lap sliding halfway onto the floor. She seemed smaller than ever. Thin, and slumped, and pale. Her hair was cut short and her eyes were watery as she peered through the television screen and the game show flickering on its surface. A small plate of colourful boiled lollies lay on a plate beside her chair. Beside it, a cup of tea waited. None of it appeared to have been touched. For the first time that morning Katie hesitated, her excitement choked.

sign

They stood for a moment, watching their aunt's slow, deliberate blinking, the slight lolling of her head. Sam could feel his mother squeeze his shoulder. She didn't need to say anything. Together they stepped forward, and Sam raised his hands.

And then he spoke.

Acknowledgements

Thank you to my wife, Laura, for being so encouraging about this project in the beginning, and to my family—all of my families—for being a source of inspiration and support every day. Thanks to my sister Beth for riding with me.

To Alan Wearne, Tony Macri and Christine Howe, my thanks for providing invaluable feedback in the early days that gave the narrative shape. For their incredibly kind words and support, thank you to Stephen Romei, Jenny Barry and Rohan Wilson. And to Julie and Gaynor at the Mildura Visitors Information Centre, thank you for answering a torrent of baffling questions with grace.

To everyone at Allen & Unwin, there are no words. Thank you for being the most generous, supportive and creative team that anyone could have hoped to collaborate with. My thanks to Christa Munns, Jennifer Thurgate and Genevieve Buzo; my endless gratitude to Ali Lavau, for her thorough, thoughtful reading and suggestions; to Hilary Reynolds for sharpening the tone and catching my mistakes; to Sarah Baker for revealing my overuse of the word 'sharpening'; and to Annette Barlow for everything—simply everything.